Helium Fall

By

Darren Robison

LEGALESE

This is a work of fiction. Names, characters, incidents, and dialogues are products of the author's imagination and are not real. Any resemblance to actual events, places or persons, living or dead, is entirely coincidental and the product of the readers over active imagination. The publisher does not have any control over and does not assume any responsibility for author or third-party websites or their content.

Helium Fall

Published by arrangement with the author

Copyright @ 2018 by Darren Robison

Cover Layout and Design: The Cover Collection at www.thecovercollection.com

All rights reserved.

No part of this book may be reproduced, scan distributed in any printed, electronic, or digita without written permission. Please do not particip or encourage piracy of copyrighted materials in vi of the author's rights. Purchase only authorized edit

ISBN: 9781730767685

DEDICATION

This book is dedicated to everyone
who encouraged me to embrace my dream.

ACKNOWLEDGMENTS

I would like to thank my beta reader team: D. Black, J. Henley, J. Shields and C. Robison. This story would not be what it is without their input. Special thanks to D. Black and C. Robison for their editorial expertise.

A special thank you to Alan and D. Black. Without their support and encouragement I would never have put pen to paper and would still be just dreaming of writing. You were and are truly a blessing to me.

Table of Contents

Chapter One 1
Chapter Two 15
Chapter Three 27
Chapter Four 37
Chapter Five 45
Chapter Six 55
Chapter Seven 63
Chapter Eight 79
Chapter Nine 87
Chapter Ten 95
Chapter Eleven 107
Chapter Twelve 115
Chapter Thirteen 135
Chapter Fourteen 143
Chapter Fifteen 157
Chapter Sixteen 173
Chapter Seventeen 183
Chapter Eighteen 193
Chapter Nineteen 209
Chapter Twenty 217
Chapter Twenty-One 225
Chapter Twenty-Two 238
Chapter Twenty-Three 247
Chapter Twenty-Four 257
Chapter Twenty-Five 269
Chapter Twenty-Six 281
Chapter Twenty-Seven 293
Chapter Twenty-Eight 305
About the Author 321

HELIUM FALL

Chapter One

Grant Goodwine could feel his skin beginning to crinkle and fry like a skillet full of bacon in the blazing sun on a hot summer morning. His head was banging like the worn out pistons in an old time car engine about out of oil. His head was drenched in sweat, he was covered in a reddish orange mud, and what appeared to be blood, was it his blood? If so, why was he bleeding, and from where? Why was he covered in mud? The pieces were not falling into place for Grant. It was then he realized he was no longer in his research shuttle, the Varizone. He was lying face up outside on the ground gazing at the shimmery silhouette of a large moon. How had he gotten here, how long had he been here, and where the hell was his shuttle? His mind was a swirl of questions and his head was banging so loud he couldn't remember what had happened.

He wondered what series of events had brought him to the situation he currently found himself. Had he gotten drunk at Landing's in New Liberty again or fallen asleep at the wheel and crashed his shuttle? The first idea was very possible. He had gotten drunk at Landing's many times over the years, but the later didn't make sense. Some weak memories were beginning to come back to him. He was traveling in his ship the Ebony Belle for a month or more on its maiden exploration voyage looking for new life-sustaining planets in the Green zone, or the Goldilocks zone as it is often called. But he wasn't currently in his ship the Ebony Belle or his shuttle, the Varizone. He remembered being in the Varizone approaching his first landing on his first unnamed planet. He would have to think about it later.

The air was hot and he ached all over, what the hell had happened? He carefully rolled over onto his left side and made a feeble attempt at self-evaluation to see if he was whole or broken. He still had both arms, both legs, and all his digits. They were scratched and bleeding, but not badly, and he had cuts on his face and body. He determined he was bruised and battered, but alive.

This minor success spurred him to move some more. He struggled onto his hands and knees, then to a staggering standing position. He worked out a few more kinks with a slow intentional stretch. Then he saw it. The Varizone was 50 yards away, smoking, scratched, and dented. Small fires burned close by. Dirt, grass, and small plants lay everywhere, apparently dislodged when the shuttle made its initial impact. There was a thirty yard long, three foot deep gouge in the soil with dirt and debris stacked up behind its final resting place. It rested off kilter. The landing gear was significantly damaged. Grant made his way towards the wreckage in a painful stagger, reminiscent of the aftermath of a drunken bar fight. Something nagged him and he could not put his finger on it.

His head felt like it would explode at any minute. The distance between him and the Varizone closed slowly and painfully. Each step harder than the last, but he had to get there, assess the damage, and find shelter from the heat. The top of his head and the tips of his ears felt blistered from the intense sun. Water was another priority, and there was something else he knew he was forgetting, but what was it? His main goal was to get to the shuttle quick, well, as fast as he could anyway. He focused on each painful step and told himself, just a little further, a few more steps and you're there, keep moving. As he approached the shuttle he remembered what was nagging him. He knew it was important. How could he forget his friend and co-pilot? Grant saw Sam Northland standing in the outer hatchway of the shuttle shouting, but Grant couldn't clearly hear what he was saying. Grant hobbled along at a quicker, slightly more painful pace. As he closed the distance he could hear Sam shouting.

"You're alive, thank the gods in heaven. Grant, I thought I'd lost you when you took off running and screaming after the damn thing."

Grant hesitantly replied, "What happened to the shuttle? Why am I covered in mud and blood? Glad to see you alive, are you hurt? Wait, what did you mean when you said, "the damn thing"? What was I chasing?"

Sam had known Grant for a long time and figured he must have taken a serious blow to the head. It was completely out of character for Grant to act so rashly. He replied, "Well, I believe it was a drone of sorts, never saw anything like it, and it fired a missile at you."

"It fired a missile at me? Why did it fire a missile at me? We have to figure out where it came from."

Sam recognized the look on Grant's face, he was serious, and it meant trouble — lots of trouble.

Grant was the captain and pilot of the Ebony Belle, as well as the lead scientist and photographer of this two man team. They worked for the Planetary Survey and Acquisition Division, PSAD. The Ebony Belle was the newest discovery ship in the PSAD fleet and rather large for just two people. It contained the newest scientific equipment in every size and shape imaginable. The lab was nearly the length of a football field and about half as wide. It was located in one of the two detachable pods. The other pod contained the sleeping quarters, a full gym with basketball court, and a half sized football field on the upper level. Grant and Sam were in route to the planet surface after their artificial Intelligence, AI, determined the atmosphere below was suitable for human habitation, although a bit higher in oxygen concentration than Earth's atmosphere. Due to the higher oxygen concentration, Grant was already beginning to feel somewhat better. His aches and pains were dissipating faster than normal and his memory was beginning to return. Once aboard the Varizone, both expressed their thankfulness to be alive. It was determined Sam was a bit bruised and battered, but physically sound and for the most part, uninjured.

Grant tasked Sam with setting up motion sensors around the shuttle's perimeter and detailing the extent of the external damage, while he assessed the internal damage with the help of their AI.

"EL 10 T, how are you faring?"

"Captain Goodwine, for ease of interaction, please call me Eliot. I am faring much better than the ship, thank you for asking. I was jostled by the explosion, but nothing is loose or broken."

"EL 10...Eliot it is then, you may call me captain."

Explosion, Grant had no recollection of an explosion, other than the missile Sam said the drone fired at him. His mind raced. "What kind of explosion, internal or external?"

In his usual calm voice Eliot replied, "External. A missile launched from a drone near the planet's surface to be precise.

Grant's face looked quizzical as he began recalling what recently transpired. He remembered hearing Eliot say they were at 2000 feet and closing, landing in 10, 9, 8...then there was an incredible bang. He remembered covering his ears and wincing in pain as the shuttle shook, veered wildly left, and plummeted the remaining distance to the planet's surface, crashing with a mind numbing thud, sending dirt and debris in all directions. The shuttle skidded to a smoking halt ten yards from a tree line, pivoting 180 degrees before stopping. Grant and Sam were caught off guard. They were tossed about the cabin like ragdolls, knocking both of them against the walls and to the floor several times.

In a delirious state, Grant exited the shuttle, running after whatever his addled brain perceived had attacked the shuttle. He remembered a bright flash, searing pain, and blackness. His next memory was waking up lying on the ground. The planet was supposedly uninhabited. Grant was amazed Eliot had not warned them about the danger below.

Grant and Sam had left Earth about a month ago and were in Hyperspace until he guessed, a day ago. They were sent to explore the SanDED system, about 85,000 light years from earth. A pretty close neighbor by universal standards. Scientists had detected a radio signal. A signal this close meant there was intelligence close by—they were not alone.

Many non-intelligent life forms were discovered over the years on planets in the Green Zone, but they never came in contact with anything more intelligence than the average house pet. The radio signal coming from the SanDED system prompted the PSAD to send out a discovery team, one consisting of Grant and Sam aboard the Ebony Belle.

Having reached their destination, they settled into synchronous orbit and planned their sojourn to the planet surface. They took a good portion of the day finishing preparations and getting their shuttle ready to head out the following morning. The Varizone was a planetary research shuttle designed for the exploration and scientific analysis of newly discovered planets. Their job was to determine if a planet could sustain life, and if it could be commercially developed or exploited for its natural resources.

Earth had long given up what resources it once provided and now relied on exploration teams to find and analyze suitable planets for resources and habitation. It was an interesting occupation often providing great amusement, depending on what a planet's flora and fauna were like and how it had evolved.

"The boss is gonna be mad at you, Grant. You just wrecked one of his brand new toys, and on its first mission."

"Sucks to be me, I suppose. Gonna suck even more for you, Sam, when I tell him you were driving and didn't see the missile coming at us and flew right into it."

"You wouldn't dare." Sam said with a wry smile. They were just playing like they always did.

They laughed and carried on with their examinations of the shuttle.

"If we can get the Varizone repaired, gather the data we came here for, and return back to the Ebony Belle to report all is well, and then neither of us has to worry."

"No problem, Grant. I'll just wave my magic wand and we'll be on our way."

Grant noted his stinging tone of sarcasm. He also knew returning to the Ebony Belle would be far more difficult, and take much more time than they were allotted.

The hot day drifted on with only an occasional break from the scorching sun as they continued their work.

Sam caught small movements in his peripheral vision and swore he saw what appeared to be a human face. He thought the heat was playing tricks on him and the sweat in his eyes was making him see things. He felt like they were being watched since they landed. He had a creepy feeling hidden eyes were peering out at him from every dark corner, and from behind every tree, bush, and rock. As the day progressed and the shadows grew longer he was convinced they were being watched. The movement was slight, and whatever it was, was small and quick to hide, if Sam even slightly inclined his head in its direction.

By late afternoon, Grant was sure he and Eliot had thoroughly gone through each and every sensor and determined they were functioning properly.

He went outside to see how Sam was coming along. As Grant stepped out of the shuttle he saw for the first time just how beautiful the planet was and how the sky shimmered like the surface of a hot road. It had a strange bluish purple tint, and for it being what he perceived as afternoon, it wasn't as bright as he remembered. He figured it must be autumn or the trees were naturally vibrant with color all year long. The crimson and deep orange hues mixed with bright yellow and green reminded him of autumn on Earth, his favorite time of year. The morning sun was scorching hot. It now felt like it was beginning to cool down, it was now bearable, and may soon become almost enjoyable.

After wandering around for a few minutes, he found Sam diligently making the repairs he could and documenting the ones he couldn't. "So how's it looking Sam?"

"It isn't as bad as I thought it was going to be, but it isn't all good either. The landing gear on the port side took the brunt of the impact and it's pretty much useless. Gonna take some serious bending and welding to get it even close to being functional again. The propulsion housing is dented pretty good, and then there's the underside of the shuttle. The right rear took the direct hit from the missile." This thing was definitely built to withstand a direct hit, but the missile dented it pretty deep. We may have to sacrifice some things to get it back to true. I guess with a little hammering and shinning up she'll be good as new and flight worthy, in oh, let's say a week, maybe two. Give or take a few days depending on what I can find in the shuttle to make the repairs."

Sam was a geologist, mechanic, and pretty much a jack of all trades. When they were younger, he and Grant tinkered with everything under the sun just to see how things worked. They were passionate to learn as much as they could and to explore new things. Passion and intrigue prompted them to attend college, where they both earned high marks in most subjects. Sam sought out degrees in geology and primitive studies. Grant went the more challenging route, earning degrees in physics and biology. Their passion for discovery brought them to flight school, the PSAD, and ultimately on this journey.

The sun was setting and the shadows were getting longer. They decided to call it quits for the day and hunker down for the night.

Grant thought he saw movement to his left and spun

quickly to catch a glimpse of whatever it may be. He was unsuccessful, yet somewhat amusing to Sam, as he chuckled a bit louder than he intended.

"Sam, did you see that? I swear I just saw something bi-pedal dart behind a tree over there."

Sam told Grant he was seeing things all day being left out in the scorching heat, alone, and vulnerable he thought his eyes were playing tricks on him and he was becoming paranoid. He almost went inside at several points to let Grant know.

Grant was unhappy Sam had not come in to let him know his concerns. "Sam, this is serious! Whoever shot us down could be sizing us up for another attack. What were you thinking? Why didn't you let me know the very first time you thought you saw something?"

In an equally serious tone Sam replied, "I thought the heat and the sweat in my eyes were playing tricks on me. I wasn't sure I saw anything anyway. It could have been a play with light, shadow, and my overactive imagination."

"Sam, we have to take care in everything we do, we have to be aware of our surroundings. It is what will keep us alive — at least long enough to get eaten by something large and scaly with a mouth full of razor sharp teeth."

They laughed out loud and decided it was truly time to head indoors. It appeared to them the sun was setting exceptionally fast. The whole environment began to rapidly change. The sound of small animals creeping through the brush, and the melodic hum and buzz of the local bugs they had heard during the day gave way to more sinister sounding bugs, and the grunts and growls of larger unseen animals.

Sam, with some trepidation asked, "Do you suppose there are large, nocturnal, carnivorous predators on this planet?" With a quick glance at each other they took off running like two young boys afraid of the dark, trying to get inside first and leave the other standing on the porch to be eaten by the imaginary monster. The sun would set within minutes and the night's orchestra began its symphony of animal and insect sounds. Reaching the hatch, Grant detached a light from inside the shuttle. He shined it across the landscape hoping to catch eye shine or something caught off guard and no longer hidden. The symphony went immediately silent. A cold chill ran down their backs. It was the most eerie lack of sound they had ever heard. Grant unconsciously turned out the light and they moved in unison back inside the shuttle.

"What just happened? I've never experienced anything like it in my entire life. I was never afraid of the dark, but I may be now."

Grant was thinking the same thing. It was the most surreal moment he had experienced, and one of the most terrifying.

"Keep an eye on those cameras Sam, we have no idea what to expect tonight. I have an unsettled feeling; we aren't going to get much sleep."

Sam nodded his agreement and silently made his way up to the bridge. From his chair, he could watch the cameras and monitor the sensors he set out earlier in the day to see what may be skulking around their site. He closed the shield over the view screen. He didn't really want to see firsthand what may be out there in the night.

The day had come and gone in a hazy hot blur and Sam wasn't ready to face anything larger than a house cat or possibly a small possum. The heat had really taken a lot out him, along with the stress of the crash, coupled with the day's events. He was ready to shower and get some sleep, but the adrenaline rush from the thrill of seeing new life for the first time kept him glued to the cameras.

"Let me know if you see anything moving out there, Sam."

The sudden burst of noise startled Sam just as he thought he saw something move in the distance at the edge of the camera's view.

"Oh my God, Grant you scared the holy crap out of me! I think I may have wet myself a little."

Grant had come onto the bridge unbeknownst to Sam who was intently watching for the slightest movement. "You are such a sissy! What do you think you're going to see out there, a T-Rex or something?"

"Well, now you've said it, yes, it is exactly what I think I might see out there. He might have some rather large friends with him, too, who knows? Right before you snuck up on me I thought I saw movement just at the edge of camera two. It was slight; it could have been a rodent or something else fairly diminutive in stature."

"Did it have sharp teeth and razors for claws, Sam?"

"Stop, I really do think I saw something."

Grant took on a more serious tone and asked Eliot to scan for life forms. "Large and small, please."

Eliot replied, "I could not read them before we landed, but I am getting readings now. There is a static charge just above the tree line. It is the reason the planet appeared to be desolate upon approach. I have adjusted my sensors. The planet is teaming with life."

This was great news, but also unsettling for Sam. His imagination went right back to the image of T-Rex and his friends strolling up to the shuttle looking for a fight or possibly a midnight snack.

"It's going to be a long night, Sam, if you keep thinking you're seeing things."

Sam could not take his eyes off camera two and with good reason, something had moved and he knew it. He wasn't going to let whatever it was come any closer than necessary to get a good look. Even though the Varizone was a research vessel, it was equipped with several large guns in case wildlife truly got wild and intended to bring harm to the ship or the crew.

"Eliot, can you please set the sentry guns to defend? I want to scare away anything venturing too close to the ship tonight. We need to meet our enemies — if that's what they are — in the daylight. Besides, it'll make Sam feel safer."

Grant continued, dripping with sarcasm, "I mean taking into consideration we are twenty-five feet off the ground, inside a large armor- covered space vehicle able to withstand a missile blast and the icy cold depths of space. I think it best to ease Sam's fears of the unknown and arm ourselves against the planetary rodents."

If Eliot were programmed to laugh he would have belly laughed.

"You're one to talk! Let's shine a light into the darkness and run like a girl into the ship, because it got all quiet."

"You were right there with me Sam, don't deny it."

"I was being pushed along by the biggest sissy on the ship. I had no choice but to get in."

They laughed, then mumbled "chicken" under their breath, only to laugh at themselves again.

"Since you're so into the cameras and finding a trespasser, I'll get a few hours of sleep."

"Works for me Grant. If I see anything significant, I'll

let you know."

"Significant being the key word, Sam. Significant! Don't wake me for a rodent unless he's 30 feet tall, covered in scales, and about to destroy the ship."

"Gotcha! Thirty foot tall rodent with scales, eating the ship, wake Grant, got it."

With a smile and a chuckle Grant headed off to get some much needed sleep. Meanwhile, Sam returned his focus to the cameras and turned on some music to view by. He was intent on capturing a glimpse of whatever was lurking in the dark.

Helium Fall

Chapter Two

Grant made his way down the hallway and entered his cabin. It was large and luxurious for a cabin on a research vessel. The room was white with grey accents and some splashes of bright colors to make it interesting. There were a couple leather chairs, a table in one corner, and the head was in another corner. It would have looked institutional, luckily there were pictures hanging on the walls. One picture was his favorite. It was the rise of Earth's full moon, over a body of shimmering water with bright oranges and yellows, and a dark back drop of the mountains on each side. He believed it was taken somewhere in the mountains of southern Missouri, of all places. Its beauty reminded him of the life he left behind a short time ago. Situated across from his bunk was his desk. It was littered with charts, drawings, and various other research items he was using since they left the spaceport at New Liberty.

The crash scattered things across the room despite the gyro keeping the desk level. The sudden impact had not given it time to properly adjust. Grant was the captain of the ship and it was a hard won battle to get there on his own. His education was thorough and he had excelled in all his classes, but at the expense of his social life. He dated but nothing ever become of them. He was married to his career before it ever started, and knew someday he would travel through space seeking new planets, and new life. A love interest left behind would nag at him, and make him second guess his decision to explore new worlds. It was his, and Sam's, dream since they were kids. Grant absentmindedly leafed through the papers on his desk with little enthusiasm, then rose, and promptly fell face first into his bunk. The day had been a long and stressful, filled with mishaps, an explosion, a crash, and a mystery guest Sam probably conjured in his own mind.

Grant drifted off to sleep, visions of Sam running, and screaming as he was chased by a T-Rex. He chuckled and fell into a deep, but troubled sleep. What if something was out there, and what if it was big enough to destroy the ship. It could possibly be small enough to enter the ship undetected, attached to their clothing, or dart in the door when they weren't looking.

Grant tossed and turned, his mind drifted to a much more serene thought. What if the life forms on this planet were intelligent? What if the life forms were intelligent, and thoughtful? What if the life forms were intelligent, thoughtful, and humanoid? His imagination was going wild. If there were humanoid life forms on this planet, what would they look like? What if there were no men on this planet and the women viewed him and Sam as gods? He woke and realized he had been around Sam too long. He was visualizing one of Sam's typical, nightly dreams, he shook his head in disgust. He drifted back to a peaceful, restful sleep.

Meanwhile, Sam was wide awake scanning the monitors for movement, trying desperately to find something, anything, moving. Sam, having attention deficit disorder, was easily distracted when Eliot reminded him he had not eaten his evening meal, and nutrition was of the utmost importance. Sam obliged and headed off to the galley to get himself a bite to eat, leaving the cameras unattended. Sam loved the galley, it was one of his favorite places on the ship, although it was nothing compared to the galley on the Ebony Belle. Sam decided on a chocolate, peanut butter and bananas protein drink. If he was going to stay up he needed to be alert and well fueled. He was gone for fifteen minutes, and upon returning to the bridge, he again swore he saw movement in one of the monitors. He hadn't been quick enough to get a good view. Drink in hand, eyes peeled on the monitors, Sam settled in for the long haul.

It was coming up on 4 am and Sam had not seen any other movement. He was a little deflated nothing had had the guts to walk within the camera view, or within range of the gun turrets mounted on the top of the shuttle. He was exhausted, his eyes were getting heavier, and heavier. The protein drink had worn off and he knew Grant would soon be up to relieve him, but it couldn't come quick enough. With his focus on the monitors, and the protective screens closed, Sam had no real idea what the planet looked like at night. Except for the brief moment just before he and Grant quickly entered the shuttle afraid for their lives, but it was just a glimpse. Sam waited for Grant to relieve him before he opened the screens, and got a look at the planet at night. Eliot was tracking small life forms, and an occasional medium dog sized creature looking much like a dog, but had six legs, and a small head. Nothing posed a threat to the Varizone.

Sam calculated the tilt of the shuttle, what it would take to bring it to level, and make life aboard much easier for all. With the shuttle askew the survey bots could not exit, and perform their tasks of collecting samples, and surveying the surroundings as planned. He was sure Grant overlooked the fact the exterior lab doors were buried two feet into the surface of the planet. The landing gear buckled during the crash making it impossible to right the shuttle without some serious assistance. He scanned the composition of the surrounding trees finding them extremely sturdy, and capable of supporting a portion of the shuttle's weight, making it possible to repair the landing gear. He determined a rock melting torch in the lab could be used to bring down a few trees. They could fashion a hoist, or lever of sorts, to lift the sagging corner, and make the needed repairs. It was late and his eyes were getting heavy.

He soon nodded off, and drifted into short, but intense dreams. There was a girl, of course, but she was different. She was covered in black clothing, with a sword neatly tucked into her belt. She carried a bow, and a quiver of arrows. It was so surreal. He had never seen anyone like her, or anything like her weapons, and then the dream faded. Again, he drifted into a dream vignette and found himself face to face with a small child, who's piercing dark eyes made him aware he was dreaming, and he woke with a start. Just in time to see movement on one of the monitors.

"Damn it! I know you're out there and I am going to catch you, you little bastard!" Sam was ticked off he had dozed, and missed their intruder yet again. The images in the dreams were haunting. The woman in black, and the child with the dark eyes, really made an impact on him. His fear of being eaten now became a fear for the woman, and what he guessed, was her child. He shook his head, rolled his shoulders wildly, and let out a big burst of air trying to clear the images from his mind. It would be his turn to sleep in ten minutes, and he couldn't wait to see what became of his dreams. Would they pan out into longer, more detailed scenes, or would they become nightmares of people getting eaten by monsters. Being a biologist you would think he had more of a backbone, and an inquisitive nature towards the fauna of the new world.

He drifted into the ether once again, and was soon startled awake by Grant who came to replace him.

"Sam, there's movement in monitor two again, hurry, hurry, hurry!" Sam bolted upright staring into the monitors trying to locate camera two.

Grant laughed with great delight. Once again he scared the crap out of Sam, with minimal effort.

Sam was not amused and was too tired to argue, and he decided to let it go, much to Grant's surprise. "Let's open the shields and see what's out there."

"Good idea, but aren't you afraid of the dark?" Grant took great joy in teasing Sam, and Sam knew it was all in good fun, always had been.

"Eliot, are you recording this? I mean the opening of the view shields, not the ribbing I'm giving Sam."

"Yes, I am as always, recording everything." Grant and Sam looked at each other with a bit of surprise.

Had Eliot let slip his little secret or was it just his programming? Either way it made them pause and think for a moment about what Eliot may have recorded over the weeks they were in the Ebony Belle. Was he gathering information to send back to headquarters, was he doing what he was programmed to do, or were they being watched? With a slight hesitation they returned to looking out the view screen, at a dark sky full of stars, moons, and probably a planet or two. The view was so different than the view from Earth. The lights from Earth's ever growing cities had long ago blotted out all, but the brightest of stars. Grant looked in amazement at the twinkling array of stars, and the numbers were mind boggling.

Sam must have been having the same moment, but from a different perspective, "Job security, that's what it is, job security."

"One day at a time Sam. Remember, we crash landed, we have limited resources to repair the shuttle, and we need to get back to the Ebony Belle."

"On that note, I'll be heading to bed. Did I tell you about the dream I had while I dozed off for a minute? Never mind, I know I didn't, but here it is. I dreamt of a woman...."

"Let me stop you right there Sam. All your dreams are of women, and this reeks of yet another escapade I have no interest in."

"This was different Grant, no nakedness, no sex, and no talking, just her standing there in all black, carrying a sword, and a bow with a quiver of arrows. She had a kid with her and they got really close. Close enough I could see the shimmer in their eyes. The color was like black mercury, and piercing, like they could see right through me. It gave me the willies, and I woke up."

"You never fail to amaze me Sam. You fall asleep on your watch, and dream of a woman with her kid. Then have the balls to tell me about it like it happens all the time. You're not making me feel very secure Sam!" Grant knew Sam slept on watch, and he had done it several times as well. Being the ship's captain he felt it was his duty to give him pause for thought. Especially after Eliot had given up his secret of recording everything.

Sam was about to defend himself, but Grant cut him off. "Go to bed Sam, and dream all you want of women, and their kids. I'll see you in a few hours."

"Thanks my friend, see you in a few." The angled floors made walking difficult. Sam shuffled down the hallway to his cabin, and like Grant, fell face first into his bunk. With the shuttle not level it was hard to move around. The beds, desks, and chairs were all attached to a swivel of sorts and remained fairly level no matter what direction the shuttle was leaning. It was disorienting, but Sam was exhausted and at the moment, didn't care about anything.

He adjusted and quickly drifted off to sleep. The woman in his earlier dream appeared again, this time he could make out more detail. She wore a leather tunic made of hide from some yet to be determined creature. It looked like it was made of scales, and didn't have much of a shine at all. The britches were the same material as the tunic, and went to mid-calf, showing her muscular legs. The clothing fit so well he could make out every curve, and ripple. Her skin was deeply tan, but it could just be the night, and no lights to show its true color. Her long black hair had an iridescent shimmer to it, it was beautiful.

Suddenly, the eyes were once again right in front of him, staring directly into his. The gaze was piercing, searching, knowing. Sam knew he was having a lucid dream. He was aware he was dreaming, and from past experience, he knew he could manipulate the dream how he wanted. He asked the child with the big eyes to back off, and it did. What happened next threw Sam's mind into a whirl. The figure the eyes were attached to quickly backed away, with a completely puzzled look on its smallish, human looking face. It moved its head from side to side. Sam was shocked when he realized the eyes belonged to the woman in leather. It was like she was right there in the room with him, watching him sleep. She quickly darted away leaving Sam's mind to wonder in complete disbelief. He knew he was still dreaming, and wanted to go tell Grant what had happened, but his body was not as responsive as the woman's was. It was still sleep paralyzed, and no movement was to be had until his mind, and body were good and ready. Sam drifted back to the deep sleep stage and dreamt no more.

Meanwhile Grant was on the bridge planning out the day's activities, with the help of Eliot. "How are we going to right the shuttle with the stuff we have? The rover is still strapped down in the bay and the door cannot be opened until the shuttle is level. Not to mention, the soil and debris we're going to have to remove from every crease and crevice. It could take days, or even weeks to make it happen."

Eliot said, "A focused stream from the rock melting torch will perform like a saw, easily cutting down nearby trees. They can be used as a fulcrum and lever, in a ratcheting sequence. Each time it raises a few feet, another support is added, increasing the height of the fulcrum, and the supports."

"Eliot, you are a genius."

"No, I am an EL-10-T."

"Whatever, you have a great plan if we can make it work."

"The idea was Sam's, we discussed it while you were sleeping. I will give you the dimensions when you're ready."

"Hold off until Sam can hear them too. He's the mechanic and chief thingy builder. I just make sure he makes things happen. What is the distance to the mountains to our south?"

"Fifteen miles."

Just then in his peripheral vision Grant caught movement in one of the monitors. He was as intent as Sam was earlier. He thought he saw a foot, a small, human like foot. It couldn't be, he began to think his mind was playing tricks on him, or possibly the oxygen in the shuttle was adjusted too thin. He kept his eyes glued to the screens and hoped to see the movement again.

Grant was wide awake now and ready to go. "Eliot can you scan the area closest to the ship? See if anything slipped by while we were talking. I swear I saw something, and I'm starting to see why Sam was so adamant."

"The scan did not show any life forms large enough to be detected by the sensors."

"Maybe we can turn on the exterior lights and force something into view. Wait, hold that thought. I do not want to be a bright beacon of light in this complete world of darkness. If there is anything intelligent out there, it will know exactly where we are, and I'm not quite ready for our location to be known. A better thought, can the cameras be switched to thermal? If so, see if anything out there is hot. "

He was surprised Sam had not thought to switch to other camera views. He was usually the first to think up alternate ideas on how to do things.

After a change of sensors and a quick scan Eliot said, "Seven life-forms are detected at a distance of one-hundred and twenty yards, moving from left to right. A small body of water is near them at the same distance."

"Excellent job Eliot, excellent. Did they appear to be bi-pedal in nature or quadrupeds?"

"A mixture of both."

Grant was surprised, "What? A mix of both? Like a family out walking their dog or something? Today is going to be interesting. I can't wait for Sam to hear the news."

No more movement was detected on the monitors.

Grant was looking forward to the morning sunrise. He left the bridge and went to the galley for a cup of coffee, Earth's finest creation in his opinion. Coffee had all but saved his life going through flight school. The sleep deprivation was bearable because of the copious amounts available for his consumption. A sobering thought came to him while he waited for it to brew. What if we're stranded here so long we run out of coffee? The thought was synonymous with Sam's vision of a T-Rex casually strolling into camp, and eating him whole. He shuddered at the thought, coffee was life. He took a short break, thoroughly enjoying his morning cup of liquid motivation, along with a pastry from the galley fridge.

Sam would soon be awake, itching to see his first sunrise on another planet.

"Eliot, what are the atmospheric readings at this time?"

"The temperature is fifty-two degrees; there is a two mile per hour easterly breeze. The oxygen levels are lower than yesterday, the helium and hydrogen levels, are higher. Now is not the time to ignite the rock torch."

"This planet is so weird, oxygen appears to rise in the evening, and the helium falls. Helium fall, I like how it sounds. Keep me posted when the levels are less volatile so we can right this tin can and not blow ourselves up by igniting the helium."

"You are aware helium in non-flammable. A hydrogen and oxygen combination is combustible and dangerous."

"What? Helium isn't flammable?"

"No, it is a noble gas and is non-flammable."

"Learn something new every day. I'm still going to call it Helium Fall. Were any of the survey bots damaged in the crash?"

"No, all were securely fastened into the bays and remain undamaged, and functional."

"Good news. Once we have the shuttle righted I want to get them out and let them do their thing. I think Sam and I will go for a hike, and see what we can find. We do have small arms on this ship, don't we?"

"Yes, in the armory."

Grant knew there were small arms in the armory; he was making conversation with Eliot to pass time. "Make note of any large objects, bodies of water, habitations, civilizations, or anything else of interest."

"There is a cave system three miles south."

"We will definitely look into the cave system! How large is it?"

"It is ten miles long and angles south-east towards the mountains. I cannot detect farther. The static haze is causing my sensors to operate outside of their normal range. I can only detect the mountains due to their size."

"We need to find the source of what is generating the haze, as quickly as possible, it's hindering our progress. It can't be a natural phenomenon, it has to be generated by something and created by something with considerable intelligence. We've never heard of such technologies, we've never even thought of creating such a thing back on Earth. It's a brilliant idea if you want to go undetected. Our radar didn't even detect it. What an idea, make it small enough to carry and you could become invisible to radar, and possibly even cameras."

The thought brought Grant upright in his chair, and froze him in thought. What if there were beings walking around the camp all night undetected by the radar, and the cameras. It was a scary thought, and one he almost regretted entertaining. It was going to have to be looked into, and a way figured out to detect the haze, and whatever may be hiding behind it. Better yet, a way needed to be figured out to capture the sneaky little bastards, if there really were any.

Chapter Three

It was time for Sam to surface, and Grant was more than ready to share his thoughts with him. Sam entered the bridge with a huge yawn, and a good stretch, mumbling something about a crazy night's sleep, and the woman of his dreams.

Grant pounced on him with his new thoughts, and began with the foot he saw on the camera.

"Whoa there big fella, I haven't had coffee, breakfast, or a good shower. You're going to have to wait a few minutes before you attack me with…wait, you saw a foot?" Sam was fully awake now, his curiosity was piqued, he had to hear more. "Go on then, tell me what happened."

Grant told him about what he thought was a foot, it was so fast he wasn't sure, and he thought possibly his mind was playing a trick on him. He watched and waited for a good portion of the early morning, and nothing else appeared. "I had an epiphany this morning while I was talking with Eliot. You know how Eliot told us the haze was a sort of static, and made the planet invisible to our sensors?"

Sam nodded, "Yes, I do remember him saying something." He wasn't really sure what he had heard, it was still early, and he needed coffee.

Grant continued, "What if the static haze could be generated by something, pocket size?" He sat in silence waiting for the idea to resonate in Sam's sleep addled mind. He closely watched Sam's face waiting for full realization to hit him.

He was sadly disappointed when Sam looked at him and asked, "What are you talking about? The haze, pocket sized? You're going to have to give me more information before I can make any kind of a coherent comment."

"Sam, what if, whatever was generating the haze could be made into a pocket sized, mobile device? It would generate a much smaller, personal haze."

Sam stared at Grant in obvious thought, one eyebrow slowly raised and then the other. Sam's mouth dropped open when full realization hit him square between the eyes, much to Grant's delight. He liked Sam's expressions, especially when he was having a moment of discovery and his mind went wild with ideas.

"So what you're saying is, you and Eliot, had a conversation while I was sleeping and it led you to the idea we have possibly been seeing someone out there, but they have been cloaked with a pocket sized haze generator?"

"Yep, that's what I'm saying."

"Holy crap Grant, if it's true they could have been right next to us and we would have had no idea. Now I'm freaked out."

"Maybe it's why we keep thinking we're seeing something, and nothing is there. We are only catching a glimpse of a foot, arm, or whatever may have slipped out of the haze."

Sam's mind went wild with ideas, and his sense of security was again challenged.

"Time to get moving Sam, we need to get this day going so we can get the shuttle righted, and get the survey bots out so they can do their thing."

"Gotta get me some coffee, shower, and change into my work clothes."

"Skip the shower Sam and wear what you've got on.

Bring some coffee with you. Let's go!"

"You're the boss, right behind you!"

"Eliot says you have an idea on how to right the shuttle. He plotted dimensions for us and will give us specifics.

"Yep, we can use the rock torch to cut down some trees, and use them as a fulcrum and lever. When the shuttle rises we add another log under it to keep it in position, and then raise it from there adding another log, and so on."

"Great idea, but how are we going to cut down flammable trees with a rock melting torch? The two do not mix well. We'll have quite the bonfire though."

"Eliot suggested we narrow the flow of the torch, and basically slice the trees down. Like a hot knife through butter."

"Eliot said like a hot knife through butter!"

With a look of consternation Grant replied, "No Sam, I added it on my own. Get the damn torch; I'll scout out some decent trees to suit our purpose."

Sam headed off to get the torch, and Grant headed to the tree line to find trees for the job. Grant stopped as he exited the shuttle. There they were, small footprints everywhere. Grant thought they may have had visitors in the night, and now he had confirmation. They must be using a device, much like he imagined, avoiding detection. Grant continued to the tree line, and thought he saw movement out of the corner of his eye. He froze in his tracks, and looked intently at where he saw the movement. Much to his surprise, he noted a slight shimmer, subtly different from the shimmer created by the haze. He kept walking towards the tree line, pretending not to have seen anything. He knew Sam would be along shortly, and with the time they spent outside the day before, surmised whatever was hiding in the haze was just observing them. If they were going to attack, they would.

Grant spotted six good trees and marked them so Sam would know what to cut. Grant ventured a short distance to explore some of the plant life. He noted in his recorder despite the high helium and hydrogen levels the plants thrived in the oxygen rich environment. The opposite of how plant life works on Earth. Hydrogen level, he had to check the hydrogen level before Sam fired up the rock torch. He ran back to where he had marked the trees.

Sam had arrived and was in the process of firing up the torch to begin cutting. "SAM! SAM!" Do not light the rock torch! We have to check the hydrogen levels. We could blow this whole place sky high if the levels are too high."

"Whew, good call Grant, I hadn't even thought about the levels."

"I only thought about it because Eliot brought it up last night when we were talking."

"Glad you caught me!"

With a touch to his collar Grant asked, "Eliot, what are the hydrogen levels? Can we fire up the torch without blowing the place up?"

"Yes, the levels are safe."

Sam fired up the torch and began to cut. It only took a few minutes using the rock torch to cut the trees needed for their little project.

"Good job Sam, good job thinking to bring a maintenance bot with you too. It can carry the trees where we need them. How did you get it out of the bay, we can't open the doors yet?"

"The bots float and move easily. I maneuvered it to the elevator, it barely fit, and brought it and the torch out through the hatch. I didn't want to carry it all the way over here."

"I am amazed at the level of genius lazy can produce."

Sam feigned a look of shock, "Lazy? I prefer creative or intelligent."

Grant chuckled to himself, and let it go.

The morning sunrise was beautiful. The sky was a deep purple, fading to a bright blue, then the shimmery light blue opal it was now.

"The sunrise was amazing, wasn't it Grant?"

"It sure was, there must be potassium chloride in gas form, it causes a purple flame when burned. The blues came from the amount of helium in the atmosphere."

Sam enjoyed the moment, "Whatever, it was amazing! I'd like to be around to see a few more. But not too many more, this place gives me the creeps."

"This place is beautiful Sam. The trees are bright orange, neon yellow, deep green, and a rich wine color. The underbrush is deep green, full, and lush. The flowering plants give off intense aromas like we've never smelled before. It's actually quite beautiful and inviting."

"Well, so far anyways." T-Rex and his buddies still lurked in back of Sam's mind.

"You got those trees in place? We need to get this thing back to level. The survey bots need out so they can do their job."

"On it boss, the maintenance bot is loading the last of the smaller logs into the cradle of the counter balance. I hope the shuttle doesn't weigh too much."

With the cradle now loaded, Sam instructed the bot to slowly pull down on the end of the lever log. The bot obeyed and the shuttle slowly began to rise, their plan was working. With several more adjustments and a lot more logs the shuttle would be where they wanted it.

They had miscalculated the number of posts they needed to keep it supported.

"Sam, we need four more logs to keep this thing level. Grab the bot and cut some more logs."

Sam headed off with the bot and began cutting several more pieces off the tree they felled earlier. On his second cut, without a doubt, he saw movement. Sam played it cool and continued cutting. Two more to go and he could high tail it back to the shuttle. As he finished his last cut, a figure stepped out from behind a tree. It was there only a brief moment, but Sam saw it, and it saw him.

Sam hollered to Grant, "GRANT! We are not alone!" As the bot gathered the remaining logs Sam kept a vigilant eye on the tree where the figure had been. He returned to the shuttle, and quickly went inside to the armory. He grabbed a small fire arm, and headed back outside.

The hunt was about to begin, but Grant saw him as he exited the shuttle. "What do you think you're doing?"

"I'm going on a little hunting trip!"

"Uh, no you're not. What did you see?"

"Grant, I saw a small figure step out from behind a tree. It looked me straight in the eyes, and I looked straight in its eyes, too. There is no doubt we both know the other was there. I'm going to hunt it down and make it talk, haze device or not."

"Sam, you'll do no such thing. We do not know if

they shot down the shuttle. They haven't attacked us, and most likely have had many opportunities to capture us, take us out, or destroy the shuttle. Our priority is getting the shuttle repaired so the bots can survey the planet. Then, we can address the issue of our visitors. Put the gun back in the armory, and let's finish this so we can assess the damage, and figure out what we need to make the repairs, deal?"

"Deal, but I'm keeping my eyes peeled. If I see anyone else, I'm done. WTF! Are those foot prints? Grant, there are footprints, everywhere. Did you know there were foot prints everywhere?"

Grant tried his best to remain calm, "Sam, they're small foot prints, and yes, I knew they were there. I saw them this morning, but didn't want, or need you freaking out. You act like this is your first mission and haven't had any training about meeting new life."

"It is my first mission, and I never thought I'd really be meeting anyone out here. I mean, I hoped I would, but not on the first planet I landed on."

"Well, we didn't really land did we? Get this finished and we can make a plan for tomorrow, and how we're going to deal with this situation."

Sam hurriedly set about getting the last logs in place. With the help of Grant and the bot it was accomplished in short order. He did a quick evaluation and determined one of the landing supports had crumpled and would have to be replaced, or somehow repaired. All in all it didn't appear to be in bad shape. The landing support, the exterior lab bay doors, and a couple of sensors were damaged in the crash. The shuttle was covered in dirt, debris, and hopefully a little cleaning would not reveal other issues. The first item up for repair was the bay doors. After an hour of digging, scraping and brushing away soil and chunks of tree, Sam was able to get the bay doors moving. Not perfectly, but functional.

Grant and Sam released the survey bots from their restraints and sent them on their merry way to begin their duties of figuring out what the planet was made of, and mapping the locations of promising finds. They programmed the bots to first survey their surrounding area and search for intelligent life.

"Sam, let's get some lunch then figure out what we need to do about our visitors."

"Yes, finally! You know I didn't get any breakfast, hell the rest of my coffee is still sitting out there on a log."

"Buck up Sam, we're going to discover intelligent life in the next few days and our lives will never be the same."

"That's what I'm afraid of Grant. I'd really like to see home again. You know, see my family, go to Landing's in New Liberty, and check out some hotties on the beach. Life as we knew it wasn't so bad."

"Sam, life as we knew it was alright but it could be great. We discover life, make it home, and we're heroes! Heroes, Sam. Let it sink in a bit."

They headed to the galley, Sam loved the galley, it was his happy place. He decided to have pasta Diavolo, garlic bread, and a nice glass of yet to be named, deep red wine.

Grant opted for an Italian sub with roasted yellow and red peppers, provolone cheese, and a touch of Italian dressing, sprinkled with parmesan cheese. A bag chips would complete the meal. For all their similarities they were totally different. It was their tradition to compare their meal choices and appreciate their differences.

"Ok Grant, we need to talk about the footprints, and what I saw in the woods. Tell me what you know, what you think, and how the hell we're going to deal with it. All kidding aside, I'm a little concerned about our current situation."

"I saw the footprints this morning as we left the shuttle, I saw movement when I was at the tree line, and noticed there was a shimmer from behind a tree, different from the shimmer created by the haze. I also realized if we had crashed early in the morning or late at night we could have blown this place to high heaven. The fire from the jets would have ignited the hydrogen. I also realized we have been very lucky to this point, and you really are a big chicken, all kidding aside."

"Seriously, you saw all of this and thought these things and you didn't tell me. What the heck Grant?"

"I didn't tell you because I didn't think we were in any real danger."

"Really Grant, we were shot out of the sky by something or someone we didn't see, we have been seeing movement, and suspect someone or something has watched us since we crashed. Now we know all of the above is true. You want me to be calm and rational? I can, as soon as you tell me what we're going to do, everything is going to be fine, we will get off this planet, and return safely home. Can you? I didn't think so."

Grant realized he had made a fundamental mistake by not telling Sam what he discovered, and he should have let Sam know everything he and Eliot had discussed. Now he had to regain Sam's trust and get him grounded, while solving their problems, and making sure they stayed alive.

"Sam please forgive me, I know I was wrong and I

should have told you what I saw this morning. I should have told you we aren't alone."

"We have been friends for a long time Grant and you should know I may not like how things are going, but I still have your back, and I know you were just trying to protect me. But from now on, please have enough faith in me to tell me what you know. I can and will handle it better if I know we're on the same page."

"I'm sorry Sam, open and honest from now on."

"So how are we going to handle the visitor situation?"

"Well, I've given it a little thought Sam, we need to try and make friends with whatever or whoever is out there."

"I say we trap one of them and make them talk."

"What would they say to us Sam? They most likely do not speak English, or anything similar."

"Then what do you suggest we do to make friends with them? Sing, dance, or offer them a bottle of wine?"

The sarcasm was apparent and Grant knew Sam had a point. "What do you say we offer them something edible, from Earth? Something we eat would hopefully be tasty for them and show we're not the enemy."

"I agree, we need to make who, or whatever it is, our ally, not our enemy."

Chapter Four

Grant and Sam set about trying to decide what would be the best food to leave for their visitors. Sam thought carrots or some lettuce.

"They're not rabbits Sam, keep thinking." The best Grant could come up with was bacon and eggs.

"OMG, Grant! Let's give them heart failure before we even meet them." They laughed and simultaneously said, "Chocolate!"

Sam said, "Everyone likes chocolate and they should be no exception. For lack of a better term the person I saw was petite and almost teen sized."

Grant agreed what he saw was small in stature and both agreed they shouldn't underestimate them. So, chocolate was gathered in the form of a bar of chocolate, a chocolate pie, and a chocolate covered banana.

"Do you think this is over kill? Where are we going to put it?"

"We'll set out a small table and leave it just a few yards from the hatch where I saw the most footprints this morning."

"Good call Grant, I'll get the table and meet you outside, better hurry, it will be getting dark soon."

"I'll be right out with the food, Sam." They headed their separate directions and gathered what they needed. The days were much shorter than an Earth day, about 10 hours of sunlight and oddly about 6 hours of darkness.

"Damn these short days," said Grant as he gathered the chocolate for their visitors. I hope they like it or we may possibly start another world's war."

The sunset was amazing. It highlighted the rich

burgundies, deep oranges, and bright yellows of the trees, played against the dark back drop of the mountains. Grant made it out of the hatch and stopped to take in the moment. Sam was already there admiring the sunset and much to Grant's surprise had brought a table cloth and a vase with some local flowers in it.

"Really, I never knew you were such a romantic."

Sam blushed a bit and replied, "In my mind they're children, and the one I saw I thought was a girl. Girls like flowers don't they?"

"Sam, I love your heart my friend, and yes, girls like flowers."

"Starting to lose the light Grant, better leave our treats and head in for the night."

"You know, we might be able to catch them on camera if we place the table over here." Grant motioned Sam about five feet to his left in perfect view of the hatch camera.

"I'm excited and concerned, Grant. What if the chocolate is poison to them? What if they see this as an act of aggression, or they feel like it's a trap and nothing ever moves, and we don't catch them on camera?"

"Simmer down, Sam. Time will tell and we can adjust to whatever happens. I say we leave this stuff here and go get some dinner."

"Uh, Grant. It's only about 4 in the afternoon. I feel like we just had lunch. These short days are wreaking havoc on my systems. Eventually we're going to be sleeping during the day and trying to work at night. Not a good combination on this rock. The gas combination keeps us from getting things done as much as the lack of daylight does."

"I know, we need to figure out something to enable

us to work later in the day and longer hours. I don't like using the bio suits unless it's an emergency. Once the bots get back with their first load of samples and their initial data, we are going to be pretty damn busy. Let's get the lab prepped so we're ready when they do get here."

The bots were programmed to explore the surrounding area for three days, or until their holds or recorders we full. They would then return to the shuttle to have their findings evaluated and processed. Sam, being the geologist, would sort, classify, and test the rock and mineral samples. Grant being the biologist would sample the plant and animal life as well as the micro life they found. Since the bots were exploring the neighborhood closest to the ship Grant figured they'd be back well before three days were up.

They readied the equipment and laid out the necessary tools, books, and chemicals they would need to process the samples. Sam marveled at the organization of everything, how it was so neat, and securely stored for the trip into space. If only he could organize his mind in the same way.

Sam was your typical kid with attention problems and got into lots of trouble at home. His parents never quite understood him and his teachers tried their best to ignore him. He didn't care much either way. He had his own beat and did things how he thought they should be done.

The world was his playground and boundaries were not his style. He wasn't the tallest or brightest, but held his own with his quick wit and willingness to 'go there' if necessary. He had a really big heart and a soft spot for kids. His mind wandered as he got things ready for the coming days.

All the necessary equipment was unpacked and the supplies arranged to facilitate a quick and thorough examination of the specimens. Sam thought of home and when he would return. Things would be different when he returned. He would be gone for a minimum of five years or the rest of his life if things went bad. He remembered he still had to make repairs to a forward thruster and repair the camouflage generator. The camo gen, how could he have forgotten, they could generate their own camouflage?

"Grant, are we stupid or what?"

"Or what, if you're really asking, but I'll bite. What's on your mind?"

"We can generate our own camouflage! It was installed just before we left New Liberty. Unfortunately it was damaged in the crash. With everything going on I totally forgot about it, until just a second ago. I was thinking about the forward thruster and a couple of small things still in need repair, and it came to me like a shovel to the face, camo gen!"

"I vaguely remember the conversation with the tech just as we were about to board the Ebony Belle. How long will it take to get it functional?"

"Given the short days it will take two days to get it working right."

"Get with Eliot and see if there might be a shortcut. We need to appear to disappear. It might draw them out if they think we've left."

"Now you're thinking Grant! They'll think we've left and uncloak, revealing who they really are, got 'em!"

"Well, until one of them sees us, our bots, or absentmindedly runs into the shuttle when they're out for a stroll."

"Good point Grant. We need to get the camo gen working and then relocate the shuttle a mile or two away from here. They won't be able to see it lift off or land."

"Now you're thinking Sam."

They were at it for a couple hours and Grant again offered to have dinner. Sam willingly accepted his invitation this time around. Everything was in its place and Sam's mind was running wild with ideas about the camo gen and moving the shuttle. They needed the bots to return from their initial exploration and check out their mappings to see where a good place to relocate might be. Over the meal they discussed Sam's ideas and Grant agreed they needed to move, soon. They formulated their plan for the morning, each knowing what needed to be done. The conversation turned to home and their life so far away in the distance. It was difficult to think about how far they had traveled, how much they had accomplished, and how much still needed to be done. Each new planet would take a minimum of three months to map out the terrain, analyze minerals, determine resource availability, and name and classify the flora and fauna. Classify basically meaning dangerous or not dangerous. Once the bots completed their initial analysis they would sojourn further and further away from the shuttle. During the first few weeks they would retrieve the bots with the rover and bring them back with their samples and data. Once they were too far away to reasonably retrieve with the rover, the shuttle would be moved to pick them up, and they would be re-homed to the new base location. First on Sam's list was to get the camo gen working. He knew it was a simple physical fix, but the wiring was another story. He hoped the specs were uploaded to Eliot before they took off.

"Sam, you're awful quiet!" Grant's voice penetrated his thoughts quickly and deeply. Sam was startled by its suddenness and jolted back to reality.

"Jesus, Grant, you could give a guy a heart attack hollering at him."

"I didn't holler Sam, you were lost in thought. You haven't eaten but a few bites of Sea Bass or the seasoned rice."

"I know, I was totally lost in thought about what I need to do tomorrow. Gotta have my priorities in order. This being our first mission I hope they don't grade us too harshly."

Grant chuckled and added, "If they do we'll both be looking for work when we return. I've crashed the shuttle, you were seeing things, and we haven't been under cover from day one. Going to have to get moving on protocol for sure."

The conversation continued as evening quickly slipped into night. Sam finished his meal and headed to the bridge to see if they had any visitors.

"Have we any takers Sam?" Not yet, nothing has moved and the monitors are quiet. Looks like we wasted a good pie and some really good chocolate."

"Hang in there Sam. I say tonight we both get some rest and see what the morning brings. We haven't been attacked, and not one scale of a T-Rex has been spotted."

"Funny, Grant, very funny! You've got jokes!"

"I've got 'em all day long buddy."

After a quick glance at the monitors, Sam headed back to the galley and strangely, craved a piece of chocolate pie. "Let's get some sleep and hit it hard tomorrow."

"Agreed! Catch you in the AM." They headed to their

cabins for a much needed shower and a good night's sleep.

Sam would most likely opt to pop in a movie and fall fast asleep in the first five minutes. Grant was the reader of the two and looked forward to a good book in the evening.

The day was an adventure. Grant's mind raced, sorting through everything and what needed to happen. His thoughts drifted to the table of food sitting outside, and whether or not their visitors would venture close enough to get a whiff of the pie or the sweet aroma of the banana. Did they have fruit and vegetables? What was their diet? Did they drink water, or milk, or some other form of beverage? Did they have their own version of alcohol? Maybe they should have left some out for them. He dismissed the idea knowing getting the natives drunk would not be a good idea so early on in their ventures. He began reading and quickly succumbed to the rigors of the day. He was exhausted even though the higher oxygen levels made him feel like a million bucks. His wounds from the crash had healed quickly; he hadn't felt this good in years. However, there was something else in the air draining his energy pretty quickly. Maybe the haze had something to do with it. He'd have to remember to give it consideration tomorrow. Until then he was quietly slipping deeper into sleep, and entering the world of dreams.

His dreams began almost immediately. He was standing at the hatch, mouth agape at something in front to him. The total disbelief on his face was apparent, and then a smile came across it just as quickly. Sam bounded out of the shuttle then froze in his tracks, eyes as big as they had ever been. They laughed in unison.

The dream quickly faded to smoke and fire. He was running towards a large rock and the sky was alive with humming as objects hurtling past him crashing into the rocks and the trees nearby. He felt his heart racing, and then there was pain. He felt pain in his dream and saw rivulets of blood running down his arm and one of his legs. His clothing was torn, he was disoriented. He felt himself passing out. Everything began to shimmer as a shadow appeared above him. A beautiful face appeared, it was the face of a woman. It was her, the woman he had dreamt of before. She motioned to others as he slipped into unconsciousness. Where was Sam, what was happening, where was he going? Grant woke up in a sweat, breathing heavily.

The dream felt so real. He felt as if he was there. He could feel the warmth of the fire and the stinging in his leg. It rattled him, but he lay back down, and prayed he wouldn't drift back into the dream, but the woman.

Sam had a similar dream but it ended quite differently. The explosions, the fire, and things whizzing past him were all the same, but he didn't pass out. He was helping people carry Grant to a safe place. He began to question who they were and where they came from, but his tired body won out and he slept, dreamless.

Chapter Five

Their morning routine went the same as always. Grant was making coffee, planning the day.

Sam was slugging down the hall in a zombie-like march to consume as much coffee as he thought his tired body would allow. He would gladly stay up all night and sleep all day.

Grant, the early bird, preferred the morning. "Good night sleep, Sam?" There was a spring in his voice.

Sam muttered, "Shh... not enough coffee, still can't think, eyes are only half functional."

Grant laughed and said, "Sam it's a miracle to see you up at this hour of the morning must have had a bad dream.

"Actually, it was a very weird dream, you were in it."

Grant looked surprised and asked what it was about.

"You were all shot up and bleeding and our visitors found you, then they found me, and we carried you to their village for some medical attention. It was all very surreal. There was a shimmer, and there she was, what a beauty."

"A beauty?" Grant was surprised at the word and shared his dream with Sam, "The beauty saved me, with your help. I passed out in the dream and didn't know where they were taking me. I wondered where you were and like you said, there was a shimmer and then there she was, a beauty."

"Coffee or not, she's mine big boy, I saw her first."

"Well I saw her best. She was almost nose to nose with me. I win!"

"Damn it, Grant, you always win."

"Story of your life Sam, story of your life. Let's eat some breakfast, down some coffee, and check on the offering we laid out last night."

Sam had forgotten about the offering and was excited to see if there were any takers during the night.

They finished their morning routine and headed to the hatch to see if anything had been sampled. Grant opened the hatch, gazed at the table, and his chin dropped. There before him was a table full of roasted meats, tuberous vegetables, and what he believed were deserts. He couldn't believe his eyes. Was he dreaming again? He smiled as big as possible at the sight. The chocolate must have been a complete success to warrant such a display of kindness.

Sam pushed his way past the stunned Grant and stopped dead in his tracks. He expected to find food on the ground and half eaten pieces of chocolate everywhere. He was dumbfounded it was all gone, and this smorgasbord was neatly in its place. To top it off, there were different flowers in Sam's vase. They slowly turned to one another and burst out laughing with joy and surprise. What a turn of events. From potential killers to the nice neighbors next door.

Sam headed to the table for a sample of the local grub and Grant called out.

"Sam stop. We do not know if they liked the chocolate or not. They could have poisoned the food. Take a couple items into the lab and run a few quick tests."

"Agreed, we can't be too careful. They may be the nice neighbors next door or they could be the serial killer neighbors you don't know about until it's too late. I'll run the tests; you get some pictures before we break down this feast." The morning gasses had dissipated quickly this morning and Grant was beginning to feel the heat. "Better hurry, everything could melt or spoil as hot as it's getting."

Grant took a couple of quick pictures and Sam whisked a couple samples to the lab.

Meanwhile, Grant surveyed the surroundings and noted a slight shimmer by a tree twenty yards away. He pretended not to see it and let his eyes continue their arc across the landscape, but he knew it was there. He bent down towards the food sitting on the table to catch a whiff of its aroma. Everything was still warm, much to his surprise. It must have been brought by whoever was hiding behind the tree.

Several minutes later Sam emerged from the shuttle with a huge grin across his face. "No known poisons and it's cooked to perfection."

"What, you already ate some?"

"Yep, once I knew it wasn't going to kill me I took a bit or two of everything. Hell, it's still warm and the fragrance is well, out of this world."

"Funny, Sam, nice one. I had just leant in to catch a whiff and noticed the heat too. So where do we begin?"

"I'd try the meat looking stuff first, and then the veggies. What an intense flavor. Probably like veggies used to taste on Earth long before everything was modified to be insect, drought, and weed resistant. Now the dessert, it's a bit wonky. I'm not sure if it's one of their fruits or if it's something unclassified. I felt a little silly after the first bite so I stopped. It was like a mini rush, sort of like the first gulp of coffee in the morning, but more intense."

"Good to know! Meat it is. Oh by the way, we're

being watched. Twenty yards ahead, to the right of the big tree. See the shimmer?"

"Grant, it's the same shimmer I saw in my dreams."

"I know Sam, me too. Been there since I came out, noticed it when you went inside."

"I'll bet it's a scout and they're going to go back to report our reactions."

"Well Sam, let's make it some good reactions then, give them a bit of a show. If these guys are friendly then we may need their help getting to the bottom of whatever is shooting off the missiles."

"We need to be a lot friendlier with them before I'm going to do anything with them." Sam was being cautious with what he thought was good reason. "We don't know anything about them except they hide in shimmery stuff and man can they cook."

"All right Sam, grab a piece of the meat, take a bite, and hold it up high, then smile pretty for our watchman. I'll do the same with some of the veggies."

They did as Grant suggested and Sam sort of waved at their watchman in the process. Much to their surprise the watchman uncloaked, smiled, and quickly cloaked again. They were stunned by the turn of events. They had just successfully communicated with an alien life form and it smiled at them.

"Sam let's get this stuff inside and into the galley. I think we have found the nice neighbors. We're going to have to figure out a way to meet them, face to face."

"Maybe we go about our business as planned and they'll uncloak in front of us at the most inopportune time and scare the snot out of us."

"Good idea, Sam, we'll go about our business and get things in order first. Then we can set about meeting them. The landing gear, camo gen, and the thruster are our main concern. We have to be able to move the shuttle to keep up with the bots. In a few days they'll be too far away to retrieve, even with the rover. Never saw anything work so hard in my life. Get with Eliot and see what needs to be done with the camo gen, I'll see what I can do with the thruster."

"Good plan boss! I'm on it." Sam was always ready to work, except in the morning and after dinner. Grant knew Sam would be on it quickly, and it would be done right. He appreciated not having to micro manage. Morning quickly became noon and noon quickly headed into the afternoon. They skipped lunch hoping to get the repairs done by day's end.

"Grant tapped his communicator, "Sam, how are things going?"

"Eliot has solved the problem and we're about twenty minutes away from having the camo gen up and running."

"Excellent news, keep up the good work buddy."

"You got it boss. I'll be up as soon as we're done."

"See you in a few. I'm just about done as well. The outer flange was mangled by a tree, and there were rocks and debris wedged inside the housing. A few more whacks with the mallet and it will be as good as new."

"I've been thinking, Grant, what would you say to a good old outdoor barbeque? We could cook up some steaks, grill some pineapple and veggies of our own, and maybe it will lure them into camp so we can have our little meeting, on our terms."

"Sam, you're a genius, but don't let it go to your head."

"Never boss, you're the man, I'm just the tool!"

Grant let out a hardy laugh at Sam; he really was a tool, but still his best friend. "What a life!"

The afternoon was beginning to wane. Grant let Sam know they had to start cooking. He knew the gas levels would start to rise as the sun began to set.

Sam gathered the grill and utensils. Grant began setting it up as Sam headed back into the shuttle.

Grant noticed a shimmer here and a shimmer there. He knew Sam's idea was truly genius. However, they may be in for more than they bargained for if the numbers kept increasing. Sam bounded out of the shuttle, food in hand, and a smile almost as big as his birthday smile. Sam loved his birthday. It gave him a sense of accomplishment. "Let the party begin!" Sam shouted as he slapped several large steaks onto the grill, along with the veggies, a couple sweet potatoes and large russets. Grant chuckled watching Sam, who had donned an apron and a chef's hat. It was Grant's good fortune Sam also managed to bring along some beverages of the alcoholic variety.

"Might I offer you a beer good sir?"

"Why sure you can my good man, I seem to be unable to refuse such a generous offer." The levity was much needed and they were both in good spirits. If their visitors did show up it was either going to be the first of its kind meeting or the end of life as they knew it. They were both hoping for good relations. They laughed and sang a few songs, at least the parts they could remember, as the food continued to cook. The food was nearly done and it reminded Grant of a backyard cookout when he was a kid. The aroma coming off the meat was mesmerizing.

Grant and Sam downed a few beers and were really

enjoying their little cookout. "I'm going to go grab some plates, eating utensils, and some of our finest cutlery, I'll be back shortly."

Sam nodded and continued to hum and sway along with the smoke. It had such an intoxicating scent, or was it the beer? Just then a small figure appeared five yards away from Sam. He choked on his beer and spit a little out in disbelief. It looked like an Earth boy about fifteen years old, with black hair, and dark shimmering eyes. His skin was tan, smooth, and looked healthy. They stood there looking at one another, neither one moving or blinking. Sam had envisioned Grant being there for their first encounter, but unless he hurried up, it was going to be Sam making first contact, alone. How wrong could this go if it was just him? He shuddered to think what might happen if he opened his mouth and started talking, so he kept it shut and kept staring.

Grant emerged from the shuttle with items in hand and headed to the table to deposit his spoils. He glanced at Sam who was not moving, singing, or anything else and then he saw the boy. Grant was the diplomat of the two. He slowly approached the small figure, just past the grill's edge. He smiled then bowed, extending his right hand in friendship. His movements were slow and deliberate. He did not want to spook their new neighbor. Being a foot and some taller than their visitor, he could have easily done so. The small figure was immediately joined by two others who uncloaked. They had small spears and short swords in their belts.

Grant stood erect and dropped his hand to his side, again not wanting to be intimidating, but also not able to help it. The first figure put his hands in front of the others and took three steps forward, towards Grant. Grant took three steps forward, and stopped. It seemed to be a game or part of a ceremony of sorts. The boy took three more steps, again Grant followed in kind. They were soon close enough to reach out and shake hands. Grant extended his hand, and as expected the boy extended his. Grant firmly, but gently grasped the boy's hand with little other movement. The boy grasped back with surprising strength. Grant smiled and the boy smiled back. He was the one standing behind the tree earlier. Grant recognized his smile and the dark eyes.

Sam, watching in silence, removed his hat and apron and stepped from behind the grill. The other visitors quickly joined the boy and all shook hands in greeting. The small group stood motionless for a brief minute, and then Sam spoke first. "Would you like to try some of our steak and other food?"

There were puzzled looks on their faces and Sam quickly produced a plate with their evening's dinner. He cut a few small pieces off the steak and other items and offered them to their visitors, who gladly sampled Sam's grilled handy work. Their visitors turned to one another, and must have really liked what they tasted.

To Grant and Sam's surprise they were speaking broken English and making gestures Grant thought meant good, and give me more.

Sam gave up his plate and the three devoured the meal in short order. They smiled, shook hands again, and cloaked, then disappeared in a shimmer.

Grant sternly spoke into his communicator, "Eliot, track them. They are most likely headed to their village!"

"It appears they are headed towards the lake."

"Good, we will pay them a visit tomorrow morning, and hopefully they will provide us with breakfast, and possibly some answers."

Sam was jubilant and could not stop smiling. "Grant, we just made contact with alien life forms! Holy crap, I just touched an alien! Gotta go wash my hands, they might have bacteria on them that can kill us." And off he went to wash, not acknowledging Grant's comment about visiting their camp, or about breakfast.

Grant gathered the rest of the food and other items and headed into the shuttle. The grill was turned off and left out to cool. Hopefully the neighbors would not steal it thinking it was left out as a gift for their taking. "Sam, you alright? Sam!"

"Right here Grant. I'm still amazed I, I mean we, were touching aliens, real aliens."

"It's a first for me too, Sam. Going to put this one in my journal for sure. Hopefully it was all caught on camera and we can prove first contact. I'm going to have a quick bite and call it a night. I have some writing to do and I need to think of the best way to proceed. We need to do some serious exploration tomorrow after we have breakfast with our new friends. I hate crashing their morning breakfast uninvited but we have to get moving. We do have a deadline to meet, and we haven't been able to communicate with PSAD since we landed."

"Agreed, we need to get things moving and I almost forgot, we can switch on the camo anytime. The locals have no idea we can blend into the surroundings sort of like they do but only with our shuttle. Why haven't we thought of making a small camo generator for personal use? We're scientists and explorers for god's sake."

"Sam, good night, I will ponder it all. You need to get some sleep too. Today was a scorcher and we have had a lot of excitement. Tomorrow is only going to be worse.

The heat and the atmosphere seem to really take it out of me."

"Me too, I thought I was the only one feeling that way. Good to know. We will need to pack some survival goodies for our trek tomorrow. I'll ponder it. Good night Grant."

"Good night Sam."

They both ate quickly and headed off to their cabins. Their day was eventful and the anticipation of tomorrow's ventures would prove to be taxing as well.

Chapter Six

Their dreams were filled with small people, vivid colors, and unusual moments. The woman crept into both of their dreams again, and both were totally smitten. Why had she not been at the gathering, where had she been? The meeting seemed important to Grant and he thought she would be there. Never the less she wasn't, and he planned to meet her in the morning, if they could find their village. His thoughts drifted back to the survey bots they let loose several days ago. He imagined they would be returning soon and he wondered what was in store for them. Had they found precious metals or gem deposits; possibly a new metal to catapult mechanical advancement into an new age, or even a new energy source they could harness and remove the need for nuclear energy. Hopefully they found a good source of water. He and Sam could use a good swim or at least a cool dip in a shallow pool.

Sam was having similar thoughts and dreams. The woman seemed to gravitate towards Sam in his dreams, and each time she got close, he got a better look. She was beautiful and athletic but slight in stature. He imagined she could read his mind or somehow slip into his subconscious. He hoped to test his theory if he became aware he was dreaming and she was in them. He would attempt to speak to her, and note her reactions.

Sam's mind drifted off to the exploration they planned for tomorrow. How were they going to find the missile base and the village in a single day? Sam had a flash of brilliance. The drone, they could use their drone to fly around and cover lots of ground keeping them safe, and hopefully find the places they needed to find in short order. Sam briefly woke, jotted down his idea, and just as quickly, fell back asleep.

Grant was the first to wake, as always. He prepared his morning coffee and decided he needed some good protein to last him the day. He opted for a protein drink, some eggs, and several pieces of toast with butter. The galley had an endless supply of anything and everything they could imagine, it brought a smile to Grant's face. The real struggle was to decide what to have each meal. It was a good thing he was only deciding for himself. He and Sam liked the same foods, just at different times. It had become a game for them at meal time to see who ate what. Sometime later Sam made his morning appearance, and as usual he was slothful and singularly focused on getting coffee before any interaction with Grant, or anything else. A bomb could go off and Sam would still get coffee before he made any attempt to seek cover or assist in any way. After a short time Sam spoke first, much to Grant's surprise. "I have a plan."

"Okay let's hear it!" Grant was curious what Sam had come up with, but had reservations as to what his plan might consist of.

"I get the girl, you take on the bad guys!" He said it with all the seriousness he could muster at that time of the morning.

Grant burst out laughing and countered, "You take on the bad guys, I'll have breakfast with the Huntress."

"Ooo, the Huntress, I like it! Seems like a fitting name for her. She does remind me of a hunter with her bow, her sword, and the tunic she wears looks light but durable."

"How did you know about the tunic, Sam? I never

mentioned she wore a tunic."

Grant, now fully engaged, looked intently at Sam. "Tell me how you knew, Sam."

"Well Grant, she has been coming to me in my dreams. Each time I get a closer, better look at her. She is slight, but athletic, her tunic is made of something scaly, and it looks tough and protective."

"Sam, we've been dreaming about the same woman." Said Grant with surprise and realization.

"I was going to try and talk with her in my dreams last night, but she didn't show up. In one of my first dreams of her, she was right in front of me, almost nose to nose and I spoke in the dream. I swear she heard me. She jolted with a startled look on her face, and then disappeared."

"We have to find their village, Sam. Our number one goal for the day, find their village."

"Oh and my real plan was to use the drone to do an aerial search of the area. Maybe we can find both the village and the missile base this morning. You know, take a drive to the village, have some breakfast and talk them into storming the bad guy's camp with us."

"Sam, that's an amazing idea!"

"Thanks, Grant!"

"Let's finish our morning routine while the gasses burn off. You get the drone ready for flight and I'll get the provisions ready for whatever trip we'll be making today."

"I'll get right on it, Grant." The pace picked up and the gasses began to dissipate in a hurry.

"It's going to be a hot one, Sam. Better dress accordingly."

"Gotcha, shorts, Hawaiian shirt, and sandals. Should I

bring sunscreen and an umbrella, too?" With no reply from Grant, Sam continued getting the drone flight ready.

Camera installed and fully charged, Sam made his way out of the lab bay into the morning light. "Grant, you weren't kidding. This is going to be a scorcher."

"I'm ready in here, Sam. Let's get the drone in the air and see what we can find."

"I've got it tapped into the video feed so I can see where I'm flying. If you see anything you want me to stop for let me know."

"Will do, Sam, let's go!" Sam successfully got the drone into the air and directed it to where they suspected the village to be.

"Grant, I'm going to follow what looks like a trail and see where we end up. Note anything we need to go back to revisit too. This is a scientific mission you know."

"Alright Sam, I will make note."

"Eliot are you recording the feed from the drone?"

"Yes, I am."

"Let me know if you spot anything out of the ordinary."

Grant really didn't care for the formality Eliot was programmed with and wished he could change it to a more light hearted voice, with a sunny disposition, but for now he was stuck with him. Not that he didn't appreciate him because he did. If it wasn't for Eliot more than likely they wouldn't be there. They all noted the lake they knew was there but it was much larger than they thought. The mountains were also much further away.

Sam had the drone cruising along at a pretty good clip when Grant shouted. "Stop, I see the village. It's about one hundred yards ahead and on the right. I sort of remember this trail leading to a low valley tucked into a grove of trees by a small stream."

"And the houses are like unopened flowers with round stones leading through a small pond in front of each one. I saw it in my dream when we were taking you for medical help."

"Creepy Sam, we've never been there, but we both remember something about it."

"Creepy indeed!"

"Alright let's fly overhead, return at a cross angle and then we'll slow it down and get in close for some more detailed video. Hopefully we'll get into their camp without being seen and make our way back without incident. I wouldn't want to sever our new friendship with distrust so early in the game. We may really need these guys before too long."

Sam was intently flying the drone as Grant instructed and the images were spectacular. The homes were tent like, but looked more like an opaque unopened white flower, lit from the inside. The little valley was in the shadows of many large trees and the village was bathed in a soft white glow from the structures.

"You don't think those are lit with bioluminescence do you, Grant? I don't see anything flickering, like a candle or a fire. They are beautiful and inviting, but with a "we don't know about electricity" sort of vibe."

"Nice observation, Sam. I don't see any power source and you're right, there are no flames or lights except for the dwellings themselves. Can you get in close to one and see if we can make out what they're made of. Sam closed in on a larger, more ornate dwelling than the others, it had a slightly different color too, light green and taller than the other dwellings, but still lit from inside. As the drone got closer Sam felt they were being watched and accelerated the drone vertically out from the tree cover then veered sharply left. An arrow narrowly missed the drone by inches and Sam knew it was time to head back to base.

"What are you doing, Sam? Why are you pulling out?"

"Uh hello, didn't you see the arrow whizz by the drone? Missed it by inches. I felt someone was watching us and pulled it up as soon as I felt it."

"Good call, Sam, way to be looking out." The battery life on the drone was draining and had enough charge to get back to the rover, as long as it didn't encounter any more arrows.

When the drone was safely back Grant asked Sam about what had happened. "What made you think we were being watched?"

"I'm not sure, but it was like in my dream. I could sense her being right there as close as or closer than you are, and I'm pretty sure she could sense me too. We may not be invited for breakfast after all."

"This weird link is going to have to be explored, Sam, it could be a good thing or it could put us in jeopardy."

"It's not like I can control it. It's like a natural connection and since she's a beauty, I'm not complaining so much."

"Gonna have to get real for a minute Sam. If they do turn on us, and know what you're thinking..." Grant let his voice trail off and Sam caught on to what wasn't being said.

"You're right, I need to be more diligent about not keeping my mind accessible and open for viewing. I am going to try to communicate with her in my dreams. I think she was trying to in the beginning."

"Just be careful. Alright, let's get the battery changed out and take a little flight the other direction. If we can find the missile base this morning then we have accomplished almost everything on our 'to do' list for the day. Well, except for breakfast and communicating with the good neighbors, now maybe the not so good neighbors."

"It will all work out, Grant, I have a feeling about this."

"I sure hope so, Sam, I sure hope so."

With the drone in the air again and headed in the opposite direction Sam noted almost immediately the terrain was much different. It was like a war zone. The ground was mostly barren and the trees and shrubs looked burnt and lifeless. Quite the contrast from the lush abode of the villagers. After a short flight, about half the distance of the village, Sam spotted their first obstacle. It was a sensor. It was clearly placed there and watching the surrounding area. Sam figured it was watching the sky as well. He flew lower to avoid the sensor, thinking the drone would fly under the detection range of the sensor. He soon discovered he was wrong. A larger more menacing drone advanced rapidly towards their drone.

Sam and Grant simultaneously said, "Time to go!"

"Get out of there Sam! At least we know the base is fairly close to us, and the sensor. I'd say about a quarter of a mile farther and we'll find the base, if it doesn't find us first."

"I'm glad the drone just ran us off and didn't fire at us. It seems strange we haven't seen anyone from the bad neighbors hanging about, shimmering."

Grant noted the sarcasm and agreed, "It is strange they haven't come to see what they shot down." Let's dock the drone and make our way toward the village."

Chapter Seven

With the lab bay doors now cleared and functioning Sam was delighted to finally get out the rover. The rover was part research vehicle, and part badass assault vehicle. Its six large all-terrain tires set it high off the ground. The two passenger cab sat low in the front with a wide sloped windshield. The powerful headlights and armaments were located above. It was powerfully rugged and sleek, yet functional. The passenger bay sat higher than the cab and could accommodate up to eight. It was designed to withstand harsh conditions on hostile worlds. Perfect for a morning romp, according to Sam. He pushed the gas pedal and popped out of the bay doors at a good clip, drove a short distance; put it into a power slide, and slung dirt and debris everywhere. It was ideal for slinging dirt and rocks flying in all directions, Sam was pleased. He loved the rover and drove it like he owned it. He slid to a halt in front of Grant with a huge smile and over the PA gave a hearty, "Howdy! You ready for this?"

Grant shook his head as he gathered the gear and headed to the rover. He knew this was going to be a bumpy ride, even if the terrain was perfectly flat and smooth. Sam was notorious for driving like a car thief being chased by the cops. It didn't matter if he was going on a long trip or a short one to the market, he owned the road. At least in his mind and with a vehicle as awesome as the rover, he felt invincible.

Once in and securely buckled up Grant gave Sam the go ahead and their journey began. "Ok Sam it's 9:30 AM and the sun sets at 5:45 PM, giving us just over 8 hours to check out the village, and anything we see on the way there, and get back to the shuttle for the night."

"All right, let's do this!" Sam slowly brought the rover up to a leisurely speed paying particular attention not to hit any large holes or rocks. From the co-pilot seat Grant gave Sam a sideways glance and Sam returned the glance with a slow head roll, and then stomped on the gas, they were off.

"Funny, Sam, very funny!"

"I thought you might appreciate the dainty take off and understand the need to fly! This baby is a beast!"

"Sam please, just get us there in one piece. Oh and YEE HAW! Can this thing go any faster?"

They laughed and Sam obliged. Not quite top speed but enough to exhilarate them and get them in the mood to travel.

"We have about two more miles to go, Sam, better be easing up a bit so we can keep from power sliding into the village and making mess of things. We are trying to make friends with them you know."

"I know we are, but this thing is so fun."

"It's also intimidating. Let's roll close to the village and park in the open so we're not invading their space, or look menacing."

"On a side note, Grant, the bots should be back this evening and you know what that means."

"Yes I do, it means a lot more work for us. We probably need to cut this short and head back to the shuttle before it gets dark."

"Here we are, it's show time."

"Keep in mind Sam; we are over a foot taller than they are and easily twice their size. Any sudden movements or gestures might be considered a sign of aggression. Better play it safe and be humble."

"I'm still packing a small firearm in my vest and one in my boot. Better safe than sorry!"

"Do not, I repeat, do not brandish either of them for any reason other than to save our lives, understood?" The serious tone from Grant made Sam truly take notice of why he was the captain and Sam was not.

"Yes sir! And no sarcasm this time."

"Thanks. So what direction do we go from here?"

"To the tree line and then down into the valley about thirty yards. Most likely we will be greeted by one of our neighbors. Hopefully the drone wasn't mistaken as an overt act."

They entered the tree line and walked about fifteen feet when everything went quiet. It was the same kind of quiet they experienced the first night when Grant shone his light over the landscape. They stooped reflexively and looked around for signs of trouble.

"Creeps me out to no end Grant. I haven't seen any bugs making noise and why do they all stop at the same time?"

"No idea, let's stop talking and proceed slowly. We are being watched."

Sam looked around and didn't see anything, and then he saw it. A slight shimmer five yards ahead to their right, and another to the left about two yards down the path.

"We come only to talk!"

The sudden burst of sound startled Sam and he ducked again. "Warn me next time for Christ's sake, I about shit myself."

"Here they come, better wipe before you stand back up. Sarcasm intended."

The neighbors were out in force this morning. There were about twenty and they did not appear to be happy about the unannounced intrusion. Several of them uncloaked, revealing themselves to be the same ones who shared their dinner. With a weak smile and a handshake they were greeted and led into the village. The other shimmery ones dispersed and were gone in the blink of an eye. The path wound farther down into the valley and Grant and Sam caught their first close up view of the village. The flower shaped dwellings were scattered throughout the area. The rock walkways up to their entrances were stunning. The stones were a light grey and the water was black, and mirror smooth. The plants and flowers made each one unique and their aroma was intoxicating. They had never seen such beauty in such an unreal setting. No one was out and about in the village with the exception of the guards and them. They were led to the larger dwelling with a greenish tint to it. It stood out from the others with its rustic vibe and choice of plants. Their guides stopped them and motioned for them to stay put. Three of the guards entered the structure leaving Sam and Grant alone with the other three.

"Grant, this is the place I saw in my dream. She is in there."

"She who?"

"The huntress!" Sam raised his eyebrows and Grant raised his as well. Were they about to meet the woman of both of their dreams or become prisoners? After a few moments their guides returned and motioned for them put something in their ears. It was an odorless, jelly-like slime, deep burgundy in color. Sam and Grant exchanged looks and took the sticks with the jelly on them and placed the stuff in their ears. It was warm and slimy, and slid deep into their ears. Sam could feel the slime moving and shook his head trying to dislodge it from his ear.

Grant was having similar difficulties and tried to pull it out with the end of the stick. Their neighbors stood smiling like this sort of thing happened every day. Once the initial shock wore off and they realized there was no retrieving the slime, they calmed down and looked at each other like, what the hell did we just do? The guides motioned for them to enter. The dwelling was far more spacious than they expected. The shape made the size deceiving and the rustic exterior was deceiving as to the dwelling contents. There before them, was who they called, the huntress. She was beautiful, but looked hard and serious. Her piercing black mercury eyes and set jaw made her look like a jungle animal. She was fit, but slight, and her hair was jet black with hints of other subtle dark colors. Her tunic caught Sam's eye after he got past her beauty, and the fear she might pounce at any moment. It was the same one he saw in his dream, only this close it had much more detail. It was made from the hide of something with scales and feathers. It was so dark it almost stole the light from the room.

"Why are you here?" The voice was much deeper and seemed to come from inside their heads. It startled them not only because it was deeper than expected, but it was in English.

"How can you speak our language?"

"The substance you put in your ears contains small organisms. They translate your language to ours and ours to yours."

Satisfied with her answer for now, Grant replied, "We are a survey team doing scientific research."

She must not have really wanted an answer to her question as she went directly to her next. "Did you send the small flyer to us?"

Grant replied, "Yes, it was us."

"Why?" The huntress was not one for many words.

"We used the drone, flyer, in order to locate your village so we could pay you a visit. We need your help."

"Do the diggers and boomers belong to you?"

"I do not know of diggers and the boomers. I assume they are the missiles that brought down our craft. No, they are not ours. We need your help and I believe you can use ours as well."

"I will determine who needs our help and who does not." She paced a few steps away in deep thought. She was as beautiful from the back as she was the front. Sam could not take his eyes off of her and his mind drifted to things of an intimate nature. He was getting lost in the depth of her swaying backside when she turned and approached him. Much to his surprise she had a smirk on her face. She got close enough he could smell her. She must have rubbed flowers and other tropical oils on herself because she smelled amazing. Sam sensed she knew he was thinking inappropriate thoughts about her. She was about five feet six inches tall and for Sam, she was the perfect height compared to his five feet eleven inches.

"You need to keep your thoughts quiet, I can hear them. It was in your dream I learned you can hear my thoughts, too. We will work on our communications another day." She had not said a word.

Sam was dumbfounded she knew what he was thinking and intrigued she wanted to work on their communications. It was a positive note and he beamed a little.

"We can speak of help over a meal, come, and join us." They were led out of the dwelling, onto a wide rock path leading to their large gathering hall.

"Sam, what was she doing when she was staring at you? I was getting worried you had done something to piss her off."

"I will fill you in later." The entire village was there and it must be their custom to breakfast together. Grant and Sam were invited to sit with the huntress and several others at a long table in the front of the room. They were unsure of their customs and waited for them to lead the way.

"Family, I see the puzzled looks and hear your troubling thoughts. They are not the enemy or it's like. They have come seeking our counsel and assistance. Let us welcome them and eat without fear." The villagers smiled and cautiously went about their business. Plates and utensils were placed before them and cups were filled with unknown liquids. The huntress, aware of their unease took small pieces of several different items and placed them on their plates. "These may be to your liking judging from what I've learned of your food. You can take more of what you like." Sam took a bite of his first sample. It was something similar to their steak and had a similar aroma. He placed the bite in his mouth, chewed twice and closed his eyes. Grant watched closely and quickly became concerned as Sam was not moving, then Sam spoke.

In his state of ecstasy Sam slowly said, "This is amazing! What is this called?"

"It is Chotuk, a medium-sized beast with four legs and no fur. It comes from the lower mountains."

Grant took a bite and knew why Sam had closed his eyes. If this was going to be his last bite of food ever, it was the best ever, and he prayed for more. Each and every bite was as good as the previous one.

Grant turned to the huntress and said, "By the way, I'm Grant and this is Sam. What do we call you?"

"I am Tayana and these are my people. I am their leader and protector." With a slight knowing smile she motioned to the side and soft music began to play.

The soothing melody instantly made Grant feel much more at ease and willing to talk freely. "How did such a beautiful woman become the leader and protector of an entire village?" Grant knew as soon as the words left his lips they seemed sexist and demeaning. It was not his intention to be insulting, and he feared the worst.

"My parent couple were the village leaders and my brother was to be next. When the diggers came there was a battle and my parents and brother were killed. I became the village leader at their death. I was much younger, but I understood things others could not. The village is like a large family and they supported me early on. They taught me our history and our culture. They taught me the ways of our people and how to be a protector. As time passed I needed their attention less and they needed mine more. I am who I am with their help and they are who they are with my help."

Grant was amazed. She did not miss a beat after his assumed insult, and he was truly relieved. "How did you become leader of Sam?"

"Well, our planet is much larger than this one and there are different occupations and ranks. We work for the Planetary Survey and Acquisition Division, PSAD. I am the captain of the ship and a scientist. Sam is a scientist and mechanic and works with me. If something goes bad then I am responsible. Sam and I are friends before we are scientists."

"What is a scientist?"

"We study life and resources on uninhabited planets to see if they are suitable for our planet. Our planet ran out of natural resources and we must explore others and utilize their resources in order to maintain life."

"Why did you think Antaya had no life?"

"It wasn't that it had no life, we did not think it had intelligent life." Again, Grant had put his foot in his mouth and awaited repercussions.

This time he did get a reaction, "You think we are not intelligent? We have harnessed the organisms in your ear to speak for us and we hide in plain sight and cannot be seen.

Not wanting to appear even ruder, he reluctantly raised his hand to signal for her to stop. With a quizzical look on her face, and much to Grant's surprise, she stopped talking.

"We did not know you were here. The static haze surrounding this planet kept our sensors from detecting you. We assumed there was no intelligent life because you didn't show up. We are truly impressed with your knowledge and wholly respect you and your people. I apologize for the way my words came out. There was no harm or insult intended."

Grant must have looked completely humbled because she looked at him for a moment and then smiled a very forgiving smile. "We are glad you are intelligent and again, we need your assistance to get back to our ship."

"Has the wine made you unable to walk so quickly?"

She said with a comical smile.

Grant noted the sarcasm and appreciated her sense of humor.

"There's wine?" Sam was listening off and on, but the word wine caught his attention. "I would love some wine." As he spoke a glass of wine was delivered to him via, for lack of better terminology, a servant. "Ah, Grant, I could get used to this lifestyle."

"Pipe down and drink your wine." They chuckled and went back to what they were doing. Grant turned back to Tayana, "The craft we have here is a small research shuttle, the Varizone. It detaches from our larger ship, the Ebony Belle, orbiting the planet as we speak."

She was intrigued they had a larger unmanned ship circling the planet and they were unable to return to it without her help. "How do you plan to get back to your larger ship and how do we help you?"

Grant was glad Tayana was listening intently, "Do you know where the boomers come from? If our shuttle takes off it will again be shot down by the missiles— boomers— and if it takes further damage we may not be able to leave at all. The static haze blocks our communications with the ship and our planet."

Tayana replied, "We know where to find the boomers. They come from the diggers. We can take you there to see."

"It would help us a lot. We need to figure out how to disable the boomers and shut off the haze. We think it is being generated by the diggers."

"The haze is how they hide from others who may want to dig here too. It seems to work well, does it not?"

"Yes, we did not detect them or you. It is a technology we do not possess on our planet. How do you hide in plain sight?"

"My father created the devices that create nothing. We made more after he was killed."

"I'm sure you know they produce a shimmer, that's how we knew you were watching us in the daylight."

Tayana looked even more puzzled and leaned towards Grant. "You can see us, shimmer? What is that?"

"The device generating the nothing, we can see an outline of a shape, sort of like how the haze reflects the light in different ways. You don't completely blend in with the surroundings. It works, but I saw a foot poke out on one of our monitors."

"You need to show me your monitors, I do not know what that is, but I must see what you mean."

"I will gladly show you when you visit our ship again. This time no sneaking around, come knock on the door." Grant gave her a reassuring smile and Tayana accepted his invitation.

As breakfast came to a close and things were being put in their places Grant noticed Sam was not in the dining hall. He hoped he had not wandered off and gotten lost. They still did not know what manner of beasts inhabited the forests.

"Your thoughts are loud as well, Grant. Sam is being given a tour of the village by a couple of the women. Would you like a tour as well?"

"Yes, as long as you're my tour guide." Grant rose from the table. His stomach was full of some of the best food he had tasted in his entire life. He hoped it would agree with his systems and not cause any issues later. So far, so good!

Tayana smiled as she slid her arm around Grant's and they began to walk. There were structures scattered throughout the village. Some mixed in with the dwellings and others stood a good distance from anything. He could not make out the rhyme or reasoning in its design. He could not get over the beauty of the dwellings and their tidy little gardens in front either. The average dwelling stood twelve feet tall and was covered in an opaque material stretched over a series of flexible ribs creating a bulge a quarter of the way up. From the bulge the dwelling tapered to a two foot diameter circle at the top. Grant assumed it was like an Earth teepee and the hole was for smoke to escape from the fire inside. However, they had determined there were no fires in the dwellings because of the helium fall. Each dwelling was surrounded by a small pond and the walkway was made of grey round stones sticking out of the water about four inches. They were in staggered patterns and sizes varied. There were various aquatic plants in the pond and what Grant believed were fish. Nothing like he had seen before. The sky and the trees reflected off the water's surface creating an illusion of great depth to the water. The interior of the dwelling was much more spacious than it looked from outside. Inside there was only one room. It was sparsely decorated with colorful bedding and more plants. The outer material sort of hummed and he wondered what caused it. He noted there was neither a kitchen nor a restroom. "Do you eat all of your meals together?"

"Yes, for the most part. It builds community and everyone has a part. We take turns serving in different capacities. You may be a server one week and a guard the next. We are all well versed in every aspect of this village. The olders teach the youngers and we all teach each other."

"Amazing, I applaud you and your village for the amount of cooperation it must take to coordinate every meal and every job."

"My planet is pretty much the opposite. We gather, but not for community, it's more to be accepted. We do not teach others, we are taught in groups by individuals and their knowledge is shared with us. There is little emotion and even less care. We live in communities, but we rarely interact with our neighbors and our families are scattered across the planet. We travel great distances to celebrate holidays and events."

"That seems cold and uninviting to me."

Grant could see Tayana was struggling with the idea of family not being together for every meal and living long distances apart. The tour was thorough and informative. Grant was thankful to have Tayana as his guide. He learned the dwellings were called pods and were living plants they lived with symbiotically. The hole in the top was so the plant could breathe and maintain its membrane. But he still had lots of questions.

His most pressing question, was, "Um, where do you go to use the restroom? I didn't see any place in the pods."

"What do you mean, restroom?" She looked puzzled but was trying hard to understand. Grant thought of how to explain a toilet or a urinal to her, but the words wouldn't come.

"Oh", she said with surprise. "You mean, where do we release our excess? There are smaller pods with room enough for one, possibly two if a little one needs help."

"I need to use a pod. If you could direct me it would be appreciated."

Tayana pointed to camouflaged pod.

Grant had not seen it before, but now saw several. "Thank you, I'll be right back."

"Be careful Grant!" The words didn't have the impact they needed to and Grant, thinking he was walking into the restroom on the shuttle stepped into the dark pod. With the slight glow of the bio-luminescence he found the toilet, but the hole was much smaller than the shuttle's. He pulled down his pants and took a seat thinking business as usual. To his complete and total surprise something cupped his parts with an unbreakable grip and something else inserted itself into his anus and his urethra. He struggled to get free but was unable to escape from the grip of whatever had him. There was no pain, just surprise. He could feel his bladder empty and the tightness of his bowels relaxing. It was over quickly and whatever was cupping his parts released him a small puff of flower scent released into the pod. Grant quickly fastened his pants and stumbled out of the pod with a shocked look on his face. Tayana was laughing hysterically knowing what had transpired inside the pod. Grant was not as amused as she was. He felt violated, manhandled by something that inserted itself into his private parts without permission. He did not want to imagine what it was or its level of cleanliness.

"What a mean trick Tayana, you could have at the very least warned me about what was going to happen."

"It would not have been as entertaining had I given away its secrets."

Grant conceded and they laughed at his misfortune. "I'll go in the woods next time and use some leaves to clean up." He was shocked and couldn't quite get his mind around what had happened. He knew it would be a pretty cool trick to play on Sam if he got the opportunity.

Grant's communicator chirped, signaling the bots had returned and were ready for processing. "Tayana, it is getting late and we must get back before nightfall. We do not breathe well when the helium levels are high. Also, our bots have returned with samples to be processed."

"You are welcome to stay here for the night. Our dwellings can produce the atmosphere you need. We can also provide you with breathing equipment, if you prefer."

He gracefully declined, knowing the samples needed tending to tonight. "Thank you, Tayana; can we meet again tomorrow to discuss how we are going to proceed with the diggers?"

"Yes, we can meet you at your camp as you are closer to them than we are."

"Thank you for being such a gracious hostess and for the hospitality. We look forward to seeing you tomorrow." He set off to find Sam and head back to their camp. Sam's communicator had sounded off too, so, it wasn't going to be hard to locate him. Grant could have used the tracking device in their communicators to find him, but wandering around the village alone taking in its beauty and feeling the cool breeze from the waterfalls was much more appealing. He made his way toward the rover and found Sam waiting there.

"Took you long enough! We have work to do and you're swooning over the huntress."

"Uh, her name is Tayana!" They laughed and boarded the rover. "Like the wind, let's get this thing moving."

Sam made a quick circle throwing grass, dirt, and rocks flying into the air. "Yee haw!"

Helium Fall

Chapter Eight

Sam was excited to see what the bots found. He knew there would be samples of all types of common things but he was excited to see the strange and unusual stuff. He hoped they found some of the gel they put into their ears to translate for them. He also hoped they captured a Chotuk. He was looking forward to testing, dissecting, and eating it for dinner in a day or two.

Meanwhile, Grant's thoughts drifted back to the village and all it entailed. He wished Sam was there so they could share the experience together.

"You disappeared after breakfast. Sam where were you today?"

"I had the best day of my life. The food was amazing and the village beautiful, most beautiful I have ever seen. A couple young ladies gave me the tour; they also gave me a bath in one of the waterfalls."

"Sam you're a dog! First meeting and you get busy with the natives."

"Well, it didn't go that far, but they look almost exactly like Earth women, with a few exceptions. They are obviously smaller and their feet are out of proportion to their bodies. Small blonde hairs cover most of their bodies, and as you know, their eyes are like black mercury. Their beauty is natural, no makeup! They have a heartier, more open sexual appetite than Earth women. They marveled at our anatomy and were shocked at our man parts.

"Now you're tooting your own horn. Making a whole tree out of a stump."

"Not fair Grant and for the record, their woman parts are smaller and have no hair."

In a mocking tone Grant replied, "So, scientifically speaking—their men are considerably less endowed than we are, and your summation is based purely on science, right?"

"Yep, based on science."

"You're a dog Sam, still a dog."

"I know!"

As they neared camp they saw the bots neatly lined up waiting to be relieved of their findings and be set free again.

Sam slowed to a stop. "Grant, what the hell is that?" There was a large four-legged creature standing beside one of the bots. Standing ten feet tall, its body was covered with black feathery scales. The legs were muscular at the top and tapered to four toed, clawed feet, giving it the appearance of a terrifying four-legged battle chicken.

"There you go, Sam, we found your T-rex, except it's a chicken."

Sam pulled the rover into camp. The giant chicken struggled to get free from its mechanical captor with no success. The bots used anti gravity to move about. When they needed to be static and not move the AG was turned off. When the bots were not floating effortlessly they had considerable weight. The battle chicken was huge, but it was no match for the bot.

"All right, Sam, let's get this party started." The bots were loaded with what Sam and Grant considered the usual type stuff. There was dirt, flowers, soil and, rock samples of all kinds, colors, and sizes. "Let's get the giant chicken processed first. I'd hate to see what happens when it gets hungry."

"Me too! Okay giant chicken, let's go." Sam instructed the bot to move the chicken through the automated processing line, and not let it loose.

They would personally inspect whatever the equipment flagged for review. "Sorry giant chicken, this is not going to be your favorite day, but it will be a day you can share with your offspring."

Sam's sarcasm made Grant chuckle a bit. "Sam, you know we're not supposed to get attached things, and I sure don't want you getting attached to, C-Rex!"

They laughed and Sam shouted, "C-Rex, stalker of men and young beautiful women. Coming to a city near you!"

Grant laughed so hard he drove his bot into another causing it to dump what appeared to be fecal debris onto the lab floor making Sam laugh even harder as he mimicked a C-Rex stomping around pecking at the ground.

"Oh my god Sam, we are messed up."

"Yep, that's why they sent us out here alone!"

"Sam, you sound like a chipmunk!"

Sam, laughing and pointing at Grant said, "So do you! Man, I'm getting light headed!"

They erupted in laughter again and Grant found it hard to breath. He noticed the bay doors were open, and it was now almost dark outside.

Sam's voice, much higher than usual due to the helium, squeaked out, "We have to get the bots in and close the doors. The helium is going to kill us if we don't hurry." He was beginning to feel light headed and thought it was from laughing too hard. In his dizzy state he hit the button for all bots to enter the staging area. The procession was fairly quick even though some of the bots were loaded down with rock and dirt samples.

"Get the damn doors closed, Sam!" Grant ran to the climate control panel. He pushed the button combination to evacuate the current air and fill the hold with the oxygen they desperately needed. Before the doors closed Grant heard the climate system sucking out the helium and other gasses and replacing it with the proper mix of oxygen and carbon dioxide.

Sam had successfully closed the doors and was sitting on the floor gasping for air. Grant was hanging onto the control panel slowly sliding to the floor himself. After what seemed an eternity, the air was clean and restored to the proper levels. They almost ended their mission a lot earlier than anticipated through asphyxiation.

"Sam, you alive? Buddy, speak to me. Grant got to his feet and made his way to where Sam was sitting on the floor, alive, but loopy. "Sam, why didn't you answer when I hollered at you?"

"I didn't want to sound like the girl you did," in the highest voice he could muster, "Sam, close the damn doors!" He sounded like a four-year old girl scared of her shadow.

"Sam, you're an ass! This wasn't a joke, we really could have died. It was close, too close. We have to be better stewards of the time in the future."

"I hear you Grant, in all honesty it was too close and we were pretty stupid for letting it get there. Next time, bots in, door closed, and then we can joke around, deal?"

"Deal!"

"Let's get C-Rex processed and out the door. We need to process the live stuff now. The other stuff can wait until later. Don't forget, we have to get some sleep so we can check out the diggers tomorrow. It's going to be an interesting day."

"Gotcha. I'm on it." Sam processed C-Rex and was impressed with the chicken's hide. It was tough as steel, light as a feather, and as flexible as his own shirt. He didn't think the feathers would go well with his pants but he could sure use a vest like Tayana's.

"Hey Grant, wanna go C-Rex hunting sometime next week? I could use a good chicken vest. I don't think the meat is suitable for us to eat, but maybe the villagers could use it."

"Sure, we can do some hunting, after we destroy the drone and its missiles. We have to be able to move the shuttle. It is of the utmost importance."

"Agreed, destroy the drone, hunt us a chicken, and get down to business." Sam's nonchalant manner often rubbed Grant a little thin but he appreciated his can do attitude.

As the night wore on they ran every living thing through the lab. Several creatures warranted closer inspection and Grant discovered one creature almost as poisonous as a brown recluse spider. However, it had ten legs, wings, and its body was the size of a large chicken egg. Their policy was to let all creatures return to their natural surroundings, alive, and as undamaged as possible.

"Sam, check this one out." Grant held up and shook the container with the spider in it to get the spider to move.

Sam reacted, "Kill it, just kill it, and save us from its horror. Jesus, you know how I feel about those things."

"Yes, and this one has ten legs, and wings."

"Oh my god, it flies? Are you kidding me?"

"No kidding Sam, this one is getting its picture posted

on the wall. I might even make a life-sized model of it for your shelf."

"Payback! Remember, and know how it can come back to haunt you? I'm sure you do and you know I'll go there!"

"I'm kidding Sam, no model."

"No pictures either, keep that thing as far from my mind as possible."

Grant chuckled, it was now imperative for him bring the spider to light sometime in the near future. He didn't care what the consequences might be, it would be worth it to hear Sam scream like a girl and run for the hills after he threw a rubber model of the ten legged winged monster at him. Live processing was almost complete and C-Rex was turned loose. They would have to collate the creatures, organisms, and other living things with the pictures and environmental readings of when and where they were found, to complete the processing. They didn't find any translating gel or small intelligent life forms, but they did have a large array of new species to catalogue when they were done processing.

Tomorrow it would be soil, rocks, and minerals. "Everything turned loose Sam? Let's call it a night."

"I have one more thing to finish up and then we can grab some dinner."

"What did you find, Sam?"

"It's a small six-legged creature about the size of a large house cat and it has suction cups on its feet. I'm having some difficulty dislodging it from the container. I don't want to hurt it, but I may have no choice."

"Did you talk to it? Maybe a little kindness will do wonders. Hey little fella, would you mind letting go of the container so we can set you free? We mean you no harm;

we only wish the best for you."

"Funny, Grant, very funny!" The creature released its grip and proceeded down the chute. They were shocked. Then, the little fella turned and waved back at them as it exited the shuttle.

"What the hell!"

"No way had that just happened, no way on Earth."

"Well Grant, we are not on Earth, and yes, it did just happen."

"What were its readings, did it test intelligent?"

"The results show it had some intelligence and is capable of understanding a variety of languages."

"Sam we have discovered another form of intelligent life on this planet, and it waved at us. We are going to be heroes if we ever get out of here."

"We are going to be heroes when we destroy the diggers, too. The young ladies told me they have tried many times to stop the diggers and boomers, but failed because they are no match for their technology. That's why they so willingly agreed to help us. They think we can destroy them and then they can return to their way of life. The diggers are mining one of their best resources."

"And you didn't bother to tell me this sooner, why?"

"Uh, I was lost in thought about the ladies and getting the bots back?"

"Whatever! Speaking of diggers, let's talk about them over dinner. I saw some footage of the digger camp one of bots recorded. It may give us some good information as to how we can shut them down."

"Hopefully without getting ourselves blown up!"

"Yes, there is that. Let's go clean up and eat." After cleaning up and removing the day's dirt, they met in the galley.

"So what's it going to be tonight, Sam?"

"I'm not currently thinking about chicken, if that's what you're asking. I'm leaning towards roast beef, mashed potatoes, and some corn. Maybe a salad and chocolate cream pie for desert. What's on your mind?"

"I'm not thinking chicken, either. I want something of the southern persuasion. Pulled pork sandwich, potato salad, some baked beans, and a big piece of chocolate cream pie. Yeah, I borrowed it from you, sounded good."

As they ate Grant showed Sam the footage of the digger camp taken by the bot and still photos of perimeter sensors.

"Those look like the same motion sensors we saw with the drone. I think we can take them down fairly easily. It should be a cake walk from there on out. We can use one of the rifles to shoot the sensor to take it out of commission and the drone won't know where we are or where to look."

"Good plan, Sam but what if shooting the sensor sets off the drone and it chooses to go free range and hunt us down?"

"Well, do you have a better idea?"

"Ok, so we shoot the sensor and see how it reacts. We take our big guns with us, just in case."

"Okay Grant, sounds like a plan to me. You do know we never stick to our plans, right?"

"Right, but we plan."

"Right."

They headed off to bed and for the first time since their crash landing they had restful sleep.

Chapter Nine

The next morning Sam was up before Grant. He fixed himself some coffee and a ham and cheese omelet. He was about halfway done eating when Grant made his way to the galley.

"What are you doing up so early?"

"Don't sound so surprised. You know it's happened before."

"Yes Sam, once, in college and I think you stayed up all night just to make it look like you were up early."

"Well, it may or may not have happened," Sam said with a wry smile.

"Some breakfast and a good cup of coffee then gather our equipment and go digger hunting." Sam liked the idea of hunting the diggers, it sounded more like a sport than a survival situation.

"I have an idea. We can use one of the maintenance bots as a decoy after we take out the sensor. If the drone does come out it will attack the first thing it finds moving."

"Not a bad idea, we can haul it closer to their camp with the rover and it might just end up saving our lives. Nice work, Sam."

"Thanks buddy!"

They had loaded the rover and were prepared for what lay ahead and were patiently waiting for Tayana and her people. "Grant do you think they stood us up?"

"I'm not sure what's going on but we have to get things moving soon. After last night we know we have to stick to a tight schedule or we could end up dead from the gas combination. If push comes to shove we have the safety of the rover this time and we can make it back to camp without passing out."

They waited another twenty minutes before Grant decided they needed to go ahead and scout out the area. Sam fired up the rover and they began their trek to the digger camp. "We need to be very careful Sam, we don't know how sensitive the sensors are and we do not want to lose the rover to one of the missiles."

"Agreed, we know the camp is about two miles ahead of us and I think we should stop half a mile short and load the equipment on the bot. It can carry the weight easier than we can and it is silent."

"Another good idea, Sam, keep 'em coming." Close to their destination, Sam began to slow the rover and look for a good hiding spot. The forest to their left looked like the best option where there were large rocks to obscure the rover from view.

"Over there, Sam."

"I see it." Sam maneuvered the rover into a large group of bushes near the large rocks, the trees made the perfect blind to hide under.

"Okay Sam, according to Tayana and our own estimates, the Diggers should be about half a mile or less straight ahead. Let's leave the equipment here for now and do some reconnaissance. We need to know what we're dealing with."

"True, we've never seen the diggers, but we have seen the drone and we know what it can do." They gathered binoculars and a wide angle field scope, then took off to find the camp and the sensors.

After trekking about a quarter of a mile Grant suddenly stopped Sam with his arm. "Sam, there is a sensor twenty yards ahead to our right, stay low and let's find some better cover." Without a word Sam obliged and slowly made his way to a rock large enough to hide behind. He took out the rifle and took aim.

"Whoa Sam, we are not shooting the sensor now, we don't have any other weapons and we are sitting ducks if the sensor sees us."

"Keep your knickers on Grant, I'm using the scope to judge the distance and see where the best place to shoot this thing will be."

"Sorry, I know how you can be with weapons and I wasn't sure what your intentions were."

"No problem, you haven't sucked all the joy out of it yet." Sam said it with a chuckle, Grant understood he had jumped the gun and felt bad for not trusting him.

"Sam, let's move to higher ground and scout out the area better."

"A step ahead of ya, Grant." They moved up a small incline to a large set of boulders nestled among dense bushes and several trees.

"Great cover, Sam. Now we can see who the diggers are and what they're up to." Both of them thoroughly scouted the mining camp for equipment, structures, and personnel. "Sam, do you not see what I'm not seeing?"

"Yep, I'm seeing a whole lot of equipment, one building, and nothing else. What gives?" The mining camp was void of life. The structure was about thirty yards away from the mining camp. It was a square building with no features, other than the array of antennas on top. "There aren't any doors or windows on the building, Grant."

"I saw it. Do you think their mining operation is automated?"

"Most likely. It would be a good idea. I'd probably do

the same thing." Sam gave it some thought in the brief time they were there. "One building to automate the equipment and one drone to protect the building and the equipment, genius!"

"I wonder what happened to Tayana and her people?" Grant was as much concerned as perplexed. They had agreed to meet in the morning so they would have time to do what they had to do to get the drone subdued and return to camp before nightfall.

"I think they chickened out. Left us to do their dirty work so they could stay safe and unharmed. Sort of leaving a bad taste in my mouth." Sam was less concerned and more ticked off they hadn't kept their word.

"Well Sam, I think it's time for some fireworks."

"Yeah buddy! Let's get this party a hoppin'."

"We're in a very secure area surrounded by boulders and covered by thick bushes and trees. If the drone does go free range it will have a difficult time finding us. So, I'm going to watch the structure to see what happens and you're going to shoot the sensor we saw on the way here."

"Let me know when you're ready and I'll take out the sensor."

"Don't you think we need to get the bigger guns, just in case?"

"Um, yes, that's a lifesaving idea Sam." After the quick trip to the rover and a much slower return with the big guns they situated themselves. They were good with their view of the area.

"Fire away, Sam!" Grant focused his binoculars on the building and Sam cracked off his first shot. With a muzzled bang and a quick flash the first bullet was away and a direct hit. The sensor exploded and pieces went flying everywhere.

"Cool!" Sam appreciated a good explosion and this one did not disappoint. "I guess it had some sort of flammable liquid in it judging by the way it blew chunks all over the place."

"Excellent shot! We have movement. The top of the building is opening. Crap, here comes the drone. It's a lot bigger than I thought it was."

"It's carrying missiles Grant and most likely more than one." Just then a missile launched from the drone to the location of the sensor sending dirt and rocks everywhere.

"Tell me I was not chasing one of those when we got shot down. What the hell was I thinking? I'm lucky to be alive!"

With thick sarcasm Sam responded, "Lucky indeed, good thing it missed or I'd be standing under a waterfall being bathed by the village beauties."

Grant gave him a scornful look and turned to look at the building again. He noticed a small bot racing out of a side opening in the building with another sensor. It took it past where the other sensor had been located making the perimeter larger and putting the pair neatly inside of it. "Uh, Sam we have a small problem. A bot from the building just placed another sensor extending the perimeter about twenty-five yards. We are now trapped inside."

"Uh Grant, we have a huge problem, DUCK!"

The drone fired a missile directly at their location. Sam could see it coming and had just enough time to warn Grant and jump behind a large boulder that was securely anchored into the ground.

Grant was not so lucky. Though he was fairly protected, he was still in the line of fire while peering around the boulder. He grasped his head as he was launched into the air along with rocks, bushes, and copious amounts of soil. The drone had traced the origin of the bullet by its trail and fired on Sam's location. Grant felt a searing pain and his heart was racing. He was thrown about forty feet into a small patch of bushes and rocks. He saw rivulets of blood running down his arm, his shirt was ripped to pieces, and his leg was bleeding. The rest of his clothing was torn and he was disoriented. He could feel himself beginning to pass out. Everything began to shimmer and a shadow came over him. Then the face of Tayana appeared. "Am I dreaming again? I had this dream a couple nights ago. You are so beautiful." He looked deeply into her eyes and for a fleeting moment the pain went away. Tayana motioned to others as he was slipped in and out of consciousness. Where was Sam, what was happening, who was grabbing him? His eyes fluttered and all was dark.

"We have to get him to the village quickly, he is seriously injured and we need to stop the bleeding." Sam was spared Grant's fate having seen the missile coming and having a split second more to prepare then take cover.

He ran to Grant and Tayana, "We need to get him to the rover, there's medical equipment on board and we can get the bleeding stopped. We can take him to the shuttle, there is a full medical lab there and everything we need."

With a stern voice Tayana said, "No, you do not understand. Those bushes when broken release a toxin and it is now all over him. We have the cure in the village, but we must move quickly."

Sam didn't hesitate. He directed the villagers to the rover. Once inside Tayana wrapped a local plant around Grant's arm and leg while Sam administered some antibiotics and pain medications. "We don't need him suffering and we need his body to fight as hard as it can, these will help with both. You can ride along and keep him secure. This is going to be a quick ride." Sam fired up the rover and gunned it. He was racing against the clock with little time to spare. "Hold on Tayana, this is going to be a little bumpy. Make sure he stays fastened in."

Tayana had no intentions of letting him loose. She was deeply concerned and afraid for Grant's life. The bush produced a toxin similar to the toxin of a box jelly fish but with different side effects. Thankfully it was not quite as powerful, but still life threatening. Grant was beginning to shake and sweat as the toxin began making its way through his body. Tayana held his hand and spoke comforting words to him knowing he was not hearing them. It gave her as much comfort as it was supposed to give him.

Helium Fall

Chapter Ten

The two mile trek went by in a flash. The village quickly came into view. Sam drove full throttle the entire trip back. "We're getting close to the village, is there somewhere I can get the rover close to where we need to be?"

"There is a trail on the north side. It will take you past the tops of the waterfalls to the far side of the village. We need to take Grant there for healing."

"Guide me please; I have no idea where I'm going." Sam was more concerned than ever. Grant was shaking violently and sweat rolled off of him like he was out lying in the hot noon sun.

"To the right Sam, it's there, by the large tree."

Sam located the tree, turned the rover, and slowed down to maneuver through the trees and across the waterfalls. The water was not as deep as expected, even though the rover would have no trouble had it been, and the rover breezed through them with haste. He took note of the beauty surrounding him. The falls were as beautiful from the top as they were from below. The sunshine filtering through the trees gave everything an ether world effect. Sam was amused at his thought and vowed to return to the falls when he had a free moment.

"Left here Sam, then down to the large pink pod."

"Left, large pink pod, got it!" Sam made his way to the pod.

They were greeted by several villagers; two he assumed were their healers. One looked much older with long grey hair and a full flowing beard swaying in the breeze. The other was a younger looking female with the same grey hair.

Tayana jumped out of the rover and began conversing with the healers, instructing them as to what had happened and what they needed to do. The villagers with Sam's help pulled Grant from the rover and moved him into the pod. The inside was much the same as the other pods. This one had dried herbs and plants hanging everywhere, and shelves with bottles of every color of liquid Sam could imagine whose purposes were known only by the healers, and most likely Tayana. They lay Grant on a soft bed and began administering poultices and creams all over his body. The younger healer began removing his torn clothing and wiping dried blood from his face and body. Grant looked pretty beat up and Sam felt bad he had not warned him faster about the missile. He knew there was nothing he could do for Grant but watch and hope the healers had the knowledge to bring him back to health. Grant began to violently convulse and had to be strapped to the bed. The healers asked Sam to please wait outside and he obliged them. Grant had to pull through, he was the brains of the two and Sam knew he couldn't complete the mission alone.

The mission would be a bust and he would be out of a job. His best friend was lying in a flower pod surrounded by waterfalls, poisoned by an exploding plant on an alien world and was being attended to by aliens the size of fifteen year olds. How much more weird could things get?

Sam shook his head in disbelief as he paced outside the medical pod. He had left the rover doors open and walked over to close them. Grant's blood was everywhere and it brought a tear to his eye. The shock from the explosion and the pain Grant must have suffered almost overwhelmed him, he couldn't lose him, and he was the closest thing he had to family. Sam began cleaning up the blood and removing other items from the rover when he heard Tayana calling for him. "Sam, Sam..."

"Over here by the rover. Is he going to be all right?"

"Sam, he is resting now. The healers have administered the antidote and are keeping a close eye on him. We should know something as early as tomorrow evening."

"He has to pull through this, he has to!"

"He is in the best hands Sam. The healers have done this before and are most certain he will be well again. Let's leave them for now and check back in later. For now we need to let nature take its course and believe for him to be well."

"All right, I am going to have to trust in the healer's knowledge and in you. He is like my brother and I cannot lose him."

Tayana felt the same fear Sam was feeling and hugged him, much to his surprise. She believed it was what he needed to help him feel better. It was awkward at first but Sam made the right adjustment, they both smiled, and felt better about the situation.

"Thank you Tayana, I was thinking I could use a hug right about now."

"I must have needed it too; it has made me feel better."

"I'm going to finish cleaning the rover then go back to our camp and clean up."

"It will be night in a few hours, you are welcome to bathe in the falls and stay here for the night. We have extra pods and you are welcome to one."

Sam was tired, worried, and could not refuse Tayana's hospitality. He graciously accepted her invitation.

"You may also join us for dinner. Bathing and a change of clothing would be appropriate, would you like some assistance?"

"Uh, sure, assistance with what?" Sam's mind went directly to the shower scene from yesterday and he definitely wanted to do it again, but he wasn't sure what she had meant and didn't want to be a complete pervert.

"With cleaning the rover and bathing. We are very open about our sexuality Sam and I'm pretty sure you enjoyed yourself yesterday."

Sam almost blushed, how did she know about the shower in the falls? Oh yeah, she can read minds. "Sure, I would like some, assistance."

With a knowing smile Tayana headed into the village. Sam returned to cleaning the rover, his mind replaying the whole day. The morning was slow as they had waited for the villagers for almost an hour before taking off to locate the mining camp. Hiding the rover, looking for the camp, and scouting the camp took a good amount of time as well. Then there was the explosion, Grant was blasted with poison, and rushed to the village. Thankfully Tayana and the villagers arrived just in time to help Grant to safety. The race to the village and the time until now seemed to happen in a flash. With only a few hours of daylight left Sam had to get moving to get the rover clean and enjoy his bath. He smiled as his assistants arrived with huge smiles, looking, and smelling amazing beyond what his senses could handle. "You ladies look amazing, and what is that scent, it is quite intoxicating. It's Kyera and Dyanta, right?"

"Hello again Sam!" Kyera's eyes twinkled as she spoke and the soft breeze gently rustled through her long black hair heightening his awareness of her beauty and what was to come. "We have been charged with assisting you with whatever you need and we do so willingly." Her giggle was seconded by Dyanta's and they happily climbed into the rover to help Sam clean. "

He briefly explained the rover to them. Dyanta only partially listening said, "It's so hard, and shiny." Obviously there was no interest in the workings of the rover, its systems or cameras. He changed his tack and directed them to remove the rest of the debris and blood from the rover, and then he needed to bathe. The women were excited by his last statement and made quick work of cleaning the rover to a sparkling shine. With the rover clean the women led Sam down pathways, to a more secluded set of falls.

Sam had a good idea about what might happen and intended to make sure it did. It had been some time since he was intimate with a woman, and now he had two. "Let the bathing begin!" His enthusiasm was rivaled by the women's. They quickly undressed and plunged into the pool. Sam marveled at how fit they were and how nearly perfect they looked. There were a few differences from Earth women, but he wasn't turned off at all. Their hands were thin and delicate and their feet were wide with well-padded soles. He guessed from not wearing shoes. Their perfectly round bottoms and firm breasts propelled Sam to strip and join them as they frolicked in the pool at the bottom of the falls. As he entered the pool the cool water and sound of the falls washed away the day's cares and he relaxed.

The women met him mid pool. Kyera threw her arms tightly around his neck and pulled her taught body snug against his. Dyanta wrapped her arms around his arm and intertwined her legs around one of his. They felt so perfect being so close to him. Their bodies were out of this world. Neither was shy and he found his man parts attended to by both of them. In kind he began to fondle their parts and as responsive as a sports car both women raised a leg to allow him full access. Sam had never been sandwiched between two beautiful women and had never had a woman so willing. He searched for their parts and remembered they were different than the female parts he was familiar with. Kyera sensing his confusion reached down and guided his hand to what felt much like a belly button. She pushed one of his fingers inside and shuddered with the discovery. Sam taking his queue from her found Dyanta's parts and she too shuddered as he slipped in a finger. They were much smaller than Earth women. Sam thought his man parts may cause them considerable discomfort upon entry. After several minutes of the women moaning and gyrating on his hands while they stroked him to the strongest erection he had had in his life, Kyera swung herself to align her body with his, raised herself up then guided him into her. It was impressively tight at first and there was little penetration but she slowly worked him in. She wrapped her legs around him and began to work her magic. Sam was lost in ecstasy. The world could have exploded and he would not care or even noticed. She began kissing him like he had never been kissed before. Dyanta caressed their bodies increasing their sensations and rubbing her body against his back. He could feel her hard nipples poke into his back and his excitement grew. If this was life on this planet he never wanted to leave, ever. Between kisses Sam muttered, "Dear god how did I get so lucky?"

"Because I chose you," was Kyera's reply. Sam and

Kyera were nearing climax, he pulled her tight, and began thrusting into her with full force. She arched her back in pleasure exposing her bare breasts causing Sam to unload what felt like a quart of his seed. She must have felt the same as she tensed her entire body then became limp in his arms, shuddering, and shaking. With a sense of manly pride he knew she had enjoyed it as much as he had. Dyanta gently pulled Kyera from his arms and floated her to the bank of the pool. Sam went to follow and she motioned for him to stay put. He knew why and wasn't sure he was up to such a challenge so soon, he needed to recharge. Dyanta, aware of his dilemma walked slowly through the shallow water towards him. The water glistening on her breasts in the waning evening light and how it trickled from her hair down her face made her look like a goddess. Sam was beginning to think he may be recharged much faster than anticipated. She was working him over with visual stimulation and he could smell her perfume wafting across the dark water. She was graceful and beautiful. Her deep brown hair with its reddish highlights draped across one of her tanned breasts and her smoky eyes set him of fire. He could feel his loins beginning to swell again, he was ready. He walked towards her and took her tightly in his arms carrying her back to the center of the pool. They kissed and again it was different than any kiss he had ever had, well, except for Kyera. There was real passion in Dyanta. She too rose up and inserted him into her. She was not as tight as Kyera and in no time she was thrusting away, panting like a long distance runner. Her vigor was remarkable and he met her thrusts with equal enthusiasm. They moaned aloud and squeezed each other tightly as they climaxed simultaneously. This time Sam felt as if he would be the one to pass out. But Dyanta beat him too it. She lay limp in his arms just as Kyera had. Sam guessed this must be what happens when they experience an orgasm, much like Earth women, and men too. Sam gently floated her to the bank beside Kyera and joined them for a short rest. He was beginning to drift off and a light rain began to fall. He lay on his back letting it tingle on his body. The sex was incredible. Lying on the bank next to the two women he had just shared the most pleasurable experience of his life with, the falling rain was the perfect ending.

He roused them and they softly smiled. "I believe it's almost time for dinner, we need to get dressed and join everyone else." Kyera and Dyanta were slow to get moving not unlike Sam who was moving slowly as well. All three had non-erasable smiles on their faces. He felt a bond with them he couldn't explain. He enjoyed watching them rise and dress, there was something about these two making his senses go crazy.

The rain began to increase as Kyera grabbed her clothing, "We are going to be soaked before we get to the dining hall. There is dry clothing in our pod." The three of them took off towards the village, clothes in hand, naked as they were at birth. The women did not seem fearful at all. Giggling and laughing as they ran. Sam decided to let go of his inhibitions and followed suit. He was captivated by the rain running off their hair and down their backs. He kept pace with them, laughing like a kid again. Was it the women, the rain, or possibly the fact he was running through the village naked. It had a sense of indecency, but also an edge of adventure. They reached Kyera's pod in short order and clamored inside to get out of the rain.

"We can rinse off in here." She led Sam to a small pool just inside the opening of the pod and handed him a large ladle. She took one for herself, scooped up the water, and poured it over herself.

In the light glow of the pod it was one of the most sensual things he had ever seen. Dyanta noticed he was excited, "Ready again? Ooo...I knew I liked you." She began pouring the water over herself as well. Sam did his best not to get too excited but was failing miserably. Missing dinner would not be a good way to look responsible so he hurriedly poured the water over himself.

The women were also aware of the time and quickly finished, leaving Sam fully at attention and wanting.

"You're teases, the both of ya'." Sam quickly rinsed, dried, and dressed in time to head to dinner with his two new loves. Who knew a large leaf would make such a good umbrella, well I guess they did Sam thought to himself. It was dinner as usual but this time Sam was not seated at the head table, he was seated with Kyera and Dyanta, much to his liking. Something was nagging at him but he shrugged it off. He knew it was customary for the village families to sit together at the same table and he found it strange he was sitting with them and their family. After the prayer and announcements the food was served and they began to eat.

Sam saw one of the healers come into the tent and whisper something to Tayana. They left the meal and Sam suspected it had something to do with Grant, so he left too. His hunch was right as he followed them to the healer's tent. He was several steps behind and had not been noticed in the rain. When he entered the tent everyone, including Grant, jumped with a start.

"Holy crap Sam, you scared the life out of me."

"You didn't do me a world of good either young

man." The healer was holding her chest in a gesture of having a heart attack. Tayana just looked at him with surprise.

"Grant, you're all right, thank God. I thought we might lose you and I couldn't live with you being gone." A tear rolled down Sam's cheek, he truly cared for Grant and was overjoyed he was well.

"Sam you're such a sap, but thank you for caring like you do. It really means a lot to me, brother."

"I am Salbola and this is my wife, Emara. We are giving him our best care. He is still not fully well but he should be within a day or two. The poison has been neutralized but the body still needs time to heal. This pod will speed up the process and he will be whole again."

The healers left the pod to join her family at dinner and Tayana urged Sam to go back as well.

"I'll come back in the morning and we can talk, if you're up to it."

"I'm looking forward to it, I have a couple things I want to tell you, go eat and have fun, I'll see you in the morning."

Sam ventured to the dining hall and was happily greeted upon his return. The meal was delicious as always and he said, "I could eat like this every day, you are so lucky! Grant and I eat synthesized food from our galley three meals a day. It does provide an excellent variety but nothing as good as this."

Kyera and Dyanta smiled and looked at each other as they giggled and led Sam back to their pod.

After the meal ended and all was taken care of, Tayana slipped over to the pod where Grant was thinking about her, this planet, and everything transpiring.

"Hello!"

"Well hello again. Come in, I was hoping you'd come back. I have a couple questions I wanted to ask you about today." Grant knew she knew what he was going to ask her.

"Grant, I am so sorry we were not there this morning, I have no excuse."

"Then why, were you hoping we would defeat them alone and you would not have to bring harm to yourself or any of the villagers? You let me get injured instead and then came to my rescue, I very much appreciate you, but you left us to go fight alone."

"Grant, I am very sorry, again, I have no excuse. I can only hang my head in shame and hope you will forgive me and my people."

Grant was not pleased with her answers, but knew persisting would only bring more tension to what was already a tense situation. "I do not hold you responsible Tayana; I just wish you had been there. I'll forgive you, this time!" He said it with a smile and Tayana sighed in relief.

"I was worried you would no longer enjoy my presence. I would be deeply troubled if that was the case."

"How could I be mad at someone so caring and so strikingly beautiful?" He noted a small blush come to her cheeks and smiled. He had scored a small victory.

"I am no beauty, but I do care very much for you. I will leave you to rest and I'll check in on you in the morning. Get some rest, Salbola and Emara will bring you some dinner."

"Good night, see you in the morning." He felt tomorrow was going to be a good day. After he ate what his body would allow, he drifted off to a dream filled sleep with visions of Tayana looming over him after the explosion and her holding his hand in the rover on the way back to the village. The way she looked at him, the things she said, and the way she said them — was he losing his mind or did she have a thing for him? He saw her standing in a pool at the bottom of a small waterfall. She was not wearing her usual black tunic and leather armor. She was wearing a thin loose garment. It clung tightly to her body as she submerged into the dark waters of the pool. She surfaced near the middle, turned, and motioned for him to join her. He did not hesitate and began removing his clothing as he approached the pool. The cool dark water was invigorating and the seductive look on her face was intoxicating. He could sense her intentions and was completely fine with them. There was something about the pool removing all of his inhibitions and increasing his desire for her. Maybe it was the water, maybe it was the setting, but most likely it was the way she was looking at him. She was alluring and any man would give his life to be with her at this moment. A loud boom startled him awake. The light rain had grown into an intense lightning filled storm. "Damn the luck!" He was ticked off the thunder had chosen that particular moment to roust him from such a perfect dream. There was more to the dream and he knew there was a deeper meaning. He drifted back into a much deeper sleep, and dreamt no more.

Chapter Eleven

The sun was still below the horizon when Grant woke from his deep, restful sleep. He wondered what time it was and how the pod kept the gasses out and the oxygen in with a hole in the top of it. He felt lucky to be alive and yet afraid to venture out of the pod knowing the gas levels were too high for him to breath properly. He began thinking about the drone and the alien compound, as he was now calling it. Would it have been a better idea to shoot the sensor with a bot nearby as a decoy, like Sam suggested? He ran the scenario through his head and thought of another brilliant idea. If they got get past the sensors undetected and hid in several different locations one of them being in line with the door the bot came out to replace the broken sensor, then they could fire their own missile into the bunker and blow it up from the inside. "Brilliant I tell ya."

Grant was still ruminating on his plan when Sam poked his head into the pod. "Hey buddy! Good to see you up and moving!"

"Uh, how is it you're breathing under these conditions? It's still early and the sun isn't up." Grant was as perplexed as he had ever been.

"Well, Kyera said the waterfalls and trees in this valley produce their own sort of gas. It acts like a barrier to the helium and hydrogen. I guess it's the density and mixture of the oxygen, helium, and hydrogen allowing the heavier oxygen-rich air to fall to the valley floor and remain in a sort of protective pocket."

"Excellent! I was just thinking I'd have to stay in here until the sun was up before I could go explore."

"You'll be doing no exploring until the healers say you can go exploring. You were practically blown up and severely poisoned all at the same time."

"I'm fine, I feel great, and I can leave when I choose to."

"Said the man in a flowery dress, with no shoes!" Gonna have to play by their rules, buddy, or look like a complete idiot."

"Damn it Sam, go find me some clothes. I'm ready to go kick some drone ass!"

"Whoa there big boy. No one is fighting a drone barefoot and in a dress. Besides, they destroyed your clothing and the tailor is making you some new ones. Um, should be done about lunch time I imagine."

"Are you kidding me? Go back to the shuttle and get some of my own clothes so we can get some payback, now!"

"Nope, not going to do it this time, Grant. I agree with the healers. You need at least another day's rest and then, if they feel you're up to it, we can scout out the situation again, this time with no explosions. We need a better plan than last time."

"Sam, I have a better plan. I was lying here thinking about what happened and what I saw but didn't get the opportunity to tell you. Getting blown up sort of put a damper on things."

"So what's your plan?" Sam was interested but not completely sure Grant was thinking clearly in his current condition.

"Right after you shot the sensor and just before the drone tried to kill us I was watching the bunker through the binoculars. Remember a bot came out to replace the sensor?"

"I vaguely remember it happening. It took the sensor further away from the bunker than it was originally."

"Correct you are. It wasn't the bot taking the sensor farther away it's the hatch opening on the side of the bunker to let the bot out. You starting to get where I'm going with this?"

"Nope, not a clue."

"Come on Sam, think! An open door means the interior of the bunker is exposed!"

Now the wheels were turning in Sam's love-soaked brain. "Oh, we could sneak inside and..."

"Stop right there. We are not sneaking into the bunker. The drone would have us dead to rights before we even made it halfway to the bunker and blow us to hell and back. Come to think of it that damn thing has tried to blow me up twice now."

"Focus Grant, you were actually headed somewhere with this."

"We get past the sensors. You on one side with the rifle, me on the other with a rocket launcher, and the maintenance bot up the middle as a decoy."

Sam took a minute to mull things over then asked, "What are you going to do with the rocket launcher? Shoot it out of the sky?"

"Nope, the bot is! We equip the bot with a small magpopper. When the drone is in range the bot launches the magpopper into the air at the drone. The explosion will send shrapnel flying in all directions. The drone is history if it's within five yards. As soon as the bot leaves the bunker and the door is left open, like it was last time, I will fire a rocket into the bunker through the open door. The rocket should destroy the controls and guidance systems controlling the drone."

"Brilliant Grant, I love this plan. I say we take some villagers with us as back up just in case we um...fail. They can be the decoys and we can run and hide." Grant noted the sarcasm and gave him his, I just came up with an amazing plan and you're crapping all over it, look.

"Really Grant, it is a good plan, but I do think we need some back up. Remember what happened last time?!"

"All right, they can come and be back up if needed. This has become personal to me, very personal. Like I said, it has tried to blow me up twice and I'm not giving it another chance."

Sam reached outside and retrieved a change of clothing for Grant. "Okay, simmer down, take off the dress and put these on. It will be breakfast soon and if you remember, the food is awesome."

Grant dressed and reluctantly headed towards the black pod. A thought struck him, "Sam if you need to use the restroom you can go first, I may be a minute."

"Restroom, where did you find a restroom? I've been peeing and taking a dump behind the bushes over past the falls. Pretty secluded, but you gotta watch what leaves you use. The wrong ones could kill ya."

Grant laughed and told him Tayana had shown him where to go when she was giving him the tour. "The black pods are unisex restrooms. You squat on the stump and do your business."

"Sweet, I need to go, thanks buddy! I'll just be a minute." Sam hurried over to the pod and Grant mumbled under his breath, "A minute, you'll be out of there in under forty five seconds, sucker!" Knowing what was about to take place he began to chuckle. Sam let out a yell making snot come out of Grant's nose. He knew

Sam was trapped by his junk and there was nothing he could do to get free. Tears were rolling down his face and he could barely breathe when Sam emerged, yanking up his pants and stumbling as he looked backwards at the pod. The expression on his face was priceless. Grant's stomach ached from the laughter and he was dizzy from a lack of oxygen.

"What a damn dirty trick. What the hell just happened?"

Through tears and a lack of breath Grant got out, "It's the restroom. I'd be more concerned about where it's been. Better yet it should be concerned about where you've been." Grant couldn't control it any longer and laughed so loud anyone still sleeping was now fully awake.

"Pay back's a bitch, Grant and oh you're gonna pay big time for this one."

Grant was almost hyperventilating. He was taking gulps of air to try and stay conscious. "Oh my god Sam, I must have looked exactly like you did after my time, whew. Still a bit light headed here, uh ha."

Sam was not amused at his delight. He pictured Grant running out of the pod tripping over his pants at his ankles and screaming, "What the hell was that, my anus was just invaded," and he began to laugh, too.

Their laughter was beginning to draw a small crowd. "Time to go, Sam." They wiped tears from their faces before they entered the gathering hall for breakfast.

Sam began to saunter off to his place with Kyera and Dyanta. "Where are you going? We are sitting with Tayana up front."

"Nope, I guess I've been adopted. I've been sitting with these two and their family for the last few meals."

"Suit yourself, I kind of like the head table. Elevated a little and makes me feel almost royal."

"I'd rather be me than be royal."

"Yes, you would, wouldn't you, dog!" Grant added the dog with a smile, Sam knew the meaning and wore it like badge of honor."

Breakfast was once again a feast and no one went hungry. They always made just the right amount of food with little if any leftovers. As the morning wore on they relaxed and planned some more on the next day's adventure.

Grant began to wonder where Tayana had gotten off to. She left unnoticed shortly after breakfast. "I wonder what Tayana is up to."

"Most likely dealing with some political mishap or possibly someone stubbed a toe and she needed to tend to them."

Sam's comment landed on deaf ears as Grant was envisioning his dream again. It was so real and she was so beautiful. But she was the leader of this village and she looked like a forest-dwelling badass. Was she really tough or did she just like dressing like she was. He didn't really want to find out, but really he sort of did.

"Earth to Grant, hello spacer!"

Grant was jerked out of his daydream by his annoying sidekick friend. "So you know, your timing sucks! What?"

"Where were you? Your eyes glazed over and you were a million miles away, lost in the ether."

"If you must know, I had a steamy dream about Tayana. There was this pool with black water by a small waterfall. She was there in a very thin gown and it clung to her as she walked deeper into the pool. I couldn't seem to help myself and headed in after her."

"You're not going to believe this, but I know where that pool is, I can take you there if you'd like. I've experienced the dark water and the sensation you described. The sound of the water, the smell of the flowers all around it, the girls swimming naked and...well, I know where the pool is anyway." Sam jerked himself out of his daydream with a slight rosy glow on his cheeks.

"Sam, is there something you want to tell me?" Grant had a feeling there was a lot more to this story. He didn't really want to hear the sordid details, but the scientist in him did want to know. Did Sam have sexual relations with an alien life form? What were the repercussions? What were the rules of engagement? Did Tayana know and what would happen if she did? Grant was concerned Sam may have broken the trust of the huntress. He may get to see her be a badass after all.

"I plead the fifth! I'd really like a fifth right about now too."

"Seriously, can you not keep your dick in your pants anywhere we go? Where is moral compass?"

"Get in the pool, Grant, get in the pool!"

"What the hell do you mean? Get in the pool."

"You'll see, soon enough."

Grant took it as a threat and scowled at Sam. He had a good idea what Sam meant, but wasn't in the mood to deal with it right now. He decided he needed to go lie down for a while and get some more rest. "I'm headed back to the med pod for a while. I think you're right, I wasn't ready to go drone hunting today. I'm not in top shape, yet."

"I'm sorry Grant, I didn't mean to piss you off or upset you. I wanted you to know the joy and pleasure I've experienced. Sharing the love, buddy!"

"I get it Sam, but I need some rest. Come get me if I'm not there for dinner." Grant slowly walked back to the med pod to lie down and hopefully dream some more. And dream he did, the same dream as the night before. It was exhilarating and exciting, but there was more to it. He could not put his finger on it. He fell into a troubled sleep.

Chapter Twelve

When morning came Grant was up and moving. He felt he had to get ahead of them for the healers give him clearance to leave the village and to get Sam off his back. He dressed and headed into the village for a morning stroll. The sun was only beginning to rise and its light was creating a dim glow across the many pools surrounding the pods whose bioluminescence added an amazing effect to the scene. The soft crush of the waterfall and the twinkles of light reflecting on its moving surface made Grant feel as if he was the one moving. He momentarily lost his balance. Under his breath he muttered, "Jesus, I hope no one saw that. They'd have me back in bed in a heartbeat." He continued his journey marveling at the setup of the village. The terraced landings where the pods rested, the waterfalls and streams flowing right through the middle of the village, and the way the community worked together. It was all a fairytale, simple and wholesome, but it was also real. Out of the corner of his eye he saw movement and noticed several villagers out and about. He guessed they were the ones preparing the morning meal. He wandered to the dining hall and wondered why Sam hadn't woken him for dinner and why he was sitting with the women, well not really wondering, as they were both very beautiful.

He was so lost in his thoughts he nearly bumped into a villager. "Whoa, my apologies friend! I was being absent minded and did not see you there." The villager looked at Grant in wonder; it was if he was being given a gift or something.

He looked like a star struck teenager at their first

concert and the star was walking past them down the red carpet.

"No worries sir! I was moving too quickly for my own good."

"What's your name? Can I assist you with your duties?" The young villager's mouth dropped open and he momentarily froze in place, to Grant's surprise. "Did I say something wrong? Is it not appropriate to help others do their duties?"

"Sir, you sit at the head table, you are not allowed to be a servant, you are to be served. I am humbled by your generosity but respectfully, no, you may not assist me." He quickly turned and whispered, "My name is Tyoka." Then hurried off and began setting a table some distance away.

Grant had not realized there was a hierarchy in the village and it was disrespectful to do anything other than what your station required. He hoped Tyoka was not offended by his offer. He decided to wander into the kitchen, the covered area outside of the dining hall, around back, out of view. As Grant rounded the corner Tayana was talking with the head cook. When she saw him, she indicated they would finish later, and walked towards him with a slight smile and bright eyes gleaming.

"Hello, welcome back to the living and walking. You have been missed at the meals."

"I have missed being here to dine with you. You look lovely this morning." He gave her a slight smile back.

"If I didn't know better I'd say you're flirting with me, sir."

He looked only slightly surprised; he was caught and didn't deny it. "I'm glad you noticed Yes, I am flirting with you, and so early in the morning. I'm a cad, what can I say?"

"You are charming and full of yourself; I like that in an alien." They laughed and began talking about where she was the previous day. She had not visited him and he missed her company. "I took a trip up to see the Digger's camp. We were not seen or detected by the sensors. I have an idea that might fit in with your plans, if you're willing to hear me."

"By all means What did you come up with?"

"The sensors are triggered by motion. Under our cloak we cannot be detected and were able to get within the perimeter of the camp. We did not push too far, but far enough to see there may be one stationed in the bunker."

"I thought it was completely automated."

"We think not. We do not intend to destroy his life, only the bunker. We came up with a plan to lure him out and stun him. We can move him to safety before you execute your plan of destroying the bunker."

"Good idea, we have no reason to take his life and he may be able to give us some valuable information."

"We can cross that bridge when we are there. I must prepare for the morning announcements. We can talk more during our meal." Tayana headed off to prepare and Grant marveled at her nerve. She might be a badass after all.

She could have been blown to bits, but still took the chance. "Mmm, my kind of woman!"

"Grant!" Sam came bounding into the dining hall, startling him back to reality. "Good to see you out of bed. Did the healers give you the go ahead to wander about?"

"Not yet, I'm not even sure they're up yet, still pretty early."

"I'm sure they'll let you go. Got some drone ass to kick this morning, then a nice lunch when we're done. Then some actual work stuff with the bots, some dinner, and then some pool time." The look on Sam's face said it all. He was addicted to the pool.

"First things first Sam, breakfast!"

"Good call, I'm starving."

After announcements and breakfast were complete the team gathered for their assault on the bunker. The healers cleared Grant, on his word he would return to them for a quick evaluation when they were done, and no blood or poison this time. Grant informed every one of the plan, what their role was, and what they needed to do, and when. "Let's get moving."

Grant and Sam got into the rover and Tayana and her crew rounded up rides of their own. "Oh my god Grant, they are riding C-Rex's. I guess this really is a chicken fight." Sam couldn't control himself and began laughing.

"Eyes on the road buddy. Don't want to die before we get there."

"I hear ya, but ya gotta admit, that was funny!"

"Just drive."

"You really are taking this personal aren't you? I probably would too if I was 0 and 2."

"Sam, you're an ass, and yes, this is personal. I got shot out of the sky and nearly blown to bits. It's time to get some payback."

"Or go 0 and 3. That would really suck!"

"Stop talking, and drive."

Sam chuckled under his breath. "0 and 3, here we come"

When they neared the mining compound Grant pointed for Sam to go East to the edge of the tree line.

"Drop me off here with the rocket launcher and some ammo, then head west to the small incline past where we were last time. You need high ground and it is the best spot. From here I have a direct shot into the bunker when their bot comes out. As long as neither of us is detected before we can get our shots off, we should be good."

Sam liked the plan and thought they had done a great job covering their bases. Tayana and some of her crew circled around the back side of the compound, while others cloaked the bot to keep it from being seen too soon. With the bot cloaked and everyone in their positions, Grant signaled for the assault to begin.

Sam took aim. Again a perfect shot took out the sensor. "Sensor down, I'm on the move south, don't want this thing following my trail again. You're up Grant."

As they guessed, the top of the bunker opened and out came the drone. "Uncloak the bot, now!" The cloak was turned off and the bot began making its way toward the bunker. The drone immediately fired a missile at the bot. It was a near miss. The bot from the bunker was programmed to replace a broken sensor and left the safety of the bunker to do its job. Once the bot moved out of Grant's line of sight he took aim at the hatch. The maintenance bot began firing at the drone. He wondered who had outfitted it with a weapon other than a magpopper, Sam.

"Sam, what the hell did you do? It was not part of the plan."

"Sorry Grant, I thought we needed a little more backup. It has to be able to defend itself so it can fire the magpopper at the right time."

Before Grant could take aim again, several more drones exited the bunker and chaos ensued. There were drones zooming everywhere, missiles being fired at random targets, villagers slipping in and out of cloak, and he still had not gotten off his shot. Several of the villagers had thrown a net over one of the drones. It was veering all different directions and came very close to Grant's hiding spot. Ten seconds later the net-covered drone crashed into mining equipment causing a huge explosion. All its missiles blew up at the same time, leaving a bus-sized crater in the ground. Dirt, dust, and debris were pushed into the air clouding Grant's view of the bunker. All hell was breaking loose. He had to get off his shot, now!

He took careful aim. While barely able to see, he fired a rocket into the bunker. "Rocket away, rocket away!" Seconds later the rocket entered the bunker through the hatch, and much to Grant's surprise and dismay, it did not explode right away. It did explode, just not where it should have.

"Rocket exited the back of the bunker. Grant, use the SHTF."

"The what?"

"Use the damn SHTF and take cover."

"Where is the SHTF?"

"For the love of God, Grant, it looks like a large cluster of grapes. Fire the damn thing now or we're all toast." He yelled into the communicators, "Take cover behind something large, do it, do it, do it!"

Grant loaded the SHTF, took aim, and once again, was fired upon by a drone. "Not this time bitch!"

Grant got off the shot and dove behind a large boulder covering his face and ears. He wasn't sure if he was on target or not, but prayed he was so he wouldn't die in a fetal position under a large rock only to be discovered by archeologists thousands of years from now. It was the loudest explosion he ever heard. It shook the rocks he was hiding behind and the deep boom rattled his chest with a vengeance. Suddenly the trees around him were decimated by something unseen. "What the hell is happening? Oh God, save me." It wasn't his finest moment, but he didn't really care. He was terrified and had no idea what was happening. As quickly as it began, it ended. He lay there for some time waiting for the smoke to clear and to be sure it was safe to venture out of hiding.

"Sam, you all right, Sam?"

"I'm here, got a few scrapes but doing well."

"Tayana, are you and your crew all right?"

"We took cover in the nick of time. A little more forewarning would have been nice."

"Tayana, I apologize, I should have given Grant more time to get his shot off, and all of you more time to take cover. Did anyone get hurt?"

"A few cuts and bruises, but we are all here."

Sam couldn't bear the thought of losing someone because he had not warned them quick enough. He almost lost his best friend in a very similar situation a couple weeks ago.

"When the smoke clears we can assess the situation and damage. I don't hear any equipment or a drone, that's a good sign. Sam?"

"I don't hear or see any drones, with the exception of one hanging in a tree by its one remaining propeller."

Grant poked his head out from around the rock. The devastation was far greater than he imagined it would be. He expected the bunker to look like Swiss cheese, and damage to nearby things, but this, was apocalyptic. There were holes in everything, the bunker, the mining equipment, drones, bots, the ground, and the trees were holey and stripped bare. What the hell was the SHTF anyway? Grant gave the okay to come out of hiding and began walking towards the bunker. Sam met him there. Tayana and crew were not far behind. "Sam, what the hell is the SHTF? Did it do all of this damage?"

"It's one of my creations, and yes, it did all of this damage. The PSAD would never develop a weapon of this caliber, or knowingly allow it on one of their research vessels. I hid it in my bag before I boarded the Ebony Belle.

"I must have missed it in armory training. What does SHTF stand for?"

Sam looked at Grant in complete awe. "You really don't know what you just fired into the bunker or what SHTF stands for. We have to have a serious discussion."

"Well, what does it stand for?"

"It stands for Shit is Hitting The Fan! It was hitting the fan and to save us all I told you to fire it into the bunker. I knew what was going to happen and I knew it wasn't going to be pretty."

"Good call. I think I'll take you up on the armory discussion, soon. I'm glad these boulders were here or we wouldn't be. Let's get our wounds tended to, and then we can explore the bunker and mining compound, agreed?"

"I'm glad no one was seriously injured, bleeding, or poisoned."

They laughed at Tayana's comment, but agreed.

"You know you like taking care of me."

"Yes, but I need you well, I want you whole."

Grant raised an eyebrow, and then smiled, she smiled back.

"Grant, the haze has stopped!"

"Yes Sam, it has."

Everyone cheered. In her excitement Tayana hugged Grant, close and almost inappropriately. She pressed her body tightly against his and lingered a moment longer than she should have. The look in her eyes was lustful. He did not mind one bit and hoped she would do it again soon. He could not get the look out of his mind; he had seen it before but now was not the time to think about it, even though he did.

"Tayana and I will search the bunker. The rest of you please gather the drones and parts, and bring them to the bunker. Be careful, there might still be live rounds on them. We will look at them later."

"You four, check out the mining equipment and see if you can figure out what they were mining.

Grant and crew headed towards what was left of the bunker. "Jesus, Sam, if I knew we had that much firepower we would have dusted this place sooner."

"I think you may have enjoyed that too much! Gonna have to keep a close eye on the armory. I don't want you out night hunting alone."

Grant smiled. As they neared the bunker Grant could not resist saying, "Sam, you have point."

"The hell I do! We go in together or we don't go in!"

Grant laughed and pushed past Sam, who was still reeling, followed closely by Tayana who stopped and looked Sam up and down, spun, glanced over her shoulder, and entered the bunker.

Sam muttered, "Well it's not fair, there's two of you." Then louder, "For the record, I was not afraid!"

Once they were inside Grant led the way. The roof of

the bunker was mostly gone and several walls were demolished. Pieces were scattered around with parts of equipment and other items. The SHTF was very thorough and did not miss much. The bunker was the dimension of a four bedroom house in an average part of town, with fifteen feet high ceilings.

"I think we're standing in the central bay."

Sam, being his usual smart ass self, said, "Your grasp of the obvious amazes me, Grant. All the mechanical stuff sort of gives it away."

"The drones were stacked in here on these odd landing pads." Grant pointed to circular landing pads arranged in a grid pattern about eight feet off the ground with a ladder leading up to the walkway surrounding them. "We need to get a count of the drones. From the look of things, there were probably nine of them. I would hate to have one of them flying around rogue, randomly blowing stuff up. Let's keep looking."

Tayana motioned they should check out the door at the other end of the bay. Once inside they realized it was what was left of living quarters. It was sparse. A bed, a table with two chairs, and a small dressing area. It looked recently used by a slob, at best. Clothing was scattered about and dirty dishes were relocated by the blast. The restroom was little more than a hole in the floor and no place to wash up. "I hope the occupant was only here when they set up the mining compound. Now would not be a good time to run into them."

Grant and Sam ignored her comment. Grant said, "Let's go check out the other end of this place. There has to be a control room or something in here." The other end of the building had two doors. The one on the left revealed nothing but daylight. They slowly opened the remaining door leading to the room in the other corner. It was fairly preserved despite the massive holes blown into everything, everywhere. "Sam, this looks it was a control room. See the cables running up the wall? They probably connected to the communications equipment on the roof and up the tower."

There was a bank of computers, a small workstation, and a chair miraculously standing, but rolled to the corner. There were drawings on the workstation and a tablet. It would take weeks if not months to decipher once they got them back to the shuttle. Sam noticed a small room behind the computer bank and peeked inside. He let out a scream like a six year old girl being chased by her brother with a snake. He mustered the courage to say, "Uh, Grant, there's a body over here."

Grant immediately rushed to see what Sam had found, "Holy crap, it is a body!"

Sam shook his head and stepped inside the room. Whatever it was, it was no longer breathing and was fairly well ventilated, like the surrounding walls. "Have either of you seen anything like this?"

"Never have I seen such a hideous thing." Tayana looked disgusted at the sight of the dead alien.

The alien was larger than a human and had four muscular arms. Its face looked swollen and Grant thought he could make out multiple eyes, but they could be holes from the blast. It was brownish green and covered in rough bumpy skin. There were no ears to speak of and its nose was flat and very broad. The mouth was wide with two full rows of razor sharp teeth. The teeth were nasty and full of food pieces. "I guess this guy forgot his toothbrush." Its elephantine feet were covered in heavy boots and the body was mostly covered with tough thick clothing. Its hands were massive and filthy.

"I can't even imagine where those have been." Sam was almost as grossed out as Tayana looked. He hadn't seen any toilet paper or towels anywhere and his imagination went wild.

"We need to get as much of this to the shuttle as we can. We can examine it later or send it back to the PSAD lab and have them do it."

"Great idea, Grant. Send our boss the stuff we don't really want to process and then fly away into space with his newest toys, not to be heard from again for several months, years, or ever, brilliant."

"Sam, don't you have somewhere you need to be?"

They laughed and Sam called some of the villagers inside to haul the alien to the shuttle. "We need to process this guy. Another intelligent life form, we hit the jackpot, Grant. That's now what, four intelligent life forms on the same planet? First trip out and bam, heroes. We will never have to work again."

"Ha, not quite so simple. We are owned by the PSAD. Whatever we find is theirs and they get all of the credit, remember who we're dealing with?"

Sam thought for a moment and realized Grant was more than likely right about this one. The PSAD was a great organization but it was run by some not so upstanding people who didn't really care about you or your life. They wanted fame and glory for themselves. The exception being Major Abram T. Aboy. He thought the world of Grant and Sam and would do most anything for them, even if he did act and sound like he didn't really like them a good portion of the time. He was really a soft hearted teddy bear when you got to know him. The drones were piled up and counted to be sure all of them were accounted for and none were rogue. "I count nine, Grant."

"I got nine, too. Thank God we got them all. I would lose my mind if there was another one out there on a seek and destroy mission and we were its targets. I've had enough crap!"

"Me too!"

"Me as well!"

"Tayana, come here and check this out." Grant, Sam, and Tayana made their way to the mining pit where the equipment had ceased operations. "They must have been controlled from inside and more than likely; the dead alien was monitoring their progress."

Grant noticed something unusual, there were no tailings from the mining operations, and the mining equipment was considerably smaller than he thought was necessary to successfully mine anything. "These must be used to get samples, sort of like our bots."

"I think you're right, but what have they been sampling?" As they approached the group gathered around the pit, there were whispers and giggles. The whole thing seemed like a joke.

Tayana picked up on it. "What foolishness are you up to? We are here for serious matters, not to make fun, and exercise as if it was play time."

"Tayana, we are not playing, look at the machinery." A gaping hole was ripped into the side of the machinery. Peering in they saw why the villagers were whispering and giggling. It was full of diamonds, rubies and other precious gems, some beautiful unknown gems were there, too.

"All right then, wow! Grant, can we be heroes now, please?"

"Sam, now we are heroes!" Grant reached in and grabbed a handful of gems, awed by their size and quality. "These machines must either vaporize the soil or singularly extract each gem without having to move mountains of soil and rock. This is amazing!"

"Grant, Tayana, this one is full of gold and other valuable metals. We will look in the other machines, too."

Other machines contained materials they had not seen before and one contained an emerald green liquid smelling like bathroom sanitizer, at least to Grant and Sam.

"This planet must have been volcanic in nature in the not too distant past, judging from what they were mining. We need to gather what was mined and take half to the village and half to the shuttle."

Grant thought he was being generous. He was shocked when Tayana said, "No, we will take nothing from these creatures. Besides, we have no need for anything here, but for decoration and adornment. You can take it all."

Grant, not knowing quite what to say, understood the subtle undertones of why she refused. These may have been the creatures that killed her family. "Tayana, I think I understand your position. We will remove the items to our shuttle for analysis."

"Thank you, Grant. You really are a hero!" He smiled and they shared a knowing look.

"Grant, I had a troubling thought." Sam paused for a few seconds gathering his thoughts.

"Well, let's hear it, don't leave us hanging."

Sam continued, "We just destroyed an alien mining operation. It was purposely hidden under a static haze in order to not be detected. It appears to be a lucrative operation and has now ceased. The radio beacon that was on the top of the tower probably got off a signal before we blew it to bits. I'm pretty sure we will have visitors of the dead alien variety very soon. I think we need to have Eliot signal for immediate assistance from the PSAD so we don't get blown to bits and the Ebony Belle taken over by these things, or worse, destroyed."

"Sam, you're right and bordering on genius sometimes, not now of course, but I will radio Eliot to make the calls. We need to get the shuttle flight worthy as quickly as we can."

"There is a slight problem with the plan. The shuttle is flight worthy but only here on the planet. The AG drive was slightly damaged in the crash."

"What do you mean slightly damaged?"

"You better be playing around because if you're not, we are screwed. The Ebony Belle is a sitting duck and we are next on the list. These aliens did not look friendly and their drones were less friendly. What do we need to do to get it flight worthy?"

"I'm going to have to test some of the materials we're gathering to see if there is anything I can use to create an alloy similar in strength to the broken part."

"Is that all? Is there anything else that needs repaired... is there any...Grant collapsed to the ground.

Everyone began to move all at once. Sam caught his head before it hit the ground with a thud. "Grant, Grant!" We need to get him back to the healers, now. Tayana help me get him into the rover." Sam carried Grant on his shoulders for over half a mile to get back to the rover. His back and legs were numb. He knew he had to get Grant back to the village as soon as he could. Tayana trotted along behind Sam, who despite Grant's heavy weight, was moving at a brisk pace and not stopping for anything. When they arrived at the rover Sam practically leapt into it with Grant still on his shoulders. He not so gently put him in the back and told Tayana to strap him in and not to let him fall off.

"Hurry Sam, his pulse is weakening and he is sweating like crazy. We need the healers fast."

Sam took off like a rocket with reckless abandon, sailing across the plains leaving a trail of dust behind them. The ride was rough but swift. Sam had a déjà vu moment. They did this exact same thing less than a week ago, only without the blood and poison this time. Sam frantically crossed the falls and raced down the hill to the healers pod, coming to an unceremonious halt right in front of their door. "It's Grant, he passed out while we were talking, then collapsed. He's sweating again." Sam was dragging him out of the rover as he spoke.

"Bring him inside quickly, we were afraid of this. Some of the poison is still in his system. It lays dormant waiting for stressful situations, and then reacts with the nervous system to immobilize its host."

"Is he going to be all right like last time?"

"Sam. We need to go and let them do their thing. Sam!"

Sam reluctantly pulled himself from the pod and walked away. He didn't know how much more of this Grant could take. He had been through the wringer since they crashed.

"Sam, you have to have faith. Salbola and Emara know what they are doing. They have seen this before and have the right herbs to treat him."

"I know, Tayana, but he was weak and I've never seen him so frail and helpless. I can't even imagine how he must have felt right before he began to pass out. He was getting angry and louder by the second and then, he was on the ground. The look on his face will haunt me. His eyes were zinging back and forth and then they rolled back into their sockets. I didn't know what to do. I didn't want him injured so I grabbed his head and made sure it didn't split like a melon when he hit the ground. I am terrified right now."

"Sam, I cannot promise he will be all right, but I can promise the healers will do their best to bring him back to full health and this time he will not get out of bed too soon, I will see to it myself."

"Thank you, I'm going to take a walk and clear my head."

"Want some company?"

"No, I think I need to be alone for a while. I have some things I need to get straight in my head before he wakes up, if he wakes up." Sam truly hurt inside and walked towards the top of the falls alone. He made it to the top he looked around at the beauty surrounding him and marveled at the similarities between there and Earth. Pines and bushes were growing between the streams and amongst the rocks. The stream, flowers in all colors lining the banks, and the reeds rustling in the breeze, gingerly dipped their leaves into the cool dark water. It was breath taking. Sam waded into the stream about knee deep with thoughts of walking to the edge and letting the water take him over the falls. Instead, he found a flat dry rock near the edge of the falls and took a seat. He felt alone and isolated in this strange world without Grant there to laugh at this stupid humor and set him straight when he really got out of hand. He was Sam's rock and his idol, always was, and always would be. He had to pull through, he had to. Sam lay back and got lost in the gurgling of the stream, the rustle of the reeds and flowers, and the swishing sound the wind made as it softly swirled past him. The caress of the breeze on his face and the rays of sunlight filtering through the trees made this one of his favorite places on this alien world. "How is it that my best friend is fighting for his life and I'm lounging around a stunning waterfall surrounded by all of this beauty? There has to be something about this place that isn't quite right."

He called Eliot "Eliot, are you there?"

"I am always here, how can I assist you?"

"Eliot, Grant was injured again. The poison had not completely left his system and he is once again struggling for his life and at the mercy of the healers' knowledge and skill. We need to get a message to PSAD regarding what we have discovered and we may have inadvertently started an inner planetary war of sorts. We need some serious back up."

"I am aware of what you have discovered, Sam. I can be of more assistance if you provide me with more information."

"We raided the bunker in the mining camp and blew it all to hell. They were mining for precious metals and gems. We discovered this when we searched the equipment, it was also destroyed in the blast. Their machinery is amazing and needs to be reverse engineered. We discovered an alien being. It is being delivered to the shuttle as we speak. He was killed by our SHTF rocket when it was launched into the bunker. There is a lot of technology here we are not familiar with and it needs to be researched in the PSAD labs. We are afraid the alien in the bunker may have sent a distress call before we blew up the bunker. If this is the case, depending on how close their planet is to this one, we have just a few days; maybe a week before they arrive to see what happened to their operation. When they see the Ebony Belle parked in orbit they will either capture it or destroy it, I can live with neither option. Please call for help and tell them it is paramount they bring battle cruisers. We have no idea what we may be up against. Oh, and tell them we have discovered four new forms of intelligent life. That will get them moving for sure."

"The message has been sent. It will take two days to make its way to the receiver in the PSAD communications hub and two days to receive their response."

"Thank you Eliot, you are a blessing."

"I am an EL 10 T, this is my programming."

Sam cocked his head to the side and said, "We are going to have to see about a personality upgrade for you when we get back to Earth."

Helium Fall

Chapter Thirteen

"Eliot, I need your help. The expansion port on the AG drive cracked when we crashed and I need to fabricate a new part. We do not have a spare here on the shuttle. Can you assist me in processing the materials we brought aboard from the mining operation? There may be something in there we can use to make a new part for the drive."

"Yes, I can assist you, where would you like to begin?"

"Let's begin with the metals, there may be something in there we can mix to make an alloy strong enough to hold until we get back to the Ebony Belle."

"This will take time and there is no guarantee a combination will be found."

Sam was fully aware of their situation and dreaded the short amount of time they had to come up with something. He and Eliot broke down each material analyzing it with a spectrogram to see what chemicals will bond and what ones may cause an explosion. This could take days and they didn't have many of them to get this done. "We have to work fast. We must be complete within the next two days or we may be in for a rude awakening."

"I will process at the limit of my capabilities."

"That's all I ask, Eliot, that's all I ask. The lab is well equipped and we will make every effort to figure this out. Our lives hang in the balance and we must repair the broken shuttle and get it flight worthy. Grant's last words are still ringing in my ears and my thoughts are everywhere, but where they should be."

"Sam, it has been six hours since we started our analysis. You have not stopped to eat, drink, or relieve yourself."

"My focus is beginning to get the better of me."

"Sam, you must rest. You are not performing at your peak and are making simple errors. Get some food, rest for a few hours, and then return, refreshed and clear minded."

"Eliot, I am going to take your advice. I have to pee so bad I may not make it to the head." Sam bolted from the lab and ran down the passageway to the head closest to the galley. Once inside he barely got into position before the pee started to flow. "Damn close Sam, too damn close!" He washed up and headed into the galley for a late dinner. It was a little past midnight and he was starving. He punched up a protein drink, a banana pudding, a couple of grilled cheese sandwiches, and some tomato basil soup. Not his best combination but it was comfort food for him and Grant was not around to keep him in check. He was exhausted and knew sleep would come quickly regardless of his brain working overtime. The soup and sandwich filled the comfort portion of the meal, the protein drink replenished his needed vitamins and minerals, and the banana pudding hit the spot, pushing him to the brink of total comfort.

"Eliot, please wake me if you come up with anything. You might want to try the green sand looking stuff mixed with the grey gooey looking stuff."

"Very technical of you, Sam, I will do my best."

Sam made his way to his quarters where he promptly collapsed onto this bed and fell asleep. The dreams did not come tonight and he slept like a rock until Eliot woke him from his much needed sleep.

"Sam, I figured out the correct combination to fabricate the part needed for the anti-gravity drive."

"Great news, I will take a quick shower, eat, and be down shortly." Sam's mind was not fully awake as he sat on the edge of his bed assimilating what he heard. In a stupor he made his way to the head, did his business, and stepped into the shower. "Holy crap that's cold," he stepped back out of the shower. The shock of the cold water brought his eyes wide open. After adjusting the temperature to his satisfaction he got back in the shower. He did some of his best thinking in the shower and this morning was no exception. Eliot found a good combination for their project, but Sam needed to know how they were going to forge the part. Once the part was forged he would install it, test the shuttle, and check on Grant. Game plan in place, he finished and headed to the galley. No comfort food this morning. Protein drink, peanut butter and jelly toast, and three over hard eggs, lightly salted with smoked pepper seasoning. "It should hold me for a while."

Sam bounded down the passageway and into the lab to find Eliot at the helm of an automated loader, beginning to smelt the materials.

"Eliot, what are you doing?"

"I am moving the process along, as you would say. I have calculated the proper temperature and time in the smelter to produce the slag we need to pour into the forms I created while you were sleeping."

"Well I'll be damned!"

"No Sam, you will be crushed if you do not move out of the way." Eliot had yet to find a sense of humor, but it was in the works, according to Sam.

As the slag began to pour into the molds, Sam

noticed an odd scent wafting through the air; it tickled his nose and made his skin super sensitive. Not a feeling he detested but something way out of the ordinary, it made him sort of uncomfortable. He couldn't quite place the feeling but it was familiar and his mind drifted to the women and the pool.

"Man, I miss Kyera and Dyanta." Shaking his head to clear his thoughts and get back on track he had a thought, "Eliot, what materials did you use to create the slag?"

"In your terms, I used the green sand looking stuff mixed with the grey gooey looking stuff, added some crushed plant material, then mixed in some clay. We have created basic metallic porcelain. It is stronger than steel and lighter than aluminum. The first batch is cooling now. We need to see how well it can be tooled or if we need to be more precise in our form design."

"Excellent work Eliot. Has it cooled enough for me to pick it up? "

"I believe it is cool enough to be picked up, with care."

Sam donned a pair of thick gloves and picked up the first piece. "It needs to be cleaned off a bit." He went to a water bath and immersed the piece. The water began to boil and he thought nothing of it since the piece was still hot from being smelted and cast. When the water began to foam he quickly pulled the piece out and gasped. "Holy crap Eliot, this thing is melting!"

"I calculated it would begin to disintegrate when you submerged it in the water. The chemicals that make it tough and light quickly separate when water is added. Making it the perfect product for space and a poor a product for a submarine."

Sam laughed, "Did you just make a joke? Dry humor

Eliot, way to go."

"I was not being funny; I was stating the facts about the application of the material."

"Either way it made me laugh. Let's get another casting and I'll see how well it can be tooled. Once I get it installed we can get the heck out of here." Sam went to see what needed to be done in order for them to take off and go find the bots.

"We are a couple of slobs! When did we make such a mess?" He began dismantling their small but cluttered camp and put everything back inside the shuttle. Eliot would be done in short order and time was running out. He took in their table and chairs, and finally their equipment and tools. It took him about an hour and it was closing in on 10 AM.

"Time to check on Eliot."

"How goes it, Eliot?"

"I have cast three pieces, two for testing and one for the final fit."

"A tooling I will go, gotta get this craft flight worthy today. If the parts can be tooled we can be in the air in an hour."

Sam took a drill to the first piece and it went through smoothly with no incident. He took the piece to a grinder to grind off the rough edges and burrs. Again, no incidents. "Great luck, Eliot, the piece took drilling and tooling well. Now I can go test fit it and adjust as needed. We can be in the air shortly if all goes well."

"Great news, Sam."

Sam made several small adjustments to the piece with a hand file and it finally slipped perfectly into place. He fastened it in and marveled at what they had accomplished in such a short time. "We are going to be airborne in about fifteen minutes; we can make it to the Ebony Belle and get the heck out of here. Eliot, have you made it back to your dock?"

"I am five minutes from a complete dock."

"Good, we take off in fifteen minutes." Sam tested the controls, cleaned up the bridge, and performed a full systems check. *What a mess, it seems like we haven't been here for at least a week. I wonder how Grant's doing, but I've got to have this ship ready to move, every minute counts. Grant's in good hands, and once he's healed, we'll be all right – I hope.* All systems checked out. "Eliot, prepare to take off, low levels first please."

"Initiating take off."

"Ten feet off the ground, beginning maneuvers." Sam swung the shuttle left, then right, rising and falling. "Take us up another forty feet please."

"Rising to fifty feet."

Sam began to fly forward, stopped, and backed the shuttle up. "All systems seem to be in working order Eliot, let's take this thing for a spin, and I don't mean flipping us over."

"What is our heading?"

"Let's go find the bots; we need to get them loaded. We will process their findings later, but for now we need to get them aboard and secured." The bots were much farther away than Sam anticipated, "Do you have the bots on your radar? I'm not seeing them on mine yet."

"They are five miles away. They traveled as planned over the last three days and are waiting for pick up."

"This will be their last mission here. The mining camp gave us a great deal of information and we are sure this is a life sustaining planet, with water, food, and other natural resources. I'm certain it will be mined. It will probably be turned into a destination planet for the wealthy as well. Let's get to the bots as quickly as we can." Sam gave the thrusters a boost and they would reach the bots in no time. He marveled at the landscape and how it went from desert to plains, to valleys to plains, and back to valleys in only a few miles. The mountains were taller than he guessed and he could see snow caps on the highest ones. "What a planet!"

"We are almost to the bots, Sam."

"Thanks Eliot, I was spacing off and daydreaming about this being a destination planet. I'll leave the landing to you and make my way to the lab bay to open the doors." The landing was textbook. "Good job Eliot! Opening the bay doors, signal the bots to return to the shuttle. We will take the live stuff and quickly process it so we can turn them loose. Don't want anything to die in here and stink the place up."

"Signal sent, bots should be on their way."

"We'll secure the rest of the bots in their docks and process at the PSAD labs. No time now to do a thorough job. Hopefully once the threat has passed they will send us back to finish up."

"No Sam. The PSAD will send miners, harvesters, and developers in your place. The processing will be completed here."

"What a sobering thought. Oh well, let's get things moving. I want to be back at the village before night fall."

Helium Fall

Chapter Fourteen

Tayana made her way to the med pod to check in on Grant. "How is he doing?"

Salbola's look was not positive, "He has not changed, and we have determined there may be something else going on inside of him. We do not have the technology to see inside of him and I fear his time is running short."

"Please say it isn't the case, he has not yet completed his mission and I have not completed mine."

The healers' gave one another a knowing look. Emara thought, *there is more to her statement than we know. I believe Tayana fell in love with Grant at their first meeting, but I'm not about to breech the subject with her.*

Salbola continued with his assessment. "His color is still ashen and he has a fever we cannot bring down. Unless Sam can get him to their ship's technologically advanced medical equipment, he may not make it.

Tayana frowned, turned, and left the pod without another word. *No, no, no not again. I have not felt this way since my parents and brother died.* Tears welled up in her eyes and she began to cry as her heart raced. *I cannot allow my emotions to take over. I cannot be the wreck I've become.* She took off towards the headwaters of the falls. *Hopefully no one saw me. I cannot let them see m, their leader, so vulnerable.* She found a secluded spot away from prying eyes as tears rolled down her cheeks. *I cannot bear the thought of losing Grant. I must find Sam and tell him he needs to get Grant back to the Ebony Belle. Maybe he's still at their camp.* She dried her eyes and returned to her pod.

She changed into her traveling clothes and grabbed her weapons. She headed for the camp on her C-Rex. Daydreaming, she thought, *there are so many things I need to say to you Grant, if and when you comes out of your deep sleep. You need to know how I feel. I pray you feel the same. I love you, Grant.*

When she arrived at camp she was shocked to find the shuttle gone. *How could it be gone? It wasn't flight worthy yesterday.* Tears began flowing again. *This is so frustrating!* She surprised her C-Rex when she voiced her frustration aloud. "Where are you Sam? Grant needs your help and you abandoned him in his darkest hour!" She dismounted her C-Rex and paced. Shaking her fist at the vacant camp she yelled, "You sorry son of a swine. You lecherous scab of a human. He needs you and you are gone, some friend you are. If and when I see you again you will feel my wrath, you will feel lots of pain. You sorry sack of Chotuk crap!"

Her C-Rex tried to break free from her hold on its reins, but was unable to back away.

Her chest heaved as she sucked in large mouthfuls of air trying to catch her breath. She realized she was screaming at the top of her lungs. She was livid. *How could he leave his friend in his deepest time of need? He is going to die if you don't return and take him to your ship in orbit.* Tears flowed freely, but she did not care. She made no attempt to wipe them away. She was alone with her C-Rex and no one was in sight, so she screamed into the air again, "Sam you animal's ass, come back now, you are a coward and a wretched man!"

Walking along side of her unhappy C-Rex, Tayana paced. She was perplexed. *What do I do?* The C-Rex tossed its head, startling a small bird as they approached the bush it was perched in. The commotion drew Tayana away from her emotions. *Maybe there are medicines or salves at the Digger's camp to help Grant hang on until Sam shows up again — if it isn't too late.*

"Come on, my trust C-Rex, the mining camp is only two miles north of here. It will take time to get there, look around, and make it back to the village, but I have to try." She remounted and prodded her C-Rex, forward. Off they went. "Just you wait and see, I'm going to punish Sam for his heinous act of cowardice — for abandoning his friend. You just wait and see."

The unhappy duo arrived at the Digger's camp in short order. Tayana tied the reins to a bush near the bombed out building and began searching for medical supplies while continuing to mutter about Sam's cowardice. *There were supplies here somewhere, where are they? I've already spent more time than I have to waste. I need to slow down and search every room carefully. This place isn't that large and I know the supplies were here somewhere. Where are they? Sam, you are in so much trouble.*

Tayana heard her C-Rex make its spooked sounds again. She stopped, realizing she was alone at the camp and had told no one where she was headed. Moving carefully forward, she finally located the room she remembered. The labels on everything were in a language she could not read, but she found bandages and tubes full of what looked like medicine, so she gathered them and made her way to the main bunker entrance.

She was almost at the exterior door and was met by something large, and she gagged at the smell. Startled, she dropped the meds. A large, very alive, alien stood at the entrance. It was an exact replica of the one killed by the SHTF missile Grant fired.

The intruder reached out to her. She defended herself with reckless abandon. Her sword whistled through the air clanging loudly on the Alien's chest armor. The alien reached out with another arm nearly missing her arm as it raced past its menacing hand. Her rage swelled along with her fear. She swung her sword harder and faster with the same clanging result as its armor covered arms. She jabbed her sword into the neck hoping to inflict pain. She jabbed once more, this time into an armpit, and the alien howled in pain. The howl was terrifying. Unnerved, she spun and ran to the hanger bay. She hid hoping the alien would not find her. Knowing she was in there, somewhere, it spoke and she understood him. Would it know where she was hiding? She quietly crouched and grabbed her bow and an arrow out of her quiver. If it advanced, she would pierce its brain.

The alien spoke again, "I mean you no harm. I am a scientist, and I am unarmed."

She knew better It had three arms, and each was a weapon. If it got a hold of her it would be her end. It did not advance and repeated, "I am not going to harm you, I need your assistance. I am injured and need care." She wanted to step out to see what condition it was in and if she might be able to help, but the warrior in her wanted to step out and fire a warning shot into a leg so it could not pursue her.

"I need your help, I am going to lie down on the floor and will not attack you if you come near, and all fight has left me."

Tayana knew this may be a ruse, but she also knew it could read the medicine bottles for her. She stepped out of hiding, bow drawn, and arrow pointed at its head. It was now lying motionless on the floor.

"Where are you hurt?"

He jolted when she spoke his language and replied, "Who are you, you speak my tongue?"

"I am Tayana, this is my world. Where are you hurt?"

I have sustained several punctures to my midsection and now I have one under my arm. I have no means to mend myself. I have also lost a limb."

"I am not a healer," Tayana replied. "I am here to find medicine for another who is injured. Can you assist me in reading these bottles? In return I will do what I can to assist you."

"I can and will."

"How did you receive these wounds?"

"I was out gathering sustenance when there was an explosion. I feared the worst and ran back to check on Greack. There was another explosion then hissing and everything began to vaporize around me. I made for a large boulder and was almost there when something pierced me and then my limb was gone. I waited for yet another explosion but one never came. I was afraid and remained in hiding until I felt it was safe to return. Then we met in the entrance, and now we are here."

Tayana lowered her bow. She crept slowly, and cautiously crept toward him. She could see where the missing limb once was and noted the blood on his clothing. She drew her sword as a precaution and moved within six feet of him. "If you can, come to a seated position, and face me."

He moved with effort to a sitting position and turned to face her. He was not a pretty thing by any means, but he did have a softer look than the other alien. "How is it I can understand you and you me?"

"There is a life-form on this world with the ability to translate languages. It is small and looks like pink gel. As filthy as this place is, it must be everywhere and apparently made its way into your ears. Who are you and why have you come to my world?"

"Delack, I am Delack. We are here to gather knowledge of your world's resources and to mine what we can of value in a short amount of time. This world is rich in minerals, gems, and metals. We need these resources. Again, I am a scientist and wish you no harm."

"Then why the boomers? They have killed many of my family and you say you mean no harm."

"The boomers, I do not understand."

"The flying things and the explosions they create. We call them boomers because of the noise they create."

"The missiles are our protection. They keep local fauna away that could interrupt our mission. They are automated and we have little control over what they seek out to destroy."

"Do they communicate with you when they have discovered or destroyed something?"

"No, they are activated when motion is detected by sensors around the perimeter. We were unaware there was intelligent life on this world."

"Well, there is! Now there are several forms of intelligent life here, if we include you. Was a distress signal sent by this place before it was destroyed?"

"I do not know the answer to your question. Like I said, I was returning when I met you. Did you capture Greack? Did he survive the explosions?"

"He did not survive."

Delack let out a wail, catching Tayana off guard. She quickly backed away keeping her sword pointed at him.

She reached for her bow and Delack saw her.

"Please, I am not going to attack. I grieve the loss of my brother. Greack was my older and meant a lot to me. He was a soldier turned miner and my mentor."

"I am sorry for your loss. I did not mean to interpret your wail as an attack; however, it did startle me. I do not know you, nor you, me. I see you are injured and I will assist you if you assist me. No harm will come to you if you keep your word not to harm me or anyone else."

"You have my word."

Tayana kept her sword close and helped Delack up and out of the bunker into the daylight. "What are these and what do they cure?" She held out the bag of medications and Delack looked inside?

"They are an assortment of minor healing aids. One will stop bleeding, another will stop fluids from escaping your facial orifices, and this one will bring you to a deep, restful sleep."

"Will any bring you back to life from a deep sleep you cannot awake from, when sweating with a high fever?"

"No, none of them will do those things. We were to be here a short time and then move on. We had no need of serious medical supplies."

Tayana's anger towards Sam grew by the minute. "Do you have means to travel?"

"No."

"Can you walk a long distance or do you require help?"

"I will require help. We are not a civilization of walkers. I am afraid my injuries will overtake me if I was to take on a journey in this condition."

Tayana sized him up and ran to a nearby pile of tree

branches. She chopped and hacked at them with a vengeance. When she was done she gathered vines and remembered seeing some animal hides in the bunker. Once everything was gathered, she fashioned a sled out of the long branches, binding them together with the vines. She covered the center with the hides from the bunker creating a comfortable, but crude seat for Delack. She attached the whole thing to her C-Rex, pointed to the sled, and motioned for Delack to have a seat. He reluctantly obliged. "The ride will be bumpy and long but you will not have to walk. You can lie back and rest. I will pull you to my village where my healers will look at you."

"Thank you! I am in your debt."

The trip back to the village was long. Delack relaxed the best he could considering he was being dragged on a crude sled behind a large chicken-like creature, ridden by a warrior woman in a black scaled tunic with dark feathers who wielded a bow and a sword. His life was truly in her hands and he knew it.

Chapter Fifteen

Sam and Eliot finished their processing and the remaining bots were loaded and secured into their docks. The flight to the village seemed to take forever. Sam was excited to tell Grant what happened and how they manufactured the part and everything else that happened since he passed out.

Nearing the village Sam got a feeling something was not right. He boosted the engines. "Eliot, land the shuttle quickly. I fear there has been a development in our absence. I think Grant is in serious trouble." Sam never experienced this kind of feeling before and was not sure if it was him being wiggy or if there really was something wrong with Grant. A few minutes later Eliot landed the shuttle. Sam bounded out and ran directly to the med pod. "How is he?"

The look on the Salbola and Emara's faces said it all, "He is not well. We cannot bring him out of sleep and his fever will not subside."

"I have to take him to the Ebony Belle, now. Help me get him in the shuttle."

Salbola said, "I fear we may be too late, Sam. Unless your technology is far more advanced than ours, he will not survive much longer."

Sam looked at them and said, "Let's move now!" They gingerly lifted Grant from the bed and carried him toward the waiting shuttle.

"Eliot, have the bay doors open and be ready to take off for the Ebony Belle as soon as the doors close."

"Yes, Sam."

Sam asked, "Would you like to assist me aboard the

Ebony Belle?"

Salbola said, "Yes, we would very much like to be part of his continued healing." The ramp to the bay was down and ready when they arrived.

"Take him to sick bay over there, there are two beds, pick either one and strap him in. You might want to strap yourselves in, too." Sam was about to hit the button to close the bay doors when he saw someone coming his way. It looked like Tayana and she was dragging something behind her?

"We are ready for lift off."

"Hold Eliot, I think Tayana is coming this way and it looks like she packed for a month long trip. Women!"

"There are two life forms, Sam. One is Tayana the other is unidentified."

Sam quickly ran to the armory. He grabbed a pistol and his trusty rifle. Tayana was closing the distance at a good pace and Sam was glad to see her. As she got closer he wasn't sure what was wrong, but her face was curled up in a snarl and she had fire in her eyes. Whoever was with her was in serious trouble for her to look that angry. Sam and Tayana connected mentally just enough for him to figure out Tayana was angry at him, not the life form with her. He sensed she was after his soul. She was so angry with him she wasn't going to stop until she nearly took his life. Sam prepared and stepped out from the shuttle. He began yelling when she was in earshot, but she was yelling too, so they cancelled each other out.

Each time he tried, she would yell, too. "Damn it woman, shut the hell up!"

At the same time Tayana yelled, "Your ass is mine you swine!" She urged her C-Rex even faster. Sam could tell it had been a long ride as the C-Rex was slowing on his own though she kept spurring it to go faster. Sam sensed she was after his hide and there was most likely nothing he could do to dissuade her from her wrath. When she reined her ride to a halt directly in front of him and jumped off before it had come to a complete stop, Sam knew there was only one thing to do. "Grant's in the med room, he needs you!"

She ran towards him and slapped him hard as she passed, never missing a step.

He turned and yelled at her, "Strap in!" Tayana had not informed him she had a passenger and Sam nearly blasted him when he climbed out of the sled. With his gun pointed at Delack's head he said, "Stop, not another step!"

From behind him he heard, "He's with me, let him in!"

Sam lowered his weapon and motioned for him to enter. "Strap in! Let's go, Eliot." With the bay doors closing behind him Sam made his way to the bridge and locked the door behind him. He didn't need a crazy woman sneaking up behind him and slitting his throat while he was concentrating on getting Grant to the Ebony Belle.

"Twenty minutes to the ship."

"Thank you, Eliot." There were times Sam was glad Eliot was emotionless and didn't give a flip about his current state of affairs. He was always the same and right now, it was comforting.

"What the hell is going on?"

Eliot began to answer. Sam cut him off, "Sorry, Eliot, it was a rhetorical question. With everything going on, I'm confused. Grant is slipping away, Tayana is a raging mad woman, there is an alien in my lab bay, and we're headed to the Ebony Bell with all of them plus two healers. Can my day get any weirder? Don't answer. Please, don't answer."

The trip would take another fifteen minutes so Sam decided to take a power nap. He needed to get some rest and he was sure he was not going to get any once they returned to the ship.

Eliot took it upon himself to intercede for Sam. He piloted the ship while Sam napped. He addressed the three Antayan's, "Hello, I am the ship's artificial intelligence EL-10T, please call me Eliot."

Not see who was speaking, Tayana and the healers hit the deck as quickly as they could move. Emara, fearful there were spirits on the ship, was terrified. Salbola cowered in the corner looking for the intruder and shook with fear. Tayana, sword in hand, was prepared for a fight.

Tayana mustered up the courage to speak, "Where are you? Show yourself!" I am unable to show myself at this time. I am part of the Ebony Belle and not a living being." The three were even more terrified now. A non-living being was speaking to them and claiming to be part of the ship.

Salbola whispered to Tayana, "What devilry is this?"

Eliot tried a different approach, "I am not a spirit and I am not going to harm you in any way. I am a friend of Grant and Sam's, we work together. I am currently in a different part of the ship talking to you over the ships inter-communications system." Their fear eased and Eliot directed them to return to their seats. He would explain more to them, if they were willing.

They sensed no harm would come to them, but with great trepidation returned to their seats. All were ready to bolt again if the need arose.

"Tayana, Sam picked up the survey bots and then came directly for Grant."

Emboldened by the knowledge no harm would come to them Tayana engaged Eliot in conversation. "But he did not tell me he was leaving. When I arrived to tell him about Grant, he was gone. What was I supposed to do? I thought he had abandoned Grant and left for the ship alone."

"He has great care for Grant and would never abandon him. He did what he had to do to make things right so he could leave your world and bring Grant back to health. You cannot fault him."

"I want to harm him anyway. He wasn't where he was supposed to be. I ran into another alien, who is now aboard this vessel."

The Emara gasped in horror and Salbola voiced his opinion, "Why is there an alien on this vessel? How do you know he will not try to kill us as we sleep? This is bad protocol, Tayana, even for you."

"Mind your station, Salbola. I would not make a rash decision and put our lives in jeopardy. You know me much better. It brings me no joy you think I have made a mistake in forming an alliance with this creature from another world."

"But he has killed many of our people. He has tried to kill Grant on two separate occasions, have you forgotten?"

"Again, and for the last time, mind your station."

Sam's voice came over the intercom, "We will be docking in five minutes, stay secured in your seats. I will let you know when you can move about."

"Take us in, Eliot. Can you remotely fire up the Belle

and have her ready when we get Grant to the med room?"

"Yes, I can and will."

"Pump up the gas levels two degrees so the healers and Tayana are comfortable breathing our air. You might add some sleeping meds to the mix too, so she will calm down. Just kidding Eliot, do not do that, yet."

He could feel the shuttle docking with the Belle and knew it was safe to unbuckle. He headed to the lab bay to tend to his guests. When he arrived he was glad to see everyone was still strapped in.

"Salbola, Emara, bring Grant and follow me. Table and all, it will float if you grab the green handle.

Tayana, bring your friend and follow us, and don't grab anything green." It was not a request it was a command. Sam was in no mood for any crap from anyone.

Once crammed into the lift, Sam directed it to take them to level five, stat. The lift was silent, smooth and fast. There was a ding and the doors slid open. "To the left and three doors down on the right."

"Eliot, is the med room ready?"

"Yes."

"Good. Increase the temperature five degrees please, then another five degrees in twenty minutes. No need to freeze us out of here so soon."

Sam heard the gentle hiss of the air handlers moving the air he requested. Sitting in space for a month, the Belle was quite cold, as expected when a ship is in hibernation. They entered the med room and the light automatically came on. Tayana and the healers were impressed and mystified at what sort of magic might be at play to make the lights act in such a manner.

"Place Grant in the room over by the wall and put our mystery guest, over here, in this room." Sam pointed to his right; Tayana escorted Delack to the room. Her look wasn't as severe as earlier and Sam detected some remorse, but he wasn't in the mood to talk with her about whatever set her off, causing her to slap him.

He went to Grant's room first and positioned him under the healing apparatus, pushed a few buttons and scanned Grant's hand so the device could read his ID imbedded between his thumb and index finger. The healing table immediately began its analysis.

"The initial analysis will take about fifteen minutes. I can explain more to you in the conference room. Eliot, please direct them to the conference room. I need to check on our other guest. You can go over there and wait for me."

Sam entered the room containing the mystery guest. "What is your issue, alien?" Sam snapped.

"I am Delack."

"I did not ask you your name; I asked you what your issue is. I need to set the apparatus to scan you, so I need to know what it needs to look for. You are not of Earth so I will have to give it some specific instructions on how to proceed with its analysis."

"I have been pierced in my midsection and one of my limbs was torn off. I cannot regenerate my limbs like other Anotokians."

"Where are you from, Delack?"

"I am from the planet Anotoke; it is a large planet over one hundred and twenty million miles from here."

Sam continued programming the machine to analyze Delack. "Unknown species, midsection, and appendages. Come over here and lie on the table. The apparatus will analyze you the best it can and determine the best course of care for you. Will you be a threat to me? Do I have to strap you to this table or will you follow my directions?"

"I have no fight in me."

Sam nodded and then realized, he was talking to an alien, in English. "How can you understand me and speak my language?" From behind him Tayana began to speak. He held up his hand to stop her. "Go ahead, Delack, explain."

"There is a biologic on the world below with the ability to translate languages. It has made its way into my ears and now translates your language to mine and mine to yours, fascinating isn't it?"

"Yes it is. I have a similar substance in my ears doing the same thing for me, thanks to Tayana."

Tayana smiled at the mention of her name. Sam did not return the smile, nor did he acknowledge her.

"Lay very still, Delack. The device will do all of the work and it will signal me when the testing is complete." Delack nodded, laid his head back and closed his eyes.

Sam led the way to the conference room conference room knowing there would be lots of questions, he was not wrong.

"Sam, will Grant be healed? Will Delack recover from his wounds? Is this how your whole world lives?"

"All right, I know this is new to some of you, well, all of you. Grant and Delack are being analyzed so the healing process can begin. I will receive notification when the scan is complete. When the scan is complete the healing will commence on its own. If it is unsure how to proceed it will notify me and I will determine how to proceed. I do not know if they will be healed or survive. We will know in about ten minutes."

"No, this is not how we live in our world, Grant and I are scientists. We travel the universe seeking out new worlds, looking for life, materials, and resources. This is our ship the Ebony Belle. She is the newest ship in our fleet and Grant and I were commissioned to pilot it into outer space. This is our home away from home. It is equipped with everything we need for the long journey we have undertaken. We have a food synthesizer that creates whatever food we desire, a pool for exercise and recreation, a fitness center, a barber shop, and our very own theatre."

The puzzled looks on their faces told Sam they had little to no idea what he was talking about. "Come on, let me show you."

They exited the conference room and Sam led them to the lift. He pressed the call button, "I hope you're ready for this." The doors opened
A moment later and they filed in.

"Level two, please." The lift doors closed with a small wisp of air and silently descended to their destination. The doors opened upon their arrival and Sam gestured for them to step out. All three stepped out and stood motionless. With a smile, Sam said, "Welcome to the grand lobby. Visitors and dignitaries enter here for meetings and festivities."

Tayana, Emara, and Salbola gazed around the room with their mouths hanging open. The white walls shimmered behind the framed pictures and the deep burgundy and grey decor. It was unlike anything they had seen before. "Make yourselves at home and explore for a minute."

The pictures on the walls fascinated Emara and Salbola. "How can they hold their pose for so long?"

"The photos are a representation of the actual person or place. They are not physically there now, but they were when the photo was taken. We will delve into that at a later time. Let's continue the tour.

Sam led the down the bench lined corridor to the lobby of the entertainment area. "Beyond these doors is another world, brace your selves."

Salbola and Emara huddled close, afraid of what awaited on the other side. They gasped as he opened the doors. "This is amazing!" Salbola's eyes were wide with wonder. He ran out onto the field; fell to the ground, and lie back looking up at the stars through the clear panels in the ceiling. "Am I in heaven? How can such a thing be in a ship flying through space? There is real grass in here, and soil, and plants. Is there a small sun as well?" He was lost in his own little dream world.

The area was a regulation football field on Earth. In one corner was a large pool and close by was the workout center and fitness room.

Emara headed straight to the pool. Its crystal clear water captivated her imagination. "I do not understand this, but I'm happy it's here."

Tayana seemed lost in her own world, too.

Sam wondered if she was imagining her and Grant running and chasing each other through the open field and frolicking in the pool alone.

Sam interrupted their day dreaming by chirping on Sam's com.

"Grant and Delack's scans are complete. I'll check on them. You can stay here if you choose or you can come with me, we can return later."

They followed Sam back to the lift.

When they got to the med room Delack was

moaning. He called out to Sam, "You did not inform me this device would stick me, and take blood and tissue samples."

"You're lucky it let you keep your clothing!" Sam said it with a smile. Delack had a surprised look on his face, "I did not know I had n option."

Grant was stripped of his clothing and now lay under covers. The healing had begun. Sam grabbed the tablet and read what was wrong with Grant. "The poison in his system caused his appendix to rupture. He is septic and the toxins are what caused him to faint. The healing apparatus will remove the poison and the toxins. It will take several days for him to be well again, but he will be well again, Tayana."

She looked at him and knew he knew.

"Now, let's check in on our other guest." Sam grabbed the tablet from Delack's healing apparatus and cocked his head sideways as if he was looking at a crooked picture. He turned his head back and then looked at Delack out of the side of his eyes.

"What, what did it say of me? Will I survive or will I perish?"

"Delack, if you allow the healing device to do its job you will be whole again. It means the hole and your insides will be repaired, and your limb will be regenerated."

"I can have my limb back? I am delighted this device will do such a wonderful thing for me."

"The sticking, the blood, and the tissue samples were to determine what the healing device need's to make you whole again. There is only one question and it is a very important question. Delack, do you want your clothing removed? It will facilitate faster healing and allow the healing to be complete."

"Remove them, but please, look away. Please turn your eyes away."

"Delack, we will leave the room and shade the windows. I will begin the healing from the main console."

"Thank you Sam, you are a kind man."

With a smile Sam and the others left the room and all of them began to giggle. "A big tough looking alien afraid someone will see his parts!" Tayana covered her parts and the laughing continued. Sam instructed the healing to begin on Delack. The procedure would knock him out, rendering him harmless.

Sam turned his attention to Tayana and the healers. "Are you hungry?"

Starving was the consensus. "Let's go to the galley. You can sample the foods we eat. I will whip up some of my favorites, and something similar to what you have fed me."

Sam went to the synthesizer and keyed in his selections. Within minutes the food came out on conveyors as Sam placed the plates, bowls, and utensils they needed on the table. "First, the dish I believe is similar to Chotuk, we call it steak, and we have a baked potato, it grows in the ground, and so does the next item, carrots. Carrots are nutritious and help with our eyesight." All three took tiny bites of the steak followed by larger bites.

"This is very close to being Chotuk." Salbola took a sampling of the potato. The look on his face was not a pleasant one. "It tastes like dirt to me."

"Oh, you can season your food with these items." Sam passed butter, sour cream, shredded cheese, and some bacon bits. "Taste them first, and then combine them as you please." Sam watched with delight as all three sampled the accoutrements. "I remember the first time I ate your food, it was a joyous event." All were having a great time and enjoyed the food. "Don't fill up yet, there is more to sample." Sam keyed in grilled cheese, tomato basil soup, and chocolate cream pie.

When he delivered it to the table Tayana breathed in deeply. "The aromas of the cooked cheese and soup are exciting my nose. What is this? I am in love with the aroma. I hope the taste is equally as delightful."

"The square thing, no that, is a grilled cheese sandwich, a delicacy on Earth and most often paired with the tomato soup, that's in the bowl."

Each tasted a sandwich and Sam thought Tayana was going to orgasm by the way she was savoring each bite.

Emara was fascinated with the chocolate cream pie and asked, "How do you eat something so beautiful?"

Sam cut the pie into pieces while his guests looked on with wonder. They were in awe when he placed the first slice on Tayana's plate. He gave the others a piece, and himself one too. He took his fork and cut off the end, placed it in his mouth, and the others followed suit. Tayana quickly took three more bites, Salbola began eating the whipped topping off the top, and Emara grabbed the pie with her hands and shoved it in her face.

Sam was beside himself. *What the hell was happening?* He grabbed pieces of pie and slung them into the refuse container. Sam's guests looked at him like he'd thrown a baby into the trash. "It's just pie!" They were licking their fingers and Salbola was licking pie off Emara's face. Tayana joined in and helped clean her up. It was the wildest thing Sam had ever seen. "Eliot, did you record what happened here?"

"Yes, I record everything happening on the ship, the shuttle, and wherever the two of you go."

"I've got to show this to Grant when he wakes up. He's going to love it." He noted they seemed high and then remembered the chocolate bars they left out for them. He felt like a drug dealer and knew he could not feed them any more chocolate products. After the meal, and after his guests came down from their high, he resumed their tour. He led them to the theatre and put a movie in for them to watch. The lion roaring at the beginning of the movie had them cowering in their seats, Sam turned down the volume some. He guessed their ears were more sensitive than his.

"It is a real beast on Earth, but this is a movie, not real. No one nor nothing can come from the screen and attack you, you are safe in here." His pep talk had little effect on them. They cringed and cowered at every car scene involving a crash. Every gunshot was reason for them to hit the floor. A woman screaming particularly caught their attention and Salbola cried out, "Where is she? She sounds to be in desperation, and in need of help."

Sam laughed and told them again it wasn't real, it was make believe, it was entertainment. Emara sat so low in her seat she practically disappeared into the cushions. This was the entertainment Sam needed to take his mind off Grant and everything else going on. Not to mention what may transpire in the next few days. He was grateful Eliot went above and beyond to get the part made so they could get off the planet. If he had not, Grant and Delack would not be here getting healed. They would be dead or close to it. Sam silently thanked God, then returned his attention to his guests and the movie.

Ninety minutes of panic and laughter later, the three of them vowed to never watch a movie again. Sam showed them there were all kinds of movies and not all of them involved scenes of mass destruction or death, and again, told them it was make believe. "The movies are not real. Yes they are real people, but they are pretending to be someone else and acting out a part in the movie."

None of them bought what he was selling. Emara asked if she could go back to the pool and take a swim.

"Sure you can, be careful; there is no lifeguard on duty. It's a joke, sorry. I will get you a suit and a towel."

Emara cocked her head this time and asked, "What are a suit and a towel?"

"Oh never mind, go take a swim." "If you get lost or into trouble just speak to the air and ask for me. The coms will connect us and we can talk."

Emara and Salbola nodded. They went their merry way to the pool leaving Sam alone with Tayana.

"Sam, I want to apologize for earlier."

"No need, I know you were concerned about Grant."

"It gave me no reason to strike your face. I was angry; I thought you had abandoned Grant in his time of need."

"Why would you think that?"

"Your shuttle was not there when I came to tell you his condition was getting worse and we needed do to something soon or he may die."

"I was retrieving the bots and trusted he was in good hands with Salbola and Emara. I had a feeling when I returned something was not right and I went straight to the med pod. They let me know his condition and we loaded him into the shuttle right before you arrived. Where did you go after you found the shuttle gone?"

"I went to the digger's compound and searched their bunker for medical supplies or something to help Grant heal. I found some stuff but it wasn't what I needed. That's when I found Delack. He was out gathering food when Grant blew up the bunker. The blast tore off his limb and punctured him. He waited for us to leave and fell unconscious. He came to and went back to the bunker and arrived as I was leaving. His sudden appearance startled me and I thought he was going to attack me. I drew my sword and defended myself. He reached out to grab me and I finally pierced the armor under his arm. He howled in pain and I ran and hid. Had it not been for the biologics in his ear giving us the ability to communicate I would have pierced his brain with an arrow. He is a scientist like you and Grant and on a similar mission."

"You mean to tell me Delack is a scientist on a mission of discovery like we are? Wow! Blows my mind. He is my equivalent in all of space and time, and of all places to meet him it is here on your world doing what I'm doing. What are the odds?" Sam was now curious to talk with Delack and pick his brain for whatever intergalactic information he could get from him.

"He is not dangerous Sam; he is like us, trying to get by and live life a day at a time."

"Everyone is dangerous in their own way Tayana. You can enter someone's mind, I have proof. You entered mine in the beginning. It can be a very dangerous thing. Grant and I have weapons training and know how to fight in hand to hand combat, making us dangerous and our minds are the most dangerous of all, Delack included. He could give us false information or lead us into a trap. My trust has not been the same since you entered my mind, I feel vulnerable and unprotected."

"Sam, I am so sorry for all I have done to make you question your trust in me. I was hurt and angry you did not let me know you were leaving to go get the bots. I thought you left because you were saving your own skin. I should have had more faith in you. I apologize for being weak and untrusting."

"I'll forgive you Tayana, if you will forgive me."

"Agreed, can we go back to how it was, so we can both have trust again?"

"Yes, I think we can."

"I want to see more of the Ebony Belle, can you take me on another tour?"

"Sure can. It will be several days before Grant and Delack are ready to get out of the med rooms and be active again. Tomorrow we need to go back to your people and prepare them for what may be coming our way. They do know you're here, right?"

"I assume they know I boarded the shuttle with you and the healers."

"I don't need anyone else slapping me when we go back. Just sayin'!" Sam gave her the deluxe tour. He took her to the engine room, Grant's quarters, the bridge, and pretty much the entire ship, with the exception of his quarters as they were a mess and he was embarrassed for her to know how he really lived. They headed back to the pool to see how the healers were doing and were shocked to find them in a naked embrace in the middle of the football field.

"They are together, like you, Dyanta and Kyera. You are life mates."

Sam's eyes got wider than they had ever been and he was at a loss for words.

"Sam, did you not know entering a woman of our

kind binds you to them for life?"

"I had no idea." Sam felt a huge knot form in his stomach and he thought he might wretch. His head was spinning and he was dumbfounded. Why had they not told him about this, why did they lure him into the pool and seduce him?

"Sam, they love you and will be forever faithful to you until death. Are they not to your liking?"

"I mean, I think they are the greatest thing that has ever happened to me, I think I love them, too. But I feel so deceived and tricked. That was such a man thing to do. Now I know how I've made several women feel in my life. I'm ashamed of myself." Sam sat with his head hanging low, pondering the situation for a while, and then said, "Is that why I'm no longer allowed to sit at the head table and have to sit with them and their family?"

"Yes, it is why. You have a family now and families are together at meals. Kyera and Dyanta are sad you have been away from them. They will want to give you many reasons to stay with them when you return." She smiled at him knowing what they would do and the pleasure they would bring him. He would never want to leave again.

Sam's attention was divided between the conversation with Tayana and the healers doing the nasty in the grass. "I feel like we have been staring at them and they keep right on going. Doesn't it make you uncomfortable?"

"Not in the slightest. We are open to intimacy and there is nothing wrong with the act or watching it happen. It is accepted and common. We do not stress about such small things and no one ever says a thing if they are watched or watching. It's like being in public and carrying on a conversation that is private, but you don't care who hears."

" I'm going to have to get used to it I guess. So, seeing other people naked is not a bad thing in your culture?"

"Not as long as you do not take action with someone who is together with another. The penalty for that is death for both parties. It has not happened in my lifetime."

"Thank God, I would never cheat on the Kyera or Dyanta. They are such beauties and such willing participants to bring me pleasure. I'm not sure how this interplanetary relationship is going to work, but I will do my best."

"Sam, you will either be here or there. They will go where you go. It is being together in our world. Being gone a day or two is one thing. Leaving the world for another is very different and requires them to travel with you. You will take them with you, if and when you leave."

"Yes ma'am!" Tayana was not giving him a choice, but he really didn't want any choices. Kyera was perfect in every way imaginable and Dyanta was the perfect wife and lover, too. He would be a fool to not take them with him. He would be a fool not to stay here with them. *Am I truly entertaining the idea of staying here with them, for the rest of my life?* "I need to walk for a while, alone. No offense, there is a lot on my mind and I need to do some sorting out."

Tayana knew what was on his mind; she was listening to his thoughts. She heard his dilemma and his revelation. "Go, a walk will do you good. I am going to check in on Grant for a minute."

"Please do not touch him or anything else. It will stop

the healing process and we will need to start it again."

"I will be careful and not touch a thing."

Sam went one way and Tayana the other. He decided to walk around the field. He took his boots and socks off, enjoying the feel of the cool grass between his toes and the soft give of the soil beneath his steps as he walked the perimeter of the field. He couldn't help but notice Emara and Salbola looked many years younger than they appeared fully dressed. Emara's body was fit and lithe. She was the typical height for a woman on her world. She was toned and firm. Her grey hair was the only thing giving her any age at all. Her skin was tanned and taut, with no discernible wrinkles anywhere. He blushed, realizing he was staring at her and Salbola.

Salbola was fit and muscular with long grey hair. His body was like a twenty-five year old and so was his stamina. "There must be something in the water around here, damn!" He stopped staring and kept walking.

He thought of Grant and considered what he was going to say to him. His earlier thoughts, and the recent development of his being together with an alien life form, or two. He had to tell him the truth and what his intentions were. But how was he going to breach the subject with the imminent threat of a galactic war looming in the near future. *Hi Grant! I'm married and staying with them so we can raise our kids together. Sorry, you'll have to fly back to Earth alone and be the lone hero.* It would not be the correct way to tackle this situation. He kept on walking and could not come to a conclusion. He hoped one would present itself when the time was right. He walked for several hours. He noticed the healers had moved to the pool. Salbola floated Emara to the steps and hauled her out onto the grass again. She was limp and Sam knew what it meant, it was good, very good for her.

Helium Fall

Chapter Sixteen

Sam made his way back to the med rooms to check on Grant and Delack and found Tayana sleeping in a chair in the conference room. He quietly checked the progress of Grant's recovery. It looked like he would be completely healed in a day, maybe two. The poison and toxins were nearly a lethal combination. It was taking some time to extract them without damaging Grant's internal organs.

He moved to Delack's room to check his progress as well. The healing apparatus was doing an amazing job rebuilding his limb and the punctures were being mended, too. The Ebony Belle was living up to her hype. She was the most advanced PSAD ship ever launched into space, well, from space. She was built in orbit around the Earth due to her size. Nearly half a mile long and a quarter mile wide, she was a large, well equipped beauty by space standards. Sam was honored to be the co-captain of such a marvelous vessel. With Tayana sleeping and the healers doing their thing, he decided to head to the bridge and call the PSAD. It would take days for a response and he thought it would be good for them to hear a voice on the other end. With Grant incapacitated they needed to know the situation.

The bridge seemed different without Grant sitting in his chair, drinking his coffee, and reading the celestial news.

"Eliot, open a channel to the PSAD, please."

"The channel is open."

"Acting Captain Sam Northland calling PSAD command. A distress message was previously sent and assistance is still needed. Grant Goodwine is temporarily incapacitated. There is intelligent life on this world and it needs to be preserved at all costs. All haste is appreciated. We are alive and surviving. Grant is undergoing healing for a ruptured appendix. Poison and toxins in his systems have nearly taken his life. We have discovered four alien life forms, three are aboard the Ebony Belle, all are allies, and assisting with our mission. We will communicate further when help is close. Northland out."

"Eliot, be listening for a reply, and their hail when they are within range to communicate openly."

"Always."

Sam was hungry again and headed to the galley for a quick bite. He was pleased and quite amused to find Tayana and the healers attempting to key chocolate cream pie into the synthesizer. In a loud booming voice he bellowed, "Hello ya junkies!"

The sudden burst of noise startled them. Tayana looked like a thief caught red handed. Her hands were shaking and she gulped for air. She would surely hyperventilate if she continued. She slid down the wall out of sight and the healers dodged back and forth trying to find a place to hide. They slammed into one another and fell to the floor, then crawled under the bar shaking with fear. Sam laughed with all his might, almost popping a vein in his neck, and nearly passed out from laughing so hard. His stomach ached and he was gasping for air with tears flowing down his face. His amusement level was clearly at a ten.

"What in the world were you three trying to do, get your chocolate fix?" Tayana stood quickly, lowered her head in shame, and plopped down in a chair at the table. The healers looked around the bar from opposite ends and stood at the same time to go sit with Tayana.

"There needs to be some ground rules around here. There will be no sneaking chocolate while you are on this ship. There will be no middle of the night journeys to the galley to break into the synthesizer and appropriate chocolate goodies for your personal and private consumption. Are we clear on this matter?"

The three looked like children being punished for taking a pie from a window. Tayana Said, "We are sorry for our greed and desire to obtain chocolate from the food machine without your knowledge."

"We have never had anything like chocolate on our world." Salbola said, "It is brown edible heaven full of incredible goodness. It is like a drug to us and we need to be watched."

"Oh, you're going to be watched, but for now let's have some real dinner and then maybe a small piece of chocolate afterwards." All agreed and Sam chose some different items for them to sample.

"Let's go Italian tonight. Let's have lasagna, garlic bread, salad, and tiramisu. You will love the desert!" The food promptly came out on the conveyors and Sam once again served his guests. "In the future, you are allowed to retrieve your own food from the conveyors."

"Where is the desert?" Emara was obviously in serious need of a chocolate fix. Sam thought after her romp on the field she might not need the chocolate.

"Try the large chunk of meat, sauce, and pasta. It is called lasagna, it is an Italian dish, and it brings me great comfort."

They all tried it and agreed it wasn't the best thing they had had, but it was delicious all the same. The garlic bread was a hit as it reminded them of meals on their world, where bread was a staple at every meal. They liked the butter and garlic, also. The salad posed a surprise for them. They were used to eating it raw and fresh without any dressing, or additions.

When Salbola tried it, his eyes lit up and he made an amazed face. He dug in and devoured his entire bowl, almost inhaling it. "Amazing, what do you call it?"

"We call it Italian dressing, because, it's Italian dressing."

"I have to have more of this at the next meal."

"We will see what we can do for ya, Salbola."

Sam smiled big at the joy he found in bringing smiles to their faces and seeing them enjoy their food like a child first experiencing sugar or the wind in their faces. They cleaned up after the meal and he directed them to where they would be staying for the night. It was a long day and Sam was tired. He knew Grant was safe and on the mend and Delack was knocked out with tranquilizers so he wouldn't be an issue and he would lock the doors of the other three so he could sleep in peace.

"Uh, Sam, how do we relieve ourselves? You do not have the facilities we have on our world."

"Well, I guess you're going to have to do it the old fashioned way. You'll have to sit on this and force the waste in your system out whatever hole it needs to come out. When you're done you'll need to use the other piece of equipment. This is how it works. He turned the handle and small jets of water erupted from the nozzles. It goes in the holes and cleans them out. It may take a little getting used to but it will get the job done. Then you dry yourself with these and throw them into the chute over there. He faced concerned looks, so he took the opportunity to explain his first adventure using their restrooms. Tayana and the healers chuckled and agreed the first experience could be rather traumatizing. "It's the thing that grabs you by your junk that shocked me the most. The probes terrified me to no end. I vowed to do my business in the woods from then on. I'd use leaves or grass, whatever was handy to clean the mess."

"It is not an option!" Tayana shuddered at the thought of using grass on her private parts. "I will try your facilities, but I may not like them. Thank you for the explanation, now I need to relieve myself."

Sam smiled, nodded gracefully, and went to his quarters. He would lock their doors later once they were asleep. The thoughts in his head needed to be put to paper so he sat down at his desk and began to write out what was on his mind. It wasn't really much but it kept nagging at him and he needed a list. A lot needed to be accomplished in a few days. He began listing the things he needed to do. Some of them were common sense, such as check on Grant, take the healers back to the village; take a dip in the pools with Kyera and Dyanta. His list was almost complete when there was a knock at his door. "Be right there." He answered the door and Emara and Salbola were standing there looking like guilty children, again. "How can I help you two?"

"Um, we, um, didn't, well, um, we didn't get."

"You didn't get dessert?"

"Yes, we did not." Salbola was nervously rubbing his hands together in anticipation. Emara was gripping his arm like it was about to fall off and he needed her assistance to keep it on.

"You two are junkies. Come with me." Sam escorted them to the galley and made them look away while he keyed in the order for one tiramisu. "You will have to share this. A whole one might take you past the point of no return!"

"Can we eat it in our quarters?"

"Oh for God sake, you horny goats, go, just go. Clean up when you're done." They hurried off to their quarters and Sam vowed to never use the room for anything, ever. The visions dancing in his thoughts were disturbing and he shook his head to clear them. "I have created two chocolate craving nymphos!"

He shuddered and went back to his quarters. This time he locked their door and sighed with great relief. He sat at his desk and finished his list. His last item was to give a case of chocolate bars to the healers before leaving. He knew he would make friends for life if he remembered them. Next to Kyera and Dyanta, the healers were the horniest people he ever met. His thoughts drifted to his wives. His wives, something he never imagined himself thinking or saying. According to their customs he had two beautiful, horny wives waiting for him when he returned to the village. It wasn't a bad thing. They had chosen him and he could not think of two more beautiful women. He was the luckiest man alive. He smiled. Then the thought of staying on their world and integrating into their lives came to mind. *Is this what I really want or do I want them to come with me back to Earth? Would it be too much for them to handle? Life on Earth is so fast paced and there is little, if any, open country or private places left for us to go and take leisurely naked dips in pools. The thought of them stripping and wanting sex in public, probably isn't going to happen on Earth. We would all end up in jail. The air was poor and the water has to be cleansed before we can drink it, let alone swim in it. My home has a pool, but it's nothing like the pure, clean, and fragrant water here. I like the water here, so crystal clear with the dark rock below making it look black as night.*

His thoughts were running rampant. He had to get some sleep. He decided to go to the med room and get a sleep aid, otherwise he would be up all night. When he entered the med room Grant and Delack were exactly where he knew they would be, asleep in their respective rooms being attended to by the healing apparatus. Grant had another day and half or so and Delack had three plus days left. Regenerating a limb took time.

He gathered his much needed sleep aid and gulped it down with a cool glass of water. "No distractions now." He had about 10 minutes, possibly less, to get his things in order and be in bed or he'd be sleeping where he fell. He would be awake in exactly 6 hours, the time it took for the sleep aid to wear off, and wake him from a deep and restful sleep.

He quickly returned to his quarters, used the facilities, hopped into bed, and pulled up the covers. In the remaining minute he prayed for tomorrow to be a smooth and easy day. He was out cold as the last word escaped his mouth. The rest of Sam's night was uneventful. He was in deep, restful sleep for six hours and nothing short of a miracle would wake him up.

He and Tayana were the first ones up and met in the galley. "Good night's sleep?"

"I was awake, thinking and hoping Grant was doing well. I tried my door but it would not open and it frustrated me so I lay back down not happy and could not fall asleep for some time."

"My apologies, Emara and Salbola came to my quarters and requested the dessert we missed at dinner. I obliged them, knowing they are chocolate addicts and I shudder to imagine what they did with that tiramisu. Not only does it have chocolate in it, it has cocoa powder, and coffee. They most likely got high on chocolate then humped all night because of the caffeine in the coffee. Caffeine is a stimulant on Earth."

"Oh, then what you're saying is they probably had the night of their lives?"

Sam laughed and said, "Well, since you put it that way, I guess they probably did. What would you like for breakfast? Never mind, I'll order a veggie omelet, hash browns, and some mixed fruit. For drinks we'll have orange juice and milk." He laughed to himself as he thought about the milk, chocolate milk. They would go insane if he introduced them to chocolate milk. *"Not gonna happen!"*

Tayana tasted the omelet. "What is the yellow stuff around the vegetables?"

"Those are eggs. Do you not have eggs on your world?"

"What are eggs?"

"This type of egg is the embryo of winged animals called chickens. Other birds and some reptiles lay eggs, too." He could tell by the look on her face she did not comprehend what he was saying. "Most animals give live birth, much like humans and I suppose you as well. The animals that give us eggs either fly or they crawl. These are from flyers."

She seemed to understand and continued to eat. The hash browns posed a problem for her also. "Some are hard and crunchy, some are soft and squishy, is this on purpose?"

"Yes, the crunchy part gives it texture and flavor, the

squishy part has not cooked as long or in the same manner. They are the same thing, but cooked differently, some have been in oil and some have not."

Without another word she continued to eat. She enjoyed the fruit and ate it all. She said the milk tasted like what they made from a plant growing near their village. The orange juice made her eyes water, but she loved the taste.

They were finishing as Emara and Salbola sauntered into the galley. They looked like they partied all night. There was still tiramisu residue on their faces.

"Rough night?" Sam couldn't resist giving them a hard time.

"What is the dessert you gave us? It nearly killed us both. Emara is nearly raw from our escapades and I can no longer feel my junk, as you call it."

Sam and Tayana laughed and clutched their sides while gasping for air. "I told you they'd been up humping all night."

Tayana's words did not come out clearly due to the gasping and laughter. She managed to get out, "Best night ever," and continued to laugh.

"It was amazing for the first two hours, and then it became painful. We could not stop and we cursed you for allowing us to consume the dessert right before we were to sleep." Salbola slumped in a chair, breathing deeply.

Emara chimed in, "I think we will pass on the chocolate dessert for a while, Sam. Maybe something with lemon or cherries next time."

It was all Sam could do not to say I told you so. He held his tongue and chuckled to himself as he prepared their breakfast. "We will be heading back to the planet in about two hours. You two need to eat and then clean up.

You've still got tiramisu on your faces." They lowered their heads and wiped their faces with their napkins. "I'm going to get ready. I will meet you all back here in two hours, agreed?"

They all agreed and Sam went to get ready. He showered and changed his clothing then checked his to do list. First up after he cleaned up, check on Grant. Then it was back to the village.

Chapter Seventeen

Grant was in the same state as before but this time his indications were so much better. The infection from the ruptured appendix was almost completely gone and the sepsis was nowhere to be found. "Another day or so buddy and you'll be good as new. I'm headed to the planet to drop off the healers and prepare them for what may be coming. I have no idea if the messages we sent made it to PSAD or not. I can only hope. Like you can hear me. Oh well, I'm off and I'll be back tonight to check on you and our other guest."

Sam gathered Tayana and the healers and loaded them into the shuttle for the trip back to the village. The healers were slightly reluctant to go and kept looking back at the galley as if they might see something chocolate left on a table somewhere for them to sneak away.

"Come on you two, the ride is over, time to go home!"

"Can we at least get one chocolate bar, or even just a piece?"

"You two are addicts, I will not fuel your addictions, and I will not oblige your habit. To the shuttle please!" Sam escorted them to the docking bay and made damn sure neither one of them snuck out while his back was turned. "Eliot, please keep a close eye on Emara and Salbola, I think they may be runners."

"Runners? We are in space, there is nowhere for them to run."

"They can slip off the shuttle without my knowledge

and have full run of the galley in my absence. You know what, I'm going to go back and lock the key panel so they can't get in without my authorization. Keep an eye on them!"

Sam hurried back to the galley and quickly locked the key panel. "No stealing chocolate from me boys and girls!" He headed back to the shuttle and much to his surprise all three of them were strapped in their seats and ready to go. "I'm not sure I trust the three of you right now. Do I need to search you for chocolate?"

They laughed and Sam said, "You know what, why don't you come to the bridge and have a look around as we head back to the village." Their eyes lit up like he had offered them chocolate.

Tayana said, "Yes please, I, I mean we, would be grateful. We have never seen our world from above and it would be a great honor to join you on the bridge."

The healers nodded and followed Sam with Tayana close behind. "Tayana, you can sit in the co-captains chair, you are royalty after all, and you two can have seats beside her. Once we leave the Ebony Belle and on our way to the surface you can unbuckle, roam around the bridge and look out the viewing screen.

"Eliot, we are ready to go, please detach from the Ebony Belle on my mark."

"You three ready?" They were giddy as children headed to the zoo for the first time; Tayana was uncharacteristically excited compared to her usual tough girl persona.

"Release the clamps, Eliot. We're away. Take us slowly to the surface. You might want to take us on a sightseeing tour as well once we enter the atmosphere. The mountains might be a nice treat."

"To the mountains."

The shuttle leveled out and Sam gave them the go ahead to unbuckle and look out the view screen at the planet below. There was complete quiet for the first few minutes.

"This does not look like our home, are you sure we have the right planet?"

"Yes, Salbola, this is the right planet. You are looking at the far side of the planet from where you live. The planet spins like a top." He made a circular motion with his finger and they seemed to understand.

"But why are we not going home?" Emara was still confused and Sam pulled up a schematic of how a planet operated and gave them a lesson in planetary travel.

"We are currently here and the village is here. If we went straight to the village we would crash nose first into the planet due to our rate of speed. We have to come in at an angle to control how fast we descend to the surface. So we enter the atmosphere about here and by the time we slow down the planet will have rotated the necessary degrees and we can safely land near the village with no problems."

"Now the boomers are gone!"

Sam faked looking offended at her comment and smiled.

Tayana was proud of herself and giggled. It was fortunate the boomers were gone and they could travel safely, at least until Delack's crew arrived.

"How will we see the village with everything moving so fast below us?"

"We'll slow down once we are in the atmosphere and you'll be able to see many things you may have never seen before."

The three of them glued their faces to the view screen in complete awe of how their planet looked form space. The deep lush green trees and plant life of the forested parts melted into the warm rusty oranges and browns of the plains and prairies. The clear cobalt, navy blues lakes and streams were brought to life in contrast to the brilliant white snow covered mountain tops. The colorful bands separating the zones were an artistic masterpiece created by a master artist, the planet itself. Even Sam got caught up in the beauty of the planet and lost track of what he was supposed to be doing.

"Sir, we are approaching the atmosphere, please strap in until we are past the turbulent outer rings."

"Strap in, quickly. We got caught up in the moment. We now have to hurry." With the last strap buckled the shuttle entered the turbulence of the outer rings. It was more than enough for Emara, who left what remained of her breakfast on the floor in front of her.

"Bots, we need a cleaner." A small bot came from seemingly nowhere, briskly cleaned the mess, and quietly returned to its hiding place to dispose of it. "It's all right Emara, I have done it many times, and it's not a big deal." The turbulence ended as rapidly as it began and Sam gave the go ahead to unbuckle again. This time he instructed them to hold onto the rails around the room for balance.

"Eliot, bring us to cruising speed, then slow to observation speed. We need to get the healers to the village, but let's take a quick spin over to the mountains first."

The mountains were large and tall; their snowcapped peaks were a great treat for them as they had never been to the tops of the mountains. They had never experienced the cold or the feeling of snow on their faces either.

"Eliot would it be possible to...Eliot, please scan the small valley to our left, I saw the flash of something metallic."

"Sir, there is a craft at that location. It has been there for some time and has no life forms anywhere near."

"Can you set us down farther down the valley? I want Tayana and the healers to experience snow for the first time."

"I have mapped out a landing location and will go there now." A few minutes later they landed and Sam was the first out. He made three small snow balls and hurled them at his three targets as they exited the shuttle. The first hit Salbola square in the chest and the other two grazed the women on the arms. All three squealed, jumped to the snow, and were surprised by the cold.

"We can only stay a short time. The temperature is low and you do not want to experience frost bite." They frolicked in the snow for a few more minutes, "Look up, then close your eyes. I have a special treat for you."

"Is it chocolate?"

"Emara, get your mind off chocolate, I think you're going to need counseling when you get back."

As they looked up and closed their eyes, Sam threw a large handful of snow high into the air so it fell as if snowing on their faces. The tingle of the cold snow and the rush of it hitting them everywhere brought them a sensation they had never experienced. They loved it. They wiped the melted snow from their faces but their smiles were non-erasable. They experienced a sensation beyond their imagination. The flight down, the snow, and now they were going to fly over their village for the first time and see where they lived. "Let's get back in the shuttle,

I'm cold and I'm sure you are too."

Through chattering teeth they agreed and climbed into the warmth of the shuttle. "To the village, Eliot."

"On our way."

"Look out the view screen, Eliot is going to fly us around the village. I think you will be amazed when you see the waterfalls and the pools and how the trees sort of hide the pods from above. The pods look like natural parts of the landscape they blend in so well."

"The pods are a natural part of the landscape; they are a living organism we live with symbiotically. There are several biologics living within the pods. The glow comes from a bioluminescent algae living on the outside and eats any bacteria that may harm the pods shell or leaves. The ponds are around each pod for water, of course, but also to grow food, fish, and flowers. We live in the pods because they are waterproof and smell wonderful. They entice you to sleep restfully."

Emara chimed in with a sideways look, "Like we need to do as soon as we get back on the ground. I have never been so tired in my life."

"Me too Emara, I believe a two day rest is in order."

"Definitely no more chocolate for you two."

Tayana got a little nervous as Sam pointed out the village on the horizon. "What if I find I have located the village in a poor location or in a dangerous one unknowingly?"

"Tayana, from what I have seen, this is a wonderful place for the village to be located. The gasses do not drop into the village at night and there is plenty of water and shelter. I found no lack of food or drinks at meals and never once did I hear a bad thing said about anything except for the boomers and diggers, of course. No need to worry, you will see soon enough you have chose wisely."

Tayana and the healers were once again glued to the view screen and holding onto the railings. The village came into view and Eliot slowed the shuttle to an easy pace allowing them to see the village in great detail.

"There is our pod and the rover is still out behind."

"The falls are so beautiful, I had no idea they were so plentiful or so many plants and flowers at the head waters."

Tayana was thinking more strategically, "We need to move the storage to the other side of the dining hall, closer to the kitchen and the servers. We can also divert some of the water to the flat area and we can grow other foods we could not before."

"Tayana, can you not see the beauty of this place and feel the magic it creates? This is as close to paradise as I have ever been, I would give my little finger to have this much beauty on Earth. We once had several islands that came very close to being perfect, but they were destroyed many years ago in a battle between our country and another. They could not have them so they destroyed them so we could not have them either, bastards!"

The beauty of the village moved each of them in their own way, but the tour had to come to an end, "Take us down Eliot."

With the shuttle safely on the ground the healers thanked Sam and took off for their pod.

"Tayana, I am going back to the mountains to check out the metallic object. Eliot said there was a power source and it might be something we can harness for your village, if you would like."

"We will see when you return."

"I will return tomorrow morning, hopefully with Grant. He should be healed and ready to go by the morning. Tell the girls I miss them and will return in the morning to see them for a brief minute."

"I will let them know, Sam."

Sam's mind raced with ideas about what the shiny object might be. Eliot indicated a craft but not what kind. It could be old mining equipment left behind by the diggers, but their equipment was flat and had no shine. Could be a crashed vessel, but there was no other intelligent life, save for the five races he knew of. His, Tayana's, Delack's, the translation biologic in his ear, and the little six-legged creature that waved as he exited the shuttle. He had no idea what Delack's ships look like, but guessed they would not be shiny, it wasn't their style. "Eliot, take us to the mountains please. When we get near, let's hover for a minute and see if there is a good place to set down and go in for a closer inspection."

As they approached Eliot informed Sam a weather system was moved in and flying into the valley would not be in their best interest. The wind gusts could easily slam them into the side of a mountain, not to mention visibility would be nearly zero once the winds picked up.

"Fine, let's set down so we can finish processing what the bots brought back." Eliot set down near a stream, Sam thought about the girls, but he had work to do. When he was done he might take a dip in the stream to cool off. Processing took a good portion of the day with some interesting discoveries. As Sam processed the finds he noted something moving out of the corner of his eye. It was bluish green with yellow spots.

"Eliot, I thought we processed all the biologics.

Something is moving over there in the third bin."

"Sam, I do not believe it is alive. I believe it is an audio kinetic."

"What do you mean audio kinetic?"

"If we stop talking and processing stops it will no longer move. It only moves when a force acts upon it. It can be physical, it can be wind, or it can be the vibrations caused by noise. In this case it is the noise."

"Can you scoop some up, isolate it and test it to be sure? The movement is creeping me out."

"Yes, Sam."

Sometime later Eliot had the pleasure of discovering a substance much like rubber. It too was a kinetic of sorts. It only moved by touch and once touched, it gained energy. After Eliot tried several times to coax it into a container, it built up enough energy to bounce around the lab bay. With each successive bounce it moved faster and faster. It was nearly a blur when Sam finally managed to get it under control by throwing a towel into its path, catching it mid-flight. The dampening effects of the towel neutralized its inertia and the substance was once again manageable.

"We're going to have to keep an eye on it. Be sure not to jostle the container."

"Agreed. This needs to be in motion resistant material for safe keeping." An absorbent rock and several different kinds of fluorescent minerals were among the other finds of interest.

With the lab bay cleared, Sam said, "Eliot, it is nearly dark and I need some rest. Let's head back to the Belle so I can check on Grant and go to bed."

While Eliot prepared the shuttle for takeoff Sam's mind drifted to the craft in the mountains. He was disappointed they were not able to explore it today. Once Grant was awake and well, it was game on.

They docked with the Belle and Sam made his way to check on Grant. All was good and Delack was making progress as well. He grabbed a quick bite from the galley, headed to his quarters, and prepared for bed. Lying on his bunk, his thoughts drifted to Grant and whether or not he would be ready to go on this little journey and how much stamina he would have. He would have to wait and see what the healing apparatus showed in the morning. If all was good, he would pump Grant full of vitamins and protein drinks.

Chapter Eighteen

Sam must have fallen asleep. His alarm was going off, it was time to get up and get moving. His eyes were heavy and his body didn't want to function properly. "Coffee, I need coffee!"

He dressed and headed to the galley for a quick bite and some much needed coffee. He chuckled at the thought of Emara and Salbola begging for chocolate and the looks on their faces when he told them no — they needed counseling. "Eggs, bacon-lots of bacon, and some toast should do the trick.

He was sure the shiny object had to be an exploration craft of some kind and he was damn sure going to find out. It had a power source that meant intelligence, in some form or another.

Breakfast complete, he went to the med room. The read out showed Grant's healing was complete. Electrolytes and fluids were already being administered so he wouldn't be groggy and stiff when he came out of the medical coma. "Time to push the button buddy, wake up and let's get this party started!" Sam pushed the button. The healing apparatus swung to the side and the bed brought Grant up to a sitting position. Sam guessed drugs were being pumped into him to wake him from his sleep. Grant slowly opened his eyes and looked around the room like he was lost, with no idea where he was, or how he had gotten there.

"Hey there buddy! How are you feeling?"

"What the hell? Did I get my ass blown up again?"

Sam laughed, "No, but you did about make me shit my pants when you passed out."

"I passed out? How, when, where?"

"We were at the bunker and you were yelling at me, then you just stopped yelling and fell to the ground – midsentence I might add."

"What happened?"

"Well, that poison in your body had a dormant residue and stress triggered it. You were definitely stressed. Your face turned red and you were not being nice, pretty uncharacteristic of you. The med apparatus detected your appendix had burst and you were septic. It was a miracle we got you back to the Ebony Belle."

"We're on the Belle, how?"

"Eliot and I did some fancy manufacturing with some of the materials we got from the bots and made a new part or two. I'll tell you more about it later. We need to get you out of here and down to the planet so we can check out something we discovered yesterday. It may turn out to be nothing but it may also turn out to be really something!"

"What do you mean, Sam?"

"When Tayana, the healers, and I were flying over the mountains, I saw a flash in the snow that looked metallic. Eliot made note of its location before we stopped to play in the snow and stand on top of their world. I thought it would be a great adventure for you and me to check out, before we get blown to bits by the aliens more than likely headed this way to wipe us off this world for destroying their mining operation and killing their lead miner. His brother isn't too pissed. He seems to be a pretty decent fellow, if you can get past his four arms and the smell."

"What the hell are you talking about Sam, four arms? We killed his brother? We're going to die? Did I fall into a worm hole or a black hole and this is the shit that happens on the other side? I don't even know what to say about any of this, except I'm starving. Have you eaten yet? Maybe some food will bring me back to my senses and all of this weirdness will go away."

"Um, probably not gonna happen, Grant."

"Whatever. Get me some clothes so we can go eat, I'm in desperate need of coffee."

Sam got him some clothing and Grant dressed quickly. "Um, Grant..."

"Jesus Christ, Sam, what the hell is that and why is it on the Belle? Did you really bring a dead alien on the ship? Are you out of your mind?"

Sam had heard just about enough and gently yelled, "You done yet?" Sam was being patient and Grant was plowing ahead like a freight train.

"If that thing starts to smell any worse, your ass is walking home."

"Grant, he is very much alive."

In a pitch only dogs and mice can hear, Grant screamed, "This f'ing thing is alive? On the Belle! You're being casual about it? Pull the plug and I'll fire him out the waste chute. Is this the sack of shit that fired on me three times, nearly killing me?"

"Nope, it was his brother, the dead one we left back at the bunker. This one is Delack and he may be able to help us with the incoming warships."

"Warships? Now we have warships coming after us? A month ago we were the only intelligent beings in the universe. Two weeks ago we found out we were wrong. Now we have warships coming to blow us to bits? Put me back under! Put me back under, now. I woke up in a different dimension and I want to go home."

"Oh my God, you big-ass baby! Simmer down and shut up for a minute. Delack is a scientist and does not have any fight in him. He may be able to talk with his people and calm them down so they won't blow us to bits. He is here because you blew off one of his limbs and blew a few holes in him with the SHTF."

Grant thought for a minute and asked, "How is it you can talk with him? Did you put the slimy stuff in his ear, too?"

"No, Tayana said most likely the biologics crawled into his ears because of the poor living conditions they were living in. I guess they like dirty places?"

"Okay, I am going to give this thing one chance and one only. I'm still pretty pissed his kind tried to kill me, over, and over."

"I think you'll like him, when you get the opportunity to speak with him."

"And maybe not!"

"Let's get some food in you before you go all girl on me."

"Not funny, Sam!"

"You need some protein buddy, let's get some bacon in you too!"

While they ate, they chatted about what had happened. Like how Sam was, for all intents and purposes, married to two beautiful alien women.

"How did this come about?"

"Well, no one told me if you are together with a woman on this world you become her life partner and I had two of them at the same time. I have been contemplating what I should do when we leave."

"Contemplating what? Taking them with you? Are you crazy?"

"Eat Grant, it will do you good. I can go be silent somewhere else."

"Now who's the big-ass baby?"

Grant's demeanor dramatically changed as they laughed. "I'm beginning to feel better and I feel my strength coming back, too. More protein, please."

Sam was pleased that Grant was making an award winning comeback and they could get on with their day. "I'll go get the shuttle ready. When you're done, come on down and we can get going. I'm pretty excited to check it out, whatever it is."

"I'll be down soon, another cup of coffee and I should be good to go."

Sam took off towards the lift and had an interesting thought. *What if the shiny thing is a craft from Earth's early explorations? They lost several ships over the years and this could be one of them.*

He readied the shuttle and chatted with Eliot about details on his plan to go to the mountain valley to investigate the craft. He and Grant would explore while Eliot entertained the girls. Eliot was not a ladies bot and refused to baby sit for him. "Plan B then, we take Tayana with us and leave the girls behind for another day, maybe one where we could be alone!" *Good plan Sam*, he thought to himself. He needed some alone time with Kyera and Dyanta. They were his drug of choice in this crazy mixed up adventure. He could not have chosen better mates on Earth if they were handpicked for him. They were beautiful, alluring, and perfect for him.

Grant was in better spirits once he finished his meal. "Let's get this can moving Sam, adventure awaits and I'm feeling good!" Grant had not felt this kind of energy for many years. The healing process had righted more wrongs than what was acutely ailing him. His joints felt better, his thinking was clearer than ever, and he felt like he could run for miles.

"What happened to you? Fifteen minutes ago you were pissy and whining. Now you can't sit down and are raring to go?"

"I guess it took a few minutes to kick in, but I feel great now. Like I said, let's get this can moving."

Eliot acknowledged and disengaged the shuttle from the Ebony Belle.

"To the planets surface my good AI!"

"Uh...yes, Sir."

Sam and Grant laughed at Eliot's response. It was highly unusual for him to add a human pause. This was one for the books. "Uh, Eliot, uh, how come you used an uh in front of your response?"

"I am learning how the two of you communicate by tracking your speech patterns. Sam's usual response is comprised of an uh, before he answers your question. I thought it was a common part of the English language."

"Eliot, it's something people use to buy time because they're not sure how to answer, or they are trying to lie or be deceptive."

"Hey, I'm not being deceptive. I'm trying to figure out how best to respond to Grant so he'll fully understand what I'm saying. I pick my words carefully."

"Sam, if Eliot could laugh, he would be, right about now. That is such a crock of crap it's funny!"

"Whatever. Better buckle up, we're headed into the atmosphere's outer ring, it could get choppy." Grant and Sam buckled in. It was choppier than usual. "Grant, I think there is a storm brewing, could hit in the late evening."

"Agreed, we need to head straight for the mountains

and get this done."

"Eliot, make for the mountains, for the spot Sam noted on the map."

"Yes, Sir, no uh this time."

"We're building a right fine smart ass in this one, aren't we?"

"Sure seems that way. Keep up the good work, Eliot!"

"Uh, Grant, I was thinking, maybe we need to take Tayana with us. She could be a great asset while we're exploring."

"Sorry, not this time. We need to get there and get back as fast as we can. Maybe next time we can all go. Tayana and I and you and the girls."

"Sounds like a plan to me!"

As they neared the spot where Sam saw the shiny object, Grant had Eliot circle the area for a closer look and to blow away some of the surrounding snow. "It is definitely a craft of some sort. Good eye, Sam! I'm not sure how you ever saw it from higher up."

"It flashed so bright I couldn't help but to see it. I'd have to be facing backwards to have missed it."

"Set us down on a fairly flat spot Eliot, as close to it as you can get. If there is something dangerous living in there I want to be able to get to safety quickly."

"Sam, let's take firearms with us as a precaution."

"Good idea, never know what might pop out of a frozen spacecraft."

Grant noted the sarcasm, but maintained his focus on the craft and their landing, a level spot about twenty yards from the craft. Both men were getting excited. They had not had an adventure like this since, well, about a month ago, but this one was different. This was one lone craft on a snow covered mountain, on a planet previously declared uninhabited. This could lead to other explorations and discoveries.

"Set her down gently Eliot, we don't want to bruise anything." The craft was nearly the size of the Varizone, but rounder and shorter. Grant noticed it originally hit farther up the valley, bounced a few times, then came to rest in its current position. It was tilted slightly, but the hatch was fully exposed. Unfortunately, it was locked tight. "Eliot, can you scan this thing and tell us more about it?"

"It is an early Genesis PB Mod 2, most likely from the early 2120's. This one is the GEMO 2."

"Do you mean to tell me this thing is one of ours?"

"Yes, it is an Earth vessel launched by the sister group of the PSAD, the collective EOAM, and short for Earth on a Mission. This was their second generation craft designed to create habitable locations on distant planets. None of the ships were accounted for when the project ended abruptly. They were simply forgotten. This particular ship was under the authority of Captain Jameson Morgan and his co-captain Anders Coke. They were one of four manually piloted ships. The rest were auto piloted. Their programming was flawed and not one report or reply was ever received from them."

"This is monumental. We need to get inside and see what we can find!"

Sam was now more gung-ho than ever. The thrill of finding historical items was making his skin crawl with delight.

"Now who's excited and can't sit down?"

Grant was mocking Sam, and Sam did not care one bit. He was fixated on getting inside the ship. "Eliot, is there a secret code to unlock the outer hatch?"

"No, there is a normal code to unlock the outer hatch." The door slide open.

Grant drew his firearm and Sam followed suit. "Get behind me Sam, there could be traps or something else."

"It's the something else that's scaring the crap out me right about now!"

Grant chuckled to himself, *sissy!* Leading, he slowly entered the craft. He thought he felt heat coming from inside. He was right; the inside of the ship was heated to a nice temperature. It was a nice change from the bitter cold outside. "Come on in Sam, it's warm in here."

"Warm isn't good, Grant. Warm means radiation or someone's home, or about to be."

"Get in here so we can close the door. Nothing is going to get you Sam; Eliot said there were no life forms detected."

"Right, not detected! It does not mean they're not here hiding under one of the cloaking things Tayana and the villagers have."

"Good point! Let's split up and check this thing out thoroughly. Let's make sure we are alone."

"Oh damn!" Sam was not thrilled as they went separate directions exploring the ship. After about fifteen minutes, Sam's communicator went off nearly causing him to discharge his weapon into a fluffy chair he had set spinning in one of the quarters. The movement at the time of the call unnerved him.

"Got a couple bodies down here Sam, they're all bones at this point. You need to come down here. Looks like the only things we might find in here are their ghosts."

"You could have gone all day without saying ghosts.

Where are you? I'll be down in a minute, gotta restart my heart."

"I'm in the lab, lower level near the rear of this thing."

"On my way." Sam hurried down the steps and down the long hallway to the rear of the ship. When he came into the lab Grant was pulling something out from under one of the piles of bones. "Jesus, Grant, no respect for the dead? Now you've cursed us 'cause it was probably one of his favorite things."

"It's only an ID badge. Sam, meet Captains Morgan and Coke."

Sam was surprised they found them after all these years, not that they were looking for them, but they were from Earth and they found them. "I guess the power source you detected was their reactor. It has been running all these years. The smell of their decomposing flesh must have been horrible early on, but over the last 200 plus years it faded away."

"This thing is air tight so it made a perfect tomb."

Sam was losing his queasiness and came closer for a better view. "Wonder what they were able to accomplish in the time they were alive?"

"Sam, check this out!" Grant held a cloaking device like Tayana's.

"Holy crap, Grant! Tayana told me they found them on some of the miners they killed and replicated others for themselves. "Do you know what this might mean? These two might be the grandfathers of Tayana's tribe. They may have been what started life on this rock!"

"Slow down Sam, who would they have mated with?"

"Maybe it was inhabited and they did what I did? It

would explain the near human appearance of the villagers."

"Yes it might, and it would explain how a culture lacking in technology has cloaking devices. But how did these two have the cloaking devices to give them?"

"Captain Coke was an electrical engineer, specializing in holographic projection or, better yet, holographic non-projection. Similar to the magicians tricks in the twentieth century, but his was far more advanced."

Grant and Sam both got up off the floor. Grant said, "Eliot, for the love of God can you please beep or something before you start talking. We're standing here looking at skeletons and you start talking in our ears, nearly startled the life out of us. I think Sam peed a little."

"Nope, but I may have had some movement in my pants."

"TMI, Sam!"

"Kidding, but it really does unnerve us sometimes."

"I will do my best to pre-address you in some manner."

"Thanks Eliot! I guess these were the creation of Captain Coke and he made enough to share? What power source are they using?"

"Bing...they use a small amount of radium as their power source. They can be powered for thousands of years with one small piece."

"Thanks for the bing, Eliot! I wasn't caught off guard at all." They laughed at Eliot's attempt to be less invasive.

"It is simply amazing! How do people think up stuff like this? This guy must have been a true genius. I'd shake his hand if it wasn't in so many pieces." said Grant.

"Ha, ha, Sam! This does start to bring some sense to this whole thing. The villagers, the cloaking devices, the near human looks, and the intelligence. They weren't dumb, but they weren't scientists either. There must have been some indigenous beings here and these two copulated with the locals creating a new species."

"From the looks of things they lived here for quite a while and made this their home away from home. The path leading up to the hatch was pretty worn and the floor is smoother at the hatchway than everywhere else. They must have done the deed and then came here not wanting to interfere with the process of things."

"They may have lived in the village for a while, but something doesn't seem right about all of this. I can't put my finger on it, but something tells me this isn't the whole story. The villagers wouldn't have so many human features in such a short time span of evolution. I'm going to have to do some research on this stuff."

Grant was perplexed by their new discovery. He now had more questions than answers. "I'm going back to the part of the ship I missed when you called me down here. I was about to go into their quarters and have a look around. Wanna join me?"

"Sure, we might find more answers there."

They made their way to the captain's quarters where they found every wall covered with drawings of the village, the planet, plants, trees, the animals, and the mountains.

"They must have been here a lot longer than we think. That's a lot of drawing and a whole lot of information."

"Sam, come check this out. If you look closer there are measurements on everything and what appear to be growth charts. I think they created this entire planet!"

"How could they have created a whole planet,

Grant?"

"Well, not the planet itself, but everything on it. They were a Genesis craft and everything they needed to populate a planet was in their payload."

"So, what you're telling me is, these two were carting around a barrel full of super-hot women seeds and dropped them off on the planet to populate a world they were supposed to create? Sounds like a fairy tale to me buddy!" Sam wasn't buying into Grant's theory even in the slightest. He wasn't so sure it wasn't true either, he needed more proof.

"You keep looking here; I'm going to the other captain's quarters to see what I can find."

"Go for it Sam, I'm camping here for a while. These drawings are amazing and I'm certain there are tons of notes on his desk and he has a Link Pad!"

"Ha, the pre-pre-precursor to our Com Pads from the looks of it. I'll holler if I find anything." Sam ventured across the corridor to the other captain's quarters, and again, was amazed by the amount of things on the walls. "This must have been Captain Coke's quarters; he has a makeshift workbench full of his experimental gadgets. What a nerd!" Sam sat at his desk and began looking through his papers, assorted drawings, and schematics. He was pretty well versed with electrical engineering and the basic concepts, but this guy was way above his level. Among the papers he found a curious map with three crosses on it. He said aloud to himself, "I wonder what your marking, treasure or graves?"

He set the paper aside and continued looking around the desktop. "Aren't you a curious little thing?" He picked up a trinket, on the back was inscribed, "Tayana." He about dropped it when he read the name. "How can this be here? The doors were sealed shut, the captains have been dead for many years, and here is a link to someone who shouldn't be known to these two." His thoughts raced as he tried to rationalize his discovery and all it implied. Continuing his search, he found a stack of photos in one of the drawers. He could not stop staring at a photo of Tayana as a young girl, being held by a man, her father? His pulse raced. He believed the man was one of the captains. The woman in the photo held an infant and wore an odd smile. "Looks like she didn't care much for the scent of the baby." He searched more, but found little else.

"Grant, are you still in there?" There was no answer from the other quarters. "Grant, uh you're starting to freak me out. Answer me buddy, I really don't want to find you dead or about to die. He quickly stepped into the room and found Grant sitting on the bed facing the wall, staring at a series of drawings and photos. "You okay, Grant? You're kind of freaking your partner out a bit. Talk to me, please."

"Sam, There is a photo of two young girls here who remind me of Kyera and Dyanta. How can there be photos of them in here?"

"Grant, I have a couple photos you're going to want to see." Sam handed him the photos and sat at the other end of the bed. Grant hung his head, "Sam, are you thinking this is, Tayana? I do not believe it is. It must have been a local he thought was cute."

Sam handed him the trinket and Grant snapped his head looking him square in the eyes. "If this is a trick, it is a very bad one and in exceptionally poor taste. This is low even for you, Sam!"

"I found them on Captain Coke's desk, Grant."

"This leads me to believe I have another part of Tayana's family story and how they were killed in a battle."

"Sam, there was no battle. They came here to live for whatever reason and left Tayana behind to run the village."

"What the hell is going on here? Are these two the father's of Tayana, Kyera and Dyanta? Wow! My mind just popped." Sam was lost in thought. Grant still looked at the items Sam gave him.

"How could this all have happened in such a short period of time? Is this really the truth? Wait, how could Tayana and the girls still be here? These two died many years ago"

"Sam, we need to go check out the location of the crosses, we might find more answers there."

"We might find a whole lot more confusion, too."

They exited the craft and made their way down the valley to a rocky overhang, underneath were three crosses. Each had its own placard with the name of the interred on it.

"What were Tayana's parents names? Can you remember?"

"I don't think she ever mentioned their names, just that they were killed in a war along with her brother."

"Sam, there are one small and two large crosses. Do you think these might be the graves of her father, mother, and brother?"

"If it is the case, your story about one of the captains being her father would be inaccurate, since they are both lying in the craft up there and not down here in the ground with the others."

"Good point Sam. Then who does the third grave

belong to?"

They thought about it for a few minutes. Sam offered, "I think one of the graves Kyera and Dyanta's mother. It makes sense if you stop and think about it. There is a small cross with a larger cross and then there is another large cross a couple feet removed from the other two. It's as if they do not belong together, but do belong together. The other two are Tayana's mom and her brother."

"Sam, you are a genius sometimes! It fits the story perfectly. But, how do we tell Tayana her whole life has been a lie and her parents abandoned her to run the village? Write down the names and we will talk with Tayana when we get back. We will ask her to tell us the story she knows. We may have to bring her here so she can see for herself. If nothing else, it might bring her closure."

"Great idea, but if she gets pissed and becomes dangerous, neither one of us have enough bullets to stop her. She is very much a badass as it is. Giving her this information may send her over the top and we are the bearers of the bad news. They always kill the messenger, Grant, always!"

"We are going to have to trust that she will accept what we present to her. When she sees it for herself, we are off the hook.

Chapter Nineteen

Grant still could not believe his eyes. He stared at the bracelet. Could this really be? He felt his blood pressure rising and began to perspire. His mind was a tangle of thoughts colliding together in pretty much the same place—Tayana. "What the hell Sam? Do you know what this means? Can you imagine the impact this will have on both worlds? If this is the truth, we have stumbled onto one of the biggest discoveries of our world. Not to mention these two yahoos might have started their own race and no one ever knew. If you hadn't found their ship we would never have known."

"I just had another brilliant thought! This is their shuttle, not their ship. Where is their ship?"

"Sam, you are on a roll!"

"Eliot, are there any other objects orbiting this planet?"

"My scanners tell me there is another ship on the other side of the planet. It has no power and there are no indications of life."

"Thanks Eliot! Sam, do you think we could take the power source from this shuttle and install it in their ship? It could recharge their fuel cells. We could evacuate the villagers to a safe distance away from here, for now."

"It would take days, maybe even weeks to get the power source out of here and to the ship."

"Let's go have a look and see what we're up against. We need to get a better idea anyway."

"These older ships didn't have the micro technology we have now Grant. Their power source is most likely gargantuan."

"On the contrary sirs, some of their technology was far superior to the technology we use today. Their fuel source shouldn't be much larger than a fifty-five gallon drum. On the other hand their converter will be nearly as large as a city bus."

"Thanks, Eliot! What happened to the bing?"

"I decided I am not a binger, Sir. I would rather pop in when I feel the need."

"Good for you, Eliot, you are evolving."

"Sam, take notes, we need to get him reprogrammed as soon as we get back."

Sam laughed and agreed. They made it to the engine room and discovered Eliot was right. The converter was the size of a bus and the fuel cell was actually slightly smaller than a fifty-five gallon drum.

"Sam, we could haul this thing out of here tomorrow and get it to their ship. Most of the fittings should be the same."

"I agree, we can get here first thing in the morning, and should have it contained for transport before noon. Sam, how are we going to tell Tayana?" Grant could not get it off of his mind.

"Grant, this is a seriously touchy situation and I have no point of reference from which to draw counsel. We're going to have to wing it, I guess."

"You know how well that works out for us, right?"

"Well, how would you go about it? Wait, don't answer that."

"What? Like, I'd say, Tayana, your dad was a lying Earthman who dumped you, then died, the end!"

"No, Sam, it is not what I am thinking. Ok, maybe a little, but this will take some finesse and nearly perfect timing."

"Why don't we show her the craft and let he make her own conclusions?"

"Let's see what other information we can dig up. Maybe it will give us more insight regarding what happened."

They thoroughly searched both captains' quarters and found nothing giving them any additional information.

"Grant, do you think they had AI like Eliot, who recorded everything? If the captain kept a daily log of activities and his thoughts we might find something to tell us why they crashed or why there are three grave markers."

"Brilliant Sam, did you have bacon for breakfast again?"

"Funny, I have bacon every morning for breakfast. Keeps my mind sharp."

"Only you Sam!"

"Ship, can you show us the last entry in the data log?"

"I will be happy to, if you enter the correct passcode." The ship's voice was female and rather sultry.

"I'd like to meet the woman they patterned her voice after."

"Sam, you're a married man!"

"I know, but I'd still like to meet her. What a voice."

Trying to stop what could be a long, drawn out conversation, Grant said "Tayana." Immediately the video began to play. "Well, that was simple." He made the right choice, and it shut Sam up for a while. The video showed the captains, two women, and a small boy. One of the women looked much like Tayana and the boy could have been Tayana's brother.

The video played on and the ship was rocked by an explosion, and then another, and another. The captains were thrown about the cabin along with the women and boy. Through the view screen they saw the ship was headed for the mountains when they lost control. The ship careened towards the mountains at a crazy speed with the captains trying to keep their balance and fly the ship as straight as possible. Another explosion rocked the ship and it dropped wildly, heading to the top of the valley. It crashed into a large snow bank and bounced off the valley walls. It nearly came to rest when yet another explosion sent them careening farther down the mountain valley, skipping like a flat rock on a clear lake. They hit a large outcropping and it jolted the ship violently, throwing the boy against the wall, killing him instantly. The two women, beaten against the walls, bled profusely from head and torso injuries as they tended to the motionless boy.

Sam could see the pain in their eyes and on their faces. "Stop, Grant, stop, I've seen enough. I see no need to go any farther. I can assume what else happened and that the graves outside are theirs."

"It breaks my heart. Tayana has no idea what happened. She thinks an invading species came down to their planet's surface, waged war, and killed her family. I haven't seen any signs of war, with the exception of the missiles, most likely launched by Delack's ancestors."

"Do you think anyone in her village knows the truth or do you suppose they made up the story because her family never returned from their trip around the planet?"

"I'm going to watch some more videos. You can go do whatever you think you need to do, but I need more information. I cannot go back to Tayana with half a story and no proof of anything."

"I hear ya! I'm going back to Captain Coke's quarters and do some more investigating. I might tinker with some of his inventions while I'm at it."

"Be careful Sam, some of his stuff could be dangerous."

"Duly noted." Sam left the captain's quarters and headed across the hall to Captain Coke's, while Grant restarted the video where they left off. Sam sat at Captain Coke's desk and marveled at the copious notes he had taken regarding many different subjects and about the life on this planet. Sam knew he had hit the jackpot when he found a recipe detailing the best way to cook Chotuk. He gathered the papers and drawings, loading them into some boxes he found stashed in a back closet. He figured he could look at them while they traveled back to Earth. He turned on the captain's computer and had Eliot hack into it, bypassing the password. There were many video files related to his experiments and several of him, with who Sam believed was, his wife and their children. One of them had dark hair, deep silver black eyes, and naturally tanned skin, much like Kyera. The other, was a pretty little girl with deep brown hair and reddish highlights. Both were covered in short blonde body hair, not furry, but the only places without it were their faces, feet, and hands. "Cute kids, probably made beautiful women, wonder what happened to them." He continued to look through photos and videos and stumbled across an audio file. "Hmm, what do we have here?" When he opened the file, the voice of Captain Coke came through crisp and clear. It was a private copy of his daily logs, the kind you don't send back to your boss. He told the story of how they were marooned and their ship was still orbiting the planet and they had no way to get back to it. He told about meeting the locals and how they became friends and then family. There was a lot of technical stuff, too. Sam figured he could have Eliot secure all of the files so he could peruse them as they traveled back to Earth or their next destination. He was about to shut it down when he heard the captain say, "Kyera and Dyanta, if you are hearing this, I am no longer alive. Know I loved you deeply. Please forgive me. Go to the video titled, my favorite family. It has the answers to most, if not all of your questions." Sam was stunned stupid. Captain Coke really was Kyera and Dyanta's father. Their mother lay in a grave some fifty yards from him. Why didn't the captains go back to the village and why did they abandon their children?

"Sam, time to go, we can come back tomorrow morning and gather what we need from here and get the fuel cell. It's getting late and the helium will begin to fall, we have to go now. We can talk on the way back to the village."

Sam snapped out of his thoughts and made his way to the bridge. "Buddy, we have to talk!"

"We sure do! Let's go." The trip back to the village wasn't long, but they had time to share their discoveries. Both were surprised at what the other found.

"They didn't return to the village because they were sick."

"Captain Coke had two daughters, Kyera and Dyanta."

"Captain Morgan was Tayana's father."

"There might be a video explaining all of this on Captain Coke's computer. I'll have Eliot transfer all the data from their ship to the Ebony Belle. We can pick up the boxes of papers when we return tomorrow."

"We need to get pictures of everything as well. We more than likely will not be coming back to this spot once we take the fuel cell."

"How are we going to tell the girls?"

"For now, we're not!"

"Sirs, I have detected several ships emerging from hyperspace about a million miles away. By my calculations they should be here in two days time."

Grant and Sam looked at each other for a brief moment, realizing this was real and things needed to happen at a much faster pace. "We have to prepare for the incoming ships."

"I sure hope our messages were heard and the PSAD is sending back up."

"Not likely, we cannot count on them to help us, we have to plan as if they will not be here in time."

"No pressure, got it, we are on our own against an enemy we know nothing about, Holy shit! Things are going to get sketchy pretty quick. We have to get the other ship fired up and running, and we have to get the villagers to a nearby planet for safety."

"The village is going to have to scramble. They need to get food and other things gathered; we have no idea how long they'll be gone."

"Almost there Sam. You gather the counsel and I'll get Tayana. We need to let them know what's happening and how fast we all need to move. Pray we can get the fuel cell to the other ship and get it installed quickly."

Helium Fall

Chapter Twenty

Eliot came in hot and quickly landed the Varizone. The men ran to the village. "Sam, have the counsel go to the dining hall. I'll find Tayana; we will meet you there shortly."

"Done, see you in a few!"

They tore off in different directions looking for who they needed to find. Grant ran straight for Tayana's pod. She was there, looking radiant and beautiful beyond reason. His abrupt appearance startled her. She reached for her sword, startling Grant, who slid to halt. "Tayana, it's me, I'm sorry to barge in like this, but it's an emergency. Several ships have come out of hyperspace and will be here within two days. We need to get the villagers out of harm's way. We will move them to the back side of a nearby planet out of view. We have no idea what may happen when the ships arrive and they discover we destroyed their mining operation, killed one of their own, and have another in a medically induced coma in our med room because we blew off a limb and ventilated his body with multiple holes. We need to get the counsel together in the dining hall and let them know what's happening."

Tayana was shocked into silence. She had feared this day for many years and secretly hoped it would never come. "All right, Grant, go to the dining hall and wait for me, I will be there in a few minutes." Grabbed her bow, quiver of arrows, and sword, she left the pod. She moved with grace and nimbleness, swiftness, and strength. Grant was left standing in silence, entertaining his thoughts, when he heard a loud trumpet sound coming from a short distance away. He ran from the pod to find Tayana blowing into the base of a large flower producing the noise. Villagers scrambled here and there, yet they appeared to be well organized and moving like they had rehearsed for this moment.

"Grant, to the dining hall and stay out of the way. The villagers have things to do while we meet with the counsel."

Grant obeyed. He did not want to be in the way of the villagers or on the receiving end of her wrath if he did not comply. She moved with such purpose and authority. She was a force to be reckoned with and he was not going to interfere. This was the Tayana he first met, she was fierce.

Grant made his way to the dining hall and found Sam already there with more than half of the counsel. The trumpet flower was pretty effective.

Tayana arrived shortly after Grant and addressed the counsel."We are now in the time we have feared. The evil has come back to take the rest of us, just as they did my family. Will we flee from our homes or will we stand and fight them?"

There was no immediate reply and Tayana's voice was now demanding, "Will we flee or fight? Answer me. Members of this counsel, show your hands to stay and fight!" About a third raised their hands and Tayana looked crushed. "Hands for those who wish to flee." There was a seething tone in her voice, as if the words burned her tongue and she was trying hard not to scream. There were more hands raised to flee than to fight. "Those who wish to flee, go, gather your things, and flee. Those who wish to fight, follow me." She left the dining hall followed by less than half of the counsel.

Grant addressed the remaining members. "We need to take only what is needed to survive, food, clothing, and water. We will transport you and your belongings to the Ebony Belle tomorrow as soon as we take care of a few things. Go tell your families and everyone else who wishes to go with us they need to prepare, now."

The rest of the counsel left the dining hall with murmurs and sideways glances. Grant and Sam didn't have time to worry about them. They had to get the fuel cell into the other ship as fast as possible. Neither knew if they were making the right decision, but they pressed forward, and helped the villagers gather their things.

Sam stopped Grant a while later, "Grant, we need a plan, something other than getting the villagers to safety."

"I know Sam. I've been giving it some thought. Depending on when the ships arrive and how many they send to the surface, I've thought of several options. If they bring a large number, depending on the time of day, early morning or late evening, we can detonate an incendiary device to set the gasses on fire. They will fry in their tracks. Then we fire on their ships with the blasting missiles we have for excavation."

"Sounds pretty sketchy, Grant. What about Tayana and the villagers? What will happen to them?

"They will burn too. Shit, didn't think about Plan B. We tell Tayana about how the mining defense missiles took out her family and hope she doesn't wage war when they get here?"

"Holy crap Grant, we are in deep shit here! I thought you were the strategist, the one who could make this work. I'm buggin' out with the villagers."

"Wait Sam, I do have an idea. If we can get Tayana to

hold off, we can use their cloaking devices, or a larger one, to cloak the village. The Anotokian's will not be able to detect them and if we need to, we can launch a surprise attack. The shuttle has armaments. We can use another SHTF if there are too many of them for us to handle."

"Now you're talkin'. If we land the shuttle behind the boulders and camo it, they won't know we're there either. The mining compound will hold a bunch of the bastards and we have the upper hand. Wait, what the heck are we saying?"

"What do you mean Sam?"

"We cannot be here, Grant. We have to be on the Ebony Belle and the...what is the name of their ship?"

"Eliot, what is the name of Captain Morgan's ship?"

"The ship's name is the Terra Aurai. It means goddess of Earth and nymphs of the breeze."

"What a fitting name. They populate a planet with plants, animals and all kinds of stuff, sort of like Earth, and then drop in beautiful women just to make it interesting. Uh yeah, I'll take a sack of those beautiful women seeds, please. 2120 must have been a really good year!"

"Indeed it must have been, but we're here now and have a war to stop, or avoid, if possible. Holy crap, Sam, we forgot about Delack. We need to get him out of the med room and pick his brain. He may be our only hope in this situation. Maybe he can offer some suggestions."

"Maybe he can tell them not to kill all of us; we were just protecting ourselves from their missiles. We don't really give a rat's ass about their mining operation."

"Even though we did completely destroy their entire mining operation and kill one of their kind?"

"Doesn't look good, does it? I remember Delack saying they are scientists and warriors. We are scientists and villagers with arrows and swords. We are so screwed!"

"Sam, we need to get back to the Belle, now!"

"It's almost sundown, and we won't be able to return tonight and assist the villagers."

"I'll let Tayana know this is urgent and we need to be out of here in ten minutes, or less."

"Get moving, I'll get the shuttle fired up and be ready to go. You have ten minutes or we will not be able to take off without lighting the place on fire."

"See you in about seven minutes." With a wink, Grant took off to find Tayana, and Sam took off towards the shuttle.

Sam called Eliot on his compad. "Eliot, fire up the shuttle and prepare to go to the Belle. We need to be off this planet in less than ten minutes, do you understand?"

"Yes Sir, I have been monitoring your conversations and have already started initial flight checks. The Varizone will be ready for takeoff when you arrive."

"We need to wait for Grant. Hopefully he can locate Tayana and let her know we are not abandoning her or the village. We need Delack awake and as coherent as possible. Once we are in the air, can you initiate the sequence to bring him out of stasis?"

"Yes, I can. But it is not advisable. If he becomes conscious before we arrive, he has the opportunity to disable the ship and block our entry."

"It's a chance we're going to have to take. He may be the only thing saving our asses from a cruel and painful death."

"There are other options. I can..."

"Eliot, stop. Right now we need to focus on getting off this planet and waking Delack up so we can talk with him. Once we are onboard the Belle have the galley prepare some food to his liking. I need you to do an analysis on his body composition and what his nutrition needs are so we can get him back to normal quickly."

"The systems check is complete and we are ready for takeoff." "Thank you Eliot, Grant should be here in four minutes."

"Grant will not be here in the allotted time. He is having difficulty finding Tayana. She is not in the village. She is near the entrance to the caves. Grant must return to the shuttle now or he will not make it."

"Grant abort, I say again, abort. Tayana is not in the village, she is at the cave entrance. You have to come back to the shuttle immediately."

"Sam, meet me at the cave entrance." Grant hopped a ride on one of the remaining C-Rexes and headed towards the cave entrance as fast as it would move.

"Eliot, make for the cave entrance, now!"

The shuttle lifted off immediately. The cave entrance was two minutes away by air and Grant would be there in three on the C-Rex.

"You're cutting it really close, Grant. Pray she doesn't go inside before we get there." Sam watched Grant race through the forest at breakneck speed and emerge onto the plains. "Man those things are fast!"

Grant held on for dear life as the C-Rex increased its speed on the plains. With nothing in its way it had free run and was really putting on a show.

"Grant, you better tighten your grip, it's about to take flight."

With a quick tap on his compad Grant replied, "No

shit!" Within minutes they were at the cave entrance, much to the surprise of Tayana and her crew of warriors. Grant skidded to a halt and jumped off the C-Rex, nearly tripping and flipping head over heels in front of everyone.

"Tayana, Sam and I are going to the Belle, we need to get Delack out of stasis and speak with him. He may be our only hope and we need to leave, now. I did not want you thinking we abandoned you when you returned to the village and we were not there. We are leaving just ahead of the helium fall and will return tomorrow morning, as fast as we can."

"We will be here, ready for the villagers to board the shuttle. We are ready for whatever battle they bring to us."

"Get some rest. We will be back in the morning."
Tayana replied, "See that you are, Earthman." Her comment and wry smile caught Grant off guard.

"Gotta go Grant, flirt with her tomorrow."

Sam's statement caught Tayana by surprise. They all smiled and nervously laughed."

"Eliot, take us to the Belle!"

"Yes, Sir."

The Shuttle took off for the Belle as Tayana and her crew disappeared into the cave.

"What do you think they're after, Grant?"

"I have no idea and I didn't have time to ask. I'm sure she has a good reason to go into the caves. Weird timing though, maybe she's exploring her options as a backup plan, in case we don't come back."

"But she didn't know we were leaving until a minute and a half ago."

"Too late to worry about it now."
They sat in silence for some time, each contemplating the

upcoming events most certain to happen. The outcome may depend on an alien scientist whose brother was killed by the people who are now asking for his assistance.

Sam was the first to break the silence, "Eliot, start the sequence to bring Delack out of stasis and start the other thing we discussed earlier."

"Yes, Sir."

"What's going on, Sam?"

"Eliot and I discussed bringing Delack out of stasis and preparing food to nourish his body and bring him to health and awareness via the quickest route. We need him awake and mentally functioning. We have a very short window of time to accomplish both."

Chapter Twenty-One

As Grant and Sam left for the Ebony Belle, Tayana and her crew made their way deep into the planet's caverns astride their C-Rexes. They made their way by torchlight down narrow passageways with high ceilings. Tayana's vague recollection of where she needed to turn and how far they needed to go, was all the information she had to rely on.

Tayana was confident as she spoke, but she was unsure of the exact way to go, "We need to go about a quarter of a mile into the cave, then make two left turns, two right turns, go another quarter mile and veer left, then we should reach our destination. Stay close, do not stray or fall behind."

The crew acknowledged her directions as they made their way deeper into the damp darkness of the cave. They did not know where they were going or why. The eerie shadows cast on the walls from their torches made the crew fearful of their fate. The looks on their faces said it all, they thought they were going to become lost and die in the caves.

"They are just shadows, stay with me!" Her fearless demeanor gave them courage to continue into the darkness.

Tayana began to doubt she accurately remembered where the correct turns were located; they were further apart than she remembered. She questioned herself, *was it two right turns then two left turns?* She was about to turn back when they emerged into a large open space. There in the middle was what she sought. Her father built the device to protect the village against anything that could or would possibly destroy their way of life. Her father was a scientist, an explorer, and a brilliant man. He sought to preserve life at all costs, especially hers.

"We need to get the device's sled attached to my C-Rex quickly. We have to get back to the village and have this installed before dawn. Let's move!"

"Aye." Was the simultaneous cry of her crew. They began hooking up the sled. Time was not on their side. The ropes attached to the sled had dried out from age and broke as soon as weight and tension was placed on them.

"Use the ropes in our packs," Tayana said, "we can still use the metal rings, and they have fared better than the ropes. We need to hurry."

They emptied their packs, replacing time-battered, rotten ropes with sturdy, strong ropes. One of the crew said, "We are almost done, Tayana. It will be close, but I'm certain we can safely make it back to the village with this rigging."

"Good, let's get moving as soon as we can. This device needs to be setup on the shrine rock and placed in a precise manner. It may take us longer than expected. Time is not our friend, and neither is this cave. There are creatures in here that would have us for a snack if we tarry too long."

With her words fresh on the crew's minds, their speed increased, and they finished replacing the ropes in short order. "We are ready now!"

"Back to the village, quickly. We need to be wary of the cave creatures. The hour is late and they know we are here. We did not enter with stealth, but we will leave with stealth, if possible."

They began their journey back to the surface. They

moved less than one hundred feet before the walls behind them began to move, as if they were melting, undulating in a crazy mix of wave and texture. Tayana had only a moment to duck and avoid being knocked off her C-Rex by a large mass of bat-like creatures making their nightly journey to the mouth of the cave to feed on insects and whatever else they could find. She nudged her C-Rex to the ground and hid beside it. The entire crew threw themselves to the ground avoiding being attacked and eaten by the ravenous flying creatures. They huddled in small groups, arms over their heads in a defensive posture, some crying, others screaming, and many flailed their swords at the flying beasts who easily avoided the sharp blades. The noise was incredibly loud. The flapping of so many wings and the clicking sounds they made to navigate their way around the caves was terrifying, especially to those who had never ventured into the caves or into any such enclosed area.

Once the creatures were past them, Tayana ordered the crew to press onward. "They are insect eaters, grow a backbone. Move forward, now!"

Tayana was driven and angry beyond her normal angry, driven self. The trek out of the cave went smoothly and quickly with Tayana urging her C-Rex at a rapid pace. Her thoughts turned to their situation. It would take precious time to get the device set up and functioning. If they failed, her people would be forced to resettle elsewhere, or worse, die. She found both outcomes unacceptable. The valley was their home. It protected them from the helium fall and provided everything they needed for a beautiful life.

Emerging from the cave Tayana cried, "To the shrine rock! We must move quickly."

Her crew hastened to reach the village before helium fall. Tayana looked back to check on the device attached behind her C-Rex. She noticed small wisps of flame coming from the sled's coated runners. Dragging the sled rapidly over the rocky trail generated friction causing sparks to ignite the small traces of hydrogen reaching ground level. Full on helium fall would occur in a few short minutes. Time was running out, but they only had a short distance to go. She pressed on, picking up the pace, driving her crew to move faster.

Five minutes later, with sled rails beginning to catch fire, they arrived at the village outskirts. They wound their way expertly between village pods and structures, taking the shortest route to the shrine in the center of the village.

As they approached, Tayana yelled at the villagers who were diligently preparing for their morning departure, "to the side, to the side!"

The villagers quickly stepped out of the crew's way, their eyes wide at the sight of the sled with flaming rails, and its secret cargo. Several curious villagers dropped what they were doing and followed the burning sled to its destination.

Coming to an abrupt halt, Tayana jumped off her C-Rex and climbed onto the shrine rock. "We need to uncover the protector, remove it from the sled, and place it where I am standing. Hurry!"

The crew, with help from several villagers, uncovered the protector, removed it from the sled, and hoisted it to the top of the rock shrine.

On her hands and knees, Tayana searched for the markings she saw many years ago. She was dismayed. Some of the markings etched into the surface of the rock had disappeared. Others markings were etched deeper into the face of the rock. She found a depression in the middle of the shrine and began frantically tracing small but perceptible lines emanating from the center. She found enough markers to know where the device needed to be set up.

"Place it here with the panel facing the falls. Easy now, this might be the only thing saving our village and us from certain destruction."

Villagers noted the sound of Tayana's voice and saw her agitated state. She sounded almost desperate. It was a tone they had never heard from her before and it made them uneasy. To them, Tayana was a strong, fierce, unflappable leader—she was their rock. She could not crack under pressure, she did not know how.

Finally the protector was in position. Tayana urged the villagers to back away while she tested it to ensure it worked properly. She wracked her brain trying to remember what she was supposed to do to make it function, then she remembered the instructions her father had given her.

She ran to her pod to search for a document. It was in a safe place, but she couldn't quite remember where. For many years, it sat on her bookcase, but when she changed pods, she put it between the pages of a book for safe keeping. She wondered, *is it in "Potters Guide to Herbs, Fields, Flowers and Fauna", or "In Times of Trouble", which book?* She turned the pages of several books and found it. Running back to the protector she prayed the device would work and her village would be safe.

The instructions indicated a water source was necessary to power the device. After looking over the instructions again, she shuttered, there was a part missing. She grabbed a torch and ran back to the sled. She searched everywhere. It was not there. She broke down and cried for the first time since her family was killed so many years ago. The stress of saving the village was becoming overwhelming. Should she just tell them all to get on the shuttle with Grant and Sam and leave? Her thoughts were a mess and she felt at a loss. One of the older women approached her and sat down beside her. Wrapping her arm around Tayana, she pulled her close. Tayana sobbed into her shoulder and held her tight.

Gently, the woman spoke, "This is not the Tayana we all know and love. We are your people; we love you, and will do whatever it takes to help you save our village. You need only to direct us and we will go."

Tayana slowly pulled away, wiping tears from her eyes, and brushing her long black hair from her face. "What I need is to find the other piece of the protector. It should have been on the sled, but I do not see it anywhere. It is silver and has a cable attached."

The woman stood and said, "Men, please search the sled and its wrappings for a small device, it is part of the protector. It is silver and has a cable attached to it or near it."

The men began their search immediately, without question.

Tayana said, "Thank you! You have no idea what it means to me."

"I do have some idea." The woman said. "You have not had a mother for a long time. Sometimes you just need a hug and a little push."

Tayana smiled, stood, and made her way back to the protector.

From a tree near where they uncovered the protector, a man called out, "It is here. It was behind a tree, out of sight." He rushed to give it to her.

Tayana, quickly regained her composure. She connected one end of the cable to the device and the other end to what appeared to be a canister full of small holes with something very heavy inside. Turning to a villager, she said, "Take this canister and place it in the center of the pool below the falls."

The villager ran to the pool, waded out to the middle where the pool was deepest, and lowered the canister into the water. He exited the pool in short order and returned to the group.

At first nothing happened. Tayana reread the instructions. She flipped a small red switch and the protector began humming, the lights turned on, and the control panel lit up brightly. Again, she urged the villagers to back away from the device. She was uncertain what would happen when she activated it. She only saw it operate once, over two hundred years ago. Some villagers backed away, some hid behind trees, and others turned sideways to reduce their profile.

"I will turn it on briefly to test if it is functioning. If it works, I will explain further." Tayana pushed the green button and a crystal clear dome began to form above the protector. She pushed another button and the dome began to expand. Its edge passed through the villagers, pods, and everything in its path with no harm. A couple villagers were spooked when the dome passed through them, but they giggled with excitement when it was past them and they were still alive. The dome was the height of the falls, encompassing the entire village.

"It is working! We can pass through the dome to

leave, but we cannot return once we have left its safety. Nothing can penetrate the dome. We are all safe if we are inside. Those who wish to stay may stay. Those who wish to go with Grant and Sam may do so with no recourse.

If you decide to stay, be prepared to do battle with whatever may come our way. If they are injured, finish them. We can shoot arrows out, but they cannot shoot anything in through the dome. If my father was correct, and I believe he was, the dome goes all the way under us. There are no edges to dig under."

The villagers clapped and cheered. The tension had abated and their thoughts turned to dinner. Tayana turned the protector off and began instructing others on how to operate it in case she was delayed or dispatched. The village women prepared a late meal with remaining rations. It may be their last meal together as a village for some time. They would have a quick breakfast, but would not all eat at the same time.

"Family, thank you! Tomorrow is the beginning of what may be our darkest hours. It may also be the beginning of our finest hours. We may be separated, but we are in unity when it comes to our lives. We are family and we will come through the other side. We may lose some of us. We may lose all of us. But we will never lose the love we have for one another. Be blessed and safe as we venture forth tomorrow. May Grant and Sam return to battle along side of us, as family! The villagers cheered. Everyone was happy and smiling. The looming battle was no longer on their minds, not for the moment, anyway. The meal began and Tayana's thoughts drifted to Grant.

Chapter Twenty-Two

Grant and Sam tried to formulate a more concise plan as they approached the Ebony Belle. "Sam, we need to talk with Delack before we make a decision on how to proceed, but we need some sort of plan before we approach him!"

"You're making this much harder than it needs to be. We let Delack know the situation and ask his opinion, and then we come up with ideas and present them."

Grant needed cold hard facts and as much information as possible to formulate a solid plan of attack, or defense, whatever was called for. He was frustrated with Sam because he was so nonchalant.

"We will be docking with the Ebony Belle in twenty seconds." Eliot counted down, until they came to a gentle stop, and heard four loud clicks. "We have docked. You may depart the Varizone."

Grant was the first to move. He quickly made his way to the hatchway opening. Sam, a bit more casual, sauntered towards the hatchway at a leisurely pace. He found Grant in the hallway as he suspected he would, waiting impatiently for the elevator to the med room.

"Nice day for a stroll, hey buddy?"

"Sam, you have to take this seriously. We're about to be wiped off the face of the universe and you say, 'hey buddy'?"

"You need to calm down. Look at yourself, waiting impatiently for an elevator, rubbing your hands together anticipating walking into a room with an alien lying on a table in stasis so you can press a button. Once the button is pressed it will be another five to ten minutes before he opens his eyes and another five to ten minutes before he can move, sit, or stand. Then, we need to get him to the galley so we can put food and nutrients into him that'll bring him back to some resemblance of normal. Tack on another twenty to thirty minutes before he can speak. So roughly an hour from now we'll be able to ask our first question and get an intelligent response. Ya getting the point?"

"Sam, you're right, I am freaking out. Mainly, because I don't want to die, but also because I haven't gone to the pools with Tayana. It's truly something I don't want to miss out on."

"So you do have feelings for her!" Sam grinned from ear to ear, he knew Grant had feelings for her, it was unmistakable. The way he smiled when he saw her, the flirting, being a stand up guy, and the complete lack of balls to ask her to go swimming for an hour. Sam knew Tayana felt the same way. Maybe not the part about the balls, or maybe she did. She was, after all, a beautiful, vibrant woman with killer instincts and a body that would make a priest blush. He saw her flicker of want pretty early on, when she was inside his mind.

"Yes, I have feelings for her. I'm completely in love with her and I'm too chicken to say anything."

"Grant, walk up to her tomorrow morning, wrap your arms around her, and plant a long wet one on her. She'll either passionately kiss you back, or vigorously cut your nuts off."

"It's the later that terrifies me!" They smiled and laughed deep belly laughs. Grant's stress diminished as he found a new perspective. He was in love and needed to let her know before either of them were dispatched by the upcoming battle. Right now, he had other things to focus on as the elevator doors opened. Stepping inside, the pair continued snickering and laughing, until Sam farted. "Jesus, Sam you couldn't have done it in the hallway? My mouth was open!"

Sam laughed and with each laugh, came a little fart. The more he laughed, the more he farted, and the more the two laughed together. "You're killing me, Sam, we're supposed to be all serious and you're over there crapping in your pants." Sam let go a juicy fart in response. Their faces were red and their eyes watered from the laughter. "We have to get a grip!" The elevator door opened on the med deck. Grant and Sam piled out laughing like two kids still in grade school.

"Oh my, we needed a good laugh!"

"Sam, do you need to wipe before we get started?"

"Maybe so!" They laughed some more as they approached the med room.

"Enough for now, we have to get serious. The process will take some time, but we need to be on top of things so it flows smoothly and quickly."   "Agreed!"

"Eliot, please have the galley prepare the concoction we discussed and have lots of fruit on hand, as well."

Eliot replied, "The process has begun."

Grant rounded the machine keeping Delack in stasis and pressed the right combination of buttons on the control panel to begin the reviving process.

"Sam, better get some appropriate clothing for our friend here. If you remember he is quite shy. I believe the synthesizer created a set of clothing to his liking."

"On my way."

Sam bounded down the hallway to the clothing synthesizer where he found a neatly folded uniform in the product tray. "Delack will be happy to see this." The clothing catalogue caught Sam's eye and he stopped to look for a minute. Silky short-sleeved shirts with flowers and birds, a nice pair of shorts to go with the shirt, and a very comfortable pair of sandals to round out the outfit. Sam envisioned a beach with palm trees, a fruity drink in his hand, and Kyera and Dyanta lounging beside him on the beach loungers, wearing skimpy bikinis. The warm ocean breeze softly blowing across his unbuttoned shirt ruffled his chest hair.

"SAM, you better get in here, NOW!"

The loud voice broke through his reverie like a hot knife through butter. The collar com jolted him back to reality and he ran to the med room. Delack was standing in the corner yelling at Grant.

"Delack, it's me, Sam. Do you remember us saving you?"

All Delack heard was a jumble of sounds and in his current state he was combative. The familiar voices were no longer there. Grant, Sam, and Delack were at a loss. Delack felt betrayed, and Grant and Sam thought Delack had lost his mind. Back to full health Delack was a formidable foe and the extra set of arms could deal some awesome damage.

Grant was trying to calm Delack and it was making him angry. "We need to get him to the galley and get food in him."

"We need to get the food up here, and into him." Without hesitation Sam bolted from the room and ran down the hall to the lift. The doors opened immediately. Sam was relieved he did not have to wait.

"Eliot, there better be a protein drink and some fruit handy when I get to the galley."

"The drink and fruit are ready for consumption."

Sam grabbed the foodstuffs and headed back to the lift. He arrived back at the med room just in time to see Delack take a powerful swing at Grant's head.

"Where the heck did you go? I'm about to get my head ripped off and you go get a snack?"

"This is for him!" Sam offered some fruit to Delack, and then backed away slowly when he approached the table. Delack's hunger was out pacing his anger. He took the fruit and eyed Sam. Sam set more fruit and the protein concoction on the table. Not taking any chances, he backed away again. He liked his head right where it was. Sam began speaking slowly and making gestures while Delack drank and ate at a rapid pace. He eyed Sam again, as if looking for more food. The fruit and the protein drink were now gone and Delack had calmed down considerably.

Sam tried again to speak with Delack. "Delack, we do not want to hurt you. We are trying to communicate with you, peacefully."

Grant was deep in thought, when he had an epiphany. The med device had healed Delack completely and removed the organisms from his ears, the ones translating speech. He hurried over to the equipment and instructed it to take some of the biologics from his ear and place them on the table near Delack. The machine began to whir. The arm moved to Grant's ear and extracted a small portion of the small, intelligent creatures. It then swung around and placed them on the table as instructed. Grant motioned to Delack to pick up some of the substance and put it in each ear.

Delack did as Grant motioned. Within seconds he understood what was being said and apologized profusely for trying to separate Grant from his head. He was also apologized to Sam for the looks he was giving him. It was then he realized Sam was holding his clothing. It was clean and rip free. Delack blushed, grabbed the clothing, and stuffed himself into them with haste. All four arms flailed trying to maneuver his large body into the new not so stretchy uniform. With a few grunts, snorts, and dear gods he finally managed to get himself dressed and presentable. "This must never be spoken of, do I make myself clear?"

Sam chuckled in agreement; Grant couldn't look at him for fear of bursting out in laughter.

"Do you agree?"

"Yes, we agree."

"Sure."

They all looked at one another and even Delack managed a weak smile.

"Down to business gentlemen." Grant acted business-like and Sam wondered what he was up to.

"Delack, we find ourselves in a precarious position. We need to ask for your thoughts on the matter."

"By all means proceed, you saved my life, I will honor my debt."

"You may not think so when we've finished our conversation. You are acutely aware we destroyed your mining operation and accidentally killed your brother, Graeck. We are deeply sorry. You are not aware, but as we speak, your brethren are massing for an attack on the planet below. If our calculations are correct they will arrive tomorrow afternoon. We do not know their intent, but we assume they are looking for a battle with whoever destroyed their operation. We guess your brother sent a signal just before he was killed. What are your thoughts on their arrival? Will they be violent, and what course of action should we take?"

Delack sat for a moment deep in thought, tilting his head from side to side. Grant was unsure if he was thinking or nodding off. He had just been brought out of stasis and had not had the opportunity to move about and get his blood flowing, except for his attempt to separate Grant from his head. Sam waited impatiently. It was a touchy situation and he was glad Grant had broached the subject, and he was the bystander.

"Sam, is there anything you would like to add to the conversation?"

Dammit Grant, he thought, *I figured I was here to observe.* "I do have something to say." This startled Sam as much as it did Grant. "We did not intend to kill your brother. We were fighting for our lives and opted for the only thing we could do to save ourselves from the missile wielding drones. They nearly killed Grant on two separate occasions. I—we, are asking for your forgiveness and request you consider us your friends regardless of what transpired in the past." Sam was honest and sincere.

Delack looked at Sam with dark, penetrating eyes. "An enemy would not have reconstructed my limb and body asking nothing in return. I am deeply indebted to you. However, are you asking me to turn my back on my people in order to save you and the people of the planet below?"

"No, we are not asking you to turn your back on your people. We are asking you to provide us information we can use to avoid a deadly confrontation. We do not wish to fight. We want to build a peaceful relationship between our worlds." Grant laid all his cards on the table. It was now up to Delack to make the next move.

"I cannot assist you in harming my people. I will assist you in communicating with them towards a friendly result."

"Thank you, Delack, we ask nothing more. Can you hail your ships and converse with them letting them know our intentions were survival and not war?"

"I will speak with them in the morning as they approach the planet. At this hour the captain is most likely sleeping. Disturbing a sleeping Anotokian captain is a death sentence."

They agreed to wait until the morning. Sam still had a few unanswered questions, "Delack, what do you plan to say to the captain of the lead ship? It is important to us to know if you are peaceful or not."

"Direct and to the point Sam, I like it. I will tell the captain there was an incident, the mining camp was destroyed, and Graeck was killed. He does not need to know you were the incident, the destroyers, and the killers. I will do my best to keep you far from their suspicions. Keep in mind, they are intelligent and know about war. They can easily sniff out a liar."

"If they know you are lying what will happen to you?"

"I will be blown to bits like the rest of you."

"Direct and to the point, I like it." Delack smiled at Sam. They seemed to share a kindred spirit and felt the friendship tightening.

"I knew what I was getting into when I signed up for this mission, as did Graeck. I hold no grudge against you. I mourn the loss of my brother; he was a warrior, and death was a constant possibility. He will be missed, but I will not seek revenge for his death. In truth, I have been treated better by you than my own people. Thank you!"

"Delack, you made it easy to like you. You are welcome here."

"Enough of the warm fuzzies," Grant said, "thank you for your kind words, but we have to make other plans regarding the Terra Aurai."

"Right you are, Grant."

"Delack, my friend, we'll let you rest for a while and come get you for dinner, say an hour or so?"

"I will see you in one hour."

Delack lay back as they left the med room and tried to rest, but none was to be had. He tried the door and was surprised to find he was not locked in. He left the med room and wandered down the hall finding the lift a short distance away. "Scientists are treated like royalty judging by the level of comfort and the way everything is decorated."

His shoes lightly squeaked as he walked the hallways. The lift was a particular joy for him. Anotokian ships only had stairs to access the many levels. He made his way to the lower level to the lab with all the equipment and the survey bots. His world had nothing like this and he was intrigued. "What could one find with such state of the art equipment? *This is amazing! What a wondrous society they must have to have this at their disposal.*

It was nearing the hour they had agreed upon for dinner. Delack made his way back to the galley. Out of the corner of his eye he caught movement and quickly turned to see what it was, nothing was there and he chalked it up to having recently come out of stasis, yet it still made him uneasy. When he arrived at the galley Grant and Sam were arriving as well.

They greeted each other with smiles, "Did you find anything interesting?"

"I found your lab, it is amazing. You will have to give me a real tour when time permits. I am enjoying the level of comfort on this vessel. We have nothing soft or pleasing. It is all metal, and a thin woven mat for our bunk."

"We will happily give you the grand tour once we are past whatever happens tomorrow. Let's enjoy some dinner, some wine, and the company of one another."

"What do you eat? I have no idea what you would like for dinner." Sam hoped they had something similar to meet his dietary requirements.

"We eat a lot of root type foods as well as the offerings of animals and birds. For a beverage, we drink something similar to your wine I believe, it is fermented with high alcohol content."

"We're going to get along fine!" Sam was sure he had the right combination for Delack, one that would satisfy them all. "Steak and potatoes it is, with a side of roasted carrots, a simple salad, and all the wine we can consume in one evening. It may be our last meal, so let's enjoy ourselves."

Grant had no problem with Sam's meal choices and hoped Delack agreed. "Go for it buddy! Let's get to eating!" The synthesizer quickly created three plates of perfectly cooked steaks, potatoes baked to perfection, and roasted carrots.

"For the wine selection I believe we will have a nice Cabernet Sauvignon, full bodied with a smoky hint of dark chocolate and red berries." It was the perfect choice for their meal.

Delack watched Grant and Sam cut into their steak. His brow furrowed and he raised one eyebrow. "What are you doing to your food?"

"What do you mean?"

"You are dissecting it before you eat it?"

"How would you eat such a meal?"

"With my hands of course, like this." Delack raised all four arms, taking the steak in two hands, a handful of carrots in another, and lifting the wine glass with the remaining hand. He tore into the steak with reckless abandon and shoved the handful of carrots into his mouth. Food flew everywhere, and juice ran down his chin and over his hands.

"How disgusting, you'll need a bath after eating this meal." Sam was appalled at the carnage he was witnessing. He wasn't a prude, but this was off the charts disgusting.

"This is how we eat on my world. We eat fast and plentifully. We may not get another meal for days."

Grant decided to be a bit more diplomatic. "In our culture, we do not eat in such a manner. We are more delicate with our food. We take one bite at a time, and we do not eat with our hands unless the type of food calls for it, such as bread or a sandwich. "He sliced off a piece of the steak, placed it in his mouth with a fork, and chewed the food thoroughly before swallowing.

"How disgusting! How can you eat in slow motion? It would take you all day to consume a meal."

They all laughed, they chose to respect their differences and continued with the meal. Grant and Sam both tore a chunk of steak off with their teeth and Delack daintily sliced off a piece of steak using a knife, and chewed.

"Last meal gentlemen, enjoy the wine. We will be asleep in no time only to wake to a new day and a new adventure."

"Sam gets this way when he drinks, don't pay any attention to him."

With a shrug Delack polished off his glass of wine and requested another. Grant showed him how to access the synthesizer and the wine began to flow. Delack was seven glasses deep when he began to feel the effects of the wine. It took a while to hit him, but it hit him like a garbage truck driver late for dinner on a hot summer day. "I think I need to lie down." Delack passed out and fell to the floor.

"Shit, I hope he didn't over do it. He has to talk with the ship's captain in the morning."

"We'll give him the hangover cure in the morning. He should be good as new—I hope. Our best hope is for him to communicate with the captain and ask him not to destroy us. What were we thinking, getting him drunk?"

They looked at one another, shook their heads and shrugged. "Time for bed, Sam." Nothing more was said. Delack was left lying on the floor, passed out like a college kid on his first real bender, snoring like a mongrel dog growling at a unlucky cat crossing its path. They went to their quarters and quickly fell into restless, dream filled sleep.

Sam dreamt of a huge battle, dead alien bodies littering the ground, a flash, a world on fire, and all life snuffed out in a swirl of flames.

Grant dreamt of Tayana riding her C-Rex, decked out in her black battle gear ready for all out war, and her people tripping and falling as they hurried to get into the shuttle. Small children separated from their parents were crying and screaming. He was surrounded by people asking what to do as he desperately tried to manage the chaotic scene in front of him, and was failing miserably.

Tossing and turning in their sleep, the visions they saw and the impending confrontation with the Anotokians made for a restless night. Deep sleep finally over took them, but morning came shortly after, too early for Grant.

"Sam we need to get moving, give Delack the hangover cure and be on our way. We have lots to do before we can find some version of calm."

"Yeah, the calm before the storm, looking forward to it. Maybe I can get in a nap."

Thick sarcasm signaled Grant not to push Sam. Neither had had any coffee or breakfast. Entering the galley they were surprised to see Delack nearly half way through a large plate of breakfast, more chipper than they had ever seen him.

"What on Earth? How is it you are not hung over and feeling like death warmed over?"

With a smile Delack replied, "We Anotokian's have very high metabolisms. The alcohol is metabolized quickly and the result is a feeling of euphoria. It is the best part of consuming too much alcohol. By the way, why did you leave me sleeping on the floor?"

Sam and Grant chuckled, "You were passed out and snoring so loud we had to leave. Besides, the two of us could not carry you anywhere. You are about a foot and a half taller than we are and most likely outweigh us by nearly a hundred pounds."

"Seventy-seven point five pounds to be precise," said Eliot.

"Eliot, is this another exercise to see how to fit in or did you truly feel the need to interject a random fact to show us your intelligence?"

"I was assisting you in relating to the weight

difference between the two species, nothing more."

"Thank you Eliot, the information was useful, as always," Sam had a soft spot for Eliot and gave him room to grow. "We need to get moving as soon as the gasses rise and the way is clear."

"Delack, would you like to join us? We have some things to accomplish this morning?"

"Yes, by all means. It would be an honor to work alongside the two of you."

"Settled then, we leave in approximately thirty-five minutes. Meet us here in the galley and we'll make our way to the planet's surface."

"Sam, do we have the tools we need and do we have torches? We will need them once we board the Terra Aurai."

"Ready and charged, tools are in the lab."

"Get cleaned up, we meet back here in thirty minutes."

"Yes, Sir." Grant looked crosswise at Sam, but proceeded to his quarters. A quick shower and a fresh change of clothing would do him good.

Chapter Twenty-Three

Thirty minutes later Grant arrived back at the galley followed closely by Sam and Delack. "Gentlemen today may be our last, so let's make it one of our best." Grant had never been good at speeches, but this one was direct and to the point. "May this be a day that makes the history books. May our names be logged in the annals of time. May women see us as gods."

They laughed and Delack added, "May what happens today, be what is supposed to happen, today."

They nodded in agreement and headed to the shuttle. "Strap in Delack, we're going to be moving quickly and maybe not gently. We have a limited amount of time and lots to do."

"Agreed, I will stay out of the way and let you do what you have to do."

"Eliot, detach us from the Ebony Belle."

"Yes, Sir, detaching in five, four...Shuttle detached. Ready for flight."

"Make for the planet's surface, pronto, please."

Eliot accelerated to max speed and charted a course for the surface.

"Bring us to the crash site first thing. We need the fuel cell out of the GEMO 2 and into the Terra Aurai as quickly as possible. Once we have that completed, we need to get it installed, get her running, and we need to crank up the heat. The villagers will need it, space is very cold and I'm sure the Terra Aurai is, too. They are not prepared for cold temps so it needs to be as comfortable as possible."

"Grant, not to be negative, but we don't even know

the condition of the Terra Aurai right now. She may be worthless and inoperable."

"Sam, please keep your crappy thinking to yourself. I have to believe the Terra Aurai is operational and will function perfectly once the fuel cell is installed. It's what's getting me through this morning."

"Heard and respected, sorry Grant."

"Are the two of you brothers? You squabble like brothers, yet have fun as brothers do when together."

Sam answered, "We are not brothers, but we might as well be. We have known each other for many years, since we were young. We squabble and argue, but we both know each other so well we forgive and forget, it's nothing personal, usually."

"Beginning entry into the atmosphere, hold tight gentlemen." Eliot, in an offbeat but familiar tone sounded just like one of the guys, for the first time ever.

"Eliot, you just sounded like one of us, congratulations!"

Grant suddenly had a weird feeling, "Eliot, did we find the Terra Aurai when we were approaching the planet?"

"The Terra Aurai did not appear on our scanners, it does not appear to be in orbit around this planet."

"What the...how can it be?"

"I believe the Terra Aurai is cloaked."

"Can you locate it?"

"Yes, I can."

"Find the Terra Aurai!" Grant was beginning to have bad feelings. He prayed Eliot could find the ship, even it if was cloaked. Why had he not thought to locate the Terra Aurai earlier? He had visions of there being no ship and no way to save the villagers. "Shake it off Grant, you've got to get a grip and trust Eliot can work a miracle." After speaking to himself out loud, Grant casually looked around. Sam was looking away, minding his own business, but not being very good at the deception. "Stop it Sam, I know you heard me. I was just gathering myself and trying to stop thinking about what might happen if Eliot cannot locate the Terra Aurai."

"Sounded like you were losing it, just sayin'! I don't remember you ever talking to yourself. But hey, if it works, by all means."

Grant gave Sam a look, and then turned his attention to the view screen. "Should be just about through the outer atmosphere."

Almost on cue Eliot announced, "We have entered the atmosphere and are making our way to the GEMO 2."

The descent was quick and the world below flashed by in an instant. Sam could barely make out the mining operation. The village flashed by just as quickly. From the ground they must have looked like a missile.

"Five miles to the GEMO 2, arresting descent and preparing to land." The Varizone shuddered from the rapid deceleration. Delack was physically drawn forward towards the view screen.

"The rapid deceleration makes you aware of the forces working against your body. Most of the time it is nearly imperceptible."

"I have been on many ships and shuttles, but this is remarkable. I truly like the feeling of deceleration, the weightlessness was exhilarating."

"I kind of like it, too." Sam smiled at Delack and they nodded their approval.

"On the ground in 10, 9, 8..."

"No explosion this time Eliot, please take all

measures to avoid being shot out of the sky."

If Eliot could have laughed he would have. Sam held back a good laugh. Grant was telling the truth, his fear was real. "We are on the ground, you may disembark."

"Sam, grab a low bot and gear. We'll most likely need it to carry the fuel cell."

"Good idea, meet you there in about three minutes."

Grant and Delack disembarked and headed to the GEMO 2. Once inside Grant located the fuel cell and began figuring out the best way to carefully remove the cell for transport. There were suits hanging in an open locker. Grant felt the suits were necessary to remove the cell, and not get poisoned from the radiation. How would they cover it while it was on the shuttle? Grant's mind raced once again.

Sam barged into the room, "Got the bot and the tools."

"Take a look and tell me what you think."

Sam looked over the fuel cell encasement and noticed the suits. "I think we need to suit up before we begin taking this thing out of here."

"Agreed, Delack, go to the shuttle and wait for us to return. It may not be safe for you to be near this without a suit. As you can guess, we do not have a giant sized four-arm suit." Delack turned and left for the shuttle.

"Let's get this thing on the bot and get moving." Without another word they positioned the bot below the fuel cell and began to open the housing.

"STOP! What the hell are we thinking? We haven't powered this thing down yet. We just about killed ourselves! Grant dropped to his knees and hung his head. "Sam, I am so sorry! I am in such a rush to make sure the villagers and Tayana are safe I almost killed us."

"Live and learn, I'll shut it down so it can start cooling. Should take about an hour to cool enough for us to move it. In the mean time let's take one last look around this ship to see if there is anything we missed. We could sure use any help we can find."

"Agreed, I'll go get Delack. You shut it down and take a quick tour."

After Grant left the shuttle Sam made his way to the bridge. "Ships AI, are you functioning?"

There was a hiss and the sound of static, a deep gravelly voice, almost haunting, came over the intercom, "I am online. How may I assist you?" It sounded like an old man just waking up from a good nap on a sun drenched porch. "This is Captain Sam Northland, are there any hidden spaces on the GEMO 2?"

After what seemed like minutes, the AI responded, "There are two. One is in the wall to the left, behind the captain's chair. It can be accessed from a button under the left arm of the captain's chair. The other is in the captain's quarters. There is a button under his desk and the space is at the head of his bunk."

"Thank you! Are there any other secrets aboard the GEMO 2?"

"There are no more secrets. Everything else has been removed." Sam was proud of himself for thinking to ask the AI about the secret spaces and wondered what may be hidden away. "AI, please shut down the fuel cell and prepare it for transport. We need it ready to go as quickly as possible."

"Yes, Sir." Sam knew once the fuel cell was shut off the AI would revert to a backup power cell to sustain it for another hundred or so years before it too would be forced to shut down. Sam found and pushed the button under the chair's arm and leapt out of the captain's chair. He noted there was an almost imperceptible irregularity along the wall behind him and with a slight push the secret space was revealed. There were a few papers along with two medium sized boxes. Each was marked, "In case of emergency." This caught Sam's attention and he opened the first box. There were two of the captain's devices wrapped in protective materials along with a note, it read: If you are reading this letter then I have passed, along with my co-captain, Captain Coke. It also means one of two things. You are a good treasure hunter and congratulations are in order, you are now a rich man. Or, you are in serious trouble, may God help you. The items in these two boxes will assist you either way. In the first box is a rudimentary cloaking device large enough to cloak an entire ship and a weapon capable of destroying a small armada of ships in the blink of an eye. The second box contains the answer to life, kidding, sort of. It is a potent accelerator needed to quickly begin life on a lifeless planet, along with instructions and appropriate warnings. Captain Coke and I developed it from our research on Earth and what we learned from our mistakes here on Antaya. It contains the best of the best, and more. Do with it as you please, but be warned, some things you do not want to get involved in without serious planning. You've been warned.

    The warning was ominous; there were life forms of an entire planet sitting in an egg-shaped vessel just two feet away from him. There was also a powerful weapon capable of mass destruction just another two feet away. He had the power of the gods lying before him. He gathered the boxes and papers, and carefully carried them to the Varizone.

"Hey, what did you find?"

Sam gave Grant a 'not now' look, "just a couple of boxes and some old papers, nothing really."

Grant picked up on the subtle look. He took leave of Delack and followed Sam to the shuttle. "What's up Sam? What was the look for?"

"After you left I asked the AI on the GEMO 2 if there were any secret places on this shuttle. It said there are two, and told me how to access them, and where they are. I followed its instructions and found the first secret place. We really need to talk more about it later this evening. You are not going to believe what we have in the Varizone as we speak."

"Is it alive? Does it have the potential to harm or kill us?"

"It is dormant and, well, yes, it does have the potential to harm or kill us, but not in its current situation. One of the things you are going to love and we can use it on the Ebony Belle. Well, we can use two of them on the Belle. We need to find the other secret place."

Grant followed Sam to the GEMO 2 captain's quarters and Sam began looking under the desk for a button, but he was not having any luck finding it. "Grant, come down here and see if you can find a button."

Obliging, Grant crawled under the desk to look for the elusive button. After about ten minutes of looking neither could find a button anywhere. Perplexed, they pondered the possibilities of where the button may be. Sam mentally retraced his steps, making hand gestures as if searching the undersurface of the desk again. Grant tried to figure out if there may be a play on words they had misinterpreted. Delack got bored and wandered to the GEMO2 to see what was up. He found the pair sitting on the floor deep in concentration. Sam looked like he had taken drugs and was trying to fondle a woman who wasn't there. Grant looked like he was taking a healthy dump and had to strain to get the last little pieces to come out.

"What, may I ask, are the two of you doing? Should I be afraid or call for help?" Sam and Grant jumped to their feet, made stupid gestures, and mumbled something. "This really isn't making my decision any easier. Call for help or run for my life?"

"Sorry, we are trying to figure out a riddle."

"What is a riddle?"

"It is a question with a specific answer, but you must discover the answer with very little information to go on as the question is designed to make you see many possibilities. You have to choose the one you think is appropriate for the given situation."

"Delightful, what is the question?"

"Where is the button under the desk?"

"I do not know without further investigation, may I look?"

Grant motioned to the desk. Delack plopped his large body onto the floor and managed to get his head and one of his arms under the desk. He pushed every square inch of the bottom of the desk and came to the conclusion; there was no button under the desk.

"Damn it, we are wasting too much time with this, we have to get the fuel cell to the Terra Aurai."

Sam had moved to captain's bunk while Delack was searching under the desk. It occurred to him that right beside him was a fold out board used as a writing surface—a desk. "I think I figured it out." Sam was bursting to see if he was correct and after thirty seconds of searching he found what he was looking for. "Gentlemen, the button!" He pointed to a small grey spot under the writing table and pushed it. There was a slight hiss and the secret place at the head of the bed popped open enough for Sam to open it fully. Inside were papers, contracts, and deeds to land, patents to inventions, and a box of data storage devices.

"Grab it all and get it to the shuttle, we have to get moving, Now!"

Sam gathered it up and took one last quick look to be sure it was all. He noticed a small sliding door on the left side. He opened it. Inside were three envelopes, one labeled for Tayana, one for Kyera, and one for Dyanta. Sam stuffed them in with the other papers and made for the shuttle.

Grant asked the AI if the fuel cell was cool enough for removal. It was. Sam returned and they donned the safety suits and began pulling the cell out of its housing. It was old and heavy. Their suits didn't make it any easier. They struggled, but finally got the cell onto the bot and rushed it to the shuttle. "Strap it in Sam, we are out of here."

With the cell securely in place, Sam made his way back to the bridge. "Eliot, have you located the Terra Aurai?"

"Yes, it was difficult as it is cloaked. It is orbiting the planet on the same path as the Ebony Belle. We will intercept it in thirty minutes. It is seven-hundred miles behind the Belle."

"Good work Eliot, make for the Terra Aurai."

Helium Fall

Chapter Twenty-Four

Thirty minutes seemed like an eternity to Grant. He had not asked Eliot for a description of the Terra Aurai and Eliot had not offered one.

Before Grant could ask, Eliot chimed in. "We have reached the Terra Aurai. I have accessed its systems and controls though they are on auxiliary power. We will dock with the ship in four minutes."

"Thank you, Eliot! Please power the ship the best you can, and get the life support systems up and running along with the climate controls. We need the Terra Aurai livable in short order."

"Yes sir, all systems are working and you will be able to board in twenty minutes."

"Sam, Delack, let's grab a quick snack and go over the plan. I do not want any hiccups."

"Agreed Grant, we basically have one shot at this and it has to go off without a hitch."

"A snack would be good, I am always hungry. I guess it's why I didn't die along with my brother and the others. I was out gathering food when the explosion happened."

"No gathering here my friend, we have plenty." Sam liked Delack and treated him like he would any other friend. Delack responded in kind.

"You two go ahead, I need to get something out of my quarters."

"All right, see you in a few." They went their separate ways and Grant quickly entered his quarters. He plopped in his chair and slid to the desk bracing his hands to bring it to an abrupt halt. "Come on Grant, pull it together. What is making you so suspicions of Delack" As if talking aloud to himself was going to give him answers. "Where was he when we found him, did he have food with him? Why didn't he hear all the earlier commotion? He just said others, plural. Was it just him and Greack? Why didn't we see him moving around? Something is off and I can't put my finger on it. He's not acting like a captive. We did keep him alive and repair him, but he's trying too hard to fit in and be one of us. Is he a spy?" He quickly jotted down his thoughts and made his way to the galley.

Sam and Delack had polished off a light salad and Delack was gnawing on a rather large chunk of ham. "This thing has a great handle; I could eat four at a time." He gripped the bone protruding from one end of the ham and waved it around like a kid with a pennant at a sporting event.

"Whoa there big fella, you're going to hurt yourself." The smile on Grant's face was great cover and Delack bought it hook, line, and sinker.

"I was just telling Sam I could eat four of these at a time because of their nice handles."

"You mean their bones?"

"Bones? Oh, you mean bones, like their skeleton?"

"Yep, you've got him by his knee and you're eating the parts closest to his butt."

Delack let out what Grant and Sam guessed was a belly laugh, but it sounded like a cross between a wolf howling and a little girl giggling. Then he blew food all over the table and snuffled in for another round of laughing. His greenish face was turning a brownish orange and Sam was beginning to get concerned he may be choking. Delack sucked in another deep breath, chuckled a little and said, "You are such a jokester, Grant, eating the parts nearest his butt. Who would serve such a wretched thing?"

"Delack, Grant was not being funny. It really is the part nearest its butt, but not part of the butt, just close." Delack turned a pretty shade of lavender, bolted from the table, and ran to a sink close by where he proceeded to cleanse his body via esophageal spasms, abdominal convulsions, and lots of spitting.

"He's blowin' chunks!" Sam was caught off guard by Delack's response to being told he was eating the part near the butt. Had they crossed a line or was Delack just not a fan of butt? "Delack, you alright? I had no idea, what's going on?"

"It is my culture not to eat anything near the face, genitals, or rectum of any living thing. How close to the rectum was I?" Sam and Grant laughed and then thought twice about carrying the joke any further. The look on Delack's face was of someone eating contaminated food and trying to figure out if he was going to live or die.

Grant took pity on him and lied, "Delack, you were a good foot and a half away from the butt."

Sam was not so merciful, "True, but the balls may have rubbed against the part you were eating."

Delack rushed back to the sink and hurled again. He grabbed a pitcher of water, downed it, and then another. Once he was sure there were no more contaminated materials in, on, or near him, he spun to face Sam. "You think this is funny?" His demeanor was no longer, hey we're buddies, it was more, now you're going to be a snack. He took two large steps towards Sam. Sam yanked his feet off the chair in front him and launched himself in the opposite direction away from Delack's menacing approach. Delack let out a war cry and ran towards Sam. Sam took off like a rabbit being chased by a large dangerous dog sliding behind one of the pillars in the galley. Sam and Grant were terrified. Delack pulled himself up to his full height and flexed the muscles in all four large muscular arms.

"Delack, we didn't know about your culture, we apologize for any offense, and we beg your forgiveness," said Sam.

Grant chimed in too, "Delack, we are sorry if we offended you. It was all in fun, we meant no harm or disrespect."

Delack began to laugh, and he laughed loud. He even slapped his knee a couple of times and then, "You two look like a couple of scared yearlings being chased by a fierce animal. Delack laughed some more as Grant and Sam stood there with their mouths open, staring at him.

"I just about crapped my pants! You are one scary son of a bitch! Oh my God, I thought you had lost it and I was about to die."

"Sam, I have never seen your kind move so fast. You were moving like the wind."

Grant slid into a chair, in shock. "Hell, I was breaking wind hoping you wouldn't come any closer."

"Grant, you all right?" Sam and Delack stopped to check on his condition. He didn't look good.

Grant said, "I'm fine. My life flashed in front of my eyes and a couple things caught my attention, seriously needing my attention. We need to finish eating and prepare to board the Terra Aurai."

They sat quietly as they finished their snack, and then made their way to the hatch connecting them to the Terra Aurai.

Delack spoke first, "Sorry I frightened you, I was playing along with your joke on me, it wasn't a joke after all, but it was funny."

Sam said, "Sorry for making you lose your lunch, twice. Sometimes I just can't control myself."

Eliot chimed in, "The hatch will be ready to open in thirty seconds. The oxygen in the ship is at normal levels. It has been dormant for two hundred years and may have a peculiar odor."

"Thanks for the heads up, Eliot, useful information." Grant was sure the next time Eliot provided information he would over share and then eventually provide the necessary amount of pertinent information.

"Sam, let's get suited up and check out the engine room. We need to make sure we can replace the fuel cell and get this thing out of sight, again. We don't need anyone accidentally bumping into it and killing an entire civilization of newly discovered life forms."

"I agree, let's make this happen. The Anotokians will be arriving early to mid afternoon and we have lots to do. Delack, keep an eye on things while we're gone. We won't be long."

"Got it, I'll just hang out here and wait."

Grant and Sam disappeared down the ramp to the hatchway into the Terra Aurai. "You ready for this?" asked Sam, looking intently at Grant.

Grant replied, "We don't have time to not be ready. We have to get this done, now, or we might as well take off and leave everyone behind to die."

Sam kept his mouth shut as they opened the hatch. A strong whoosh of stagnant air raced past them. It smelled of an old trunk full of clothing stored in a moldy basement for many years.

Grant caught a whiff too and made a grimace at the smell. "I hope the smell goes away before we get the villagers on here."

Sam nodded. The layout of the ship was very similar to the Ebony Belle. They made quick time finding the engine room.

"There it is! Now all we need to do is get the tools, remove the old fuel cell, and replace it with the new one."

"A step ahead of ya, Grant. I brought some tools and I should be able to get the housing around the fuel cell removed so we can pull the old cell out."

"You work on it and I'll get the new cell."

"Got it, I should be done by the time you get back." Grant headed back to the Varizone for the replacement cell. Sam began working on the housing and discovered he didn't need tools. All he had to do was press a button on the back of the housing and the fuel cell door opened, automatically exposing the fuel cell. It notified him the fuel cell was deactivated, the fuel cell door was open, and it was ready for removal. They tore the housing apart to remove the fuel cell on the GEMO 2, had they been more patient they may have saved valuable time. The Terra Aurai was a well appointed ship. As Sam pondered the consequences of their actions he discovered a hoist system to automatically remove the old cell. He activated the apparatus and it began doing its job with precision and efficiency. The apparatus plucked the old cell out and then placed it in another device, a recharging station. Sam's suspicions were correct. When the apparatus finished its move, the door on the new device closed, lots of lights came on, and a graduated bar showing the level of charge was visible, indicating the cell was being charged. Sam decided to go help Grant since his task had taken roughly five minutes. He made his way to the lab where Grant should already have the other cell detached from its restraints and ready to move. He was going to be surprised Sam was so efficient and was there to help. The door to the lab opened and the sound of metal on metal rang out across the bay. Sam saw Delack raise a large wrench and crash it down on something metallic. He ran over to see what was going on and found Grant bloody and trying his best to defend himself against the much larger and stronger Delack.

In his loudest voice Sam yelled, "What the hell is going on here?" Catching Delack off guard, it allowed Grant the opportunity to deliver a blow momentarily incapacitated Delack. Sam rushed over and grabbed some of binding cable they used to secure larger items. Delack qualified as a larger item. Once bound, Sam looked at Grant, and ran to grab a med kit. "You look like hell buddy, what happened?"

Through deep breaths and what sounded like wheezing, Grant informed him Delack was not their friend. He had attacked him when he caught him trying to destroy the fuel cell. "I'm pretty certain he broke several of my ribs and I may have a punctured lung. Son of a bitch is a lot faster than he looks and he isn't a scientist, he's military. He hadn't counted on us being back so soon. When I walked in on him, he spun on me and sent me flying before I could say anything. I knew something wasn't right about him. When I left during our break I went to my quarters to try and figure out what I was missing, I just had a feeling."

"Good thing you caught him before he could do much damage. Why didn't you call me on the com?"

Kind of hard to do when you're flying through the air and then trying to not be beat to death with a wrench."

"Good point. Eliot, why didn't you let me know Grant was in trouble?"

"I was unaware."

"How could you be unaware, you hear and see everything?"

"The cameras and microphones were disabled when Grant was making his way back to the lab to retrieve the fuel cell."

"I was diagnosing the issue and had not come to a conclusion as to the cause of the outages until moments ago, when you returned to the lab. Informing you was my next task, but your inquiry did not allow me to proceed."

"Thank you Eliot, I knew you were on top of things. I just didn't want to see our captain nearly beaten to death and no one know why."

"Thanks for the concern, Sam. Let's get this piece of crap out of here and to the brig."

"We have a brig?"

"Yes, we have a brig. It's the room next to the med room." Sam had a weird look on his face and Grant had to practically draw him a picture. "Sam, it's the room we never use until needed and the room never has its door open because we never use it. It is right next to the med room and has the word 'Brig' on the door."

"Oh, that room!" Sam had no idea they had a brig, but assisted in taking Delack there. Dragging three hundred and fifty pounds of dead weight was a chore. It took them much longer than anticipated. "Alright, so we have a brig, right next to the med room, who knew? Keep him bound and hopefully he isn't strong enough to break out."

"Not going to happen, Sam. These cells are escape proof, even if the power goes out."

"Good to know. I really don't want to have to worry about his big ass sneaking up on me with a wrench in his hands. I can't believe I was starting to like him, I was even beginning to trust him."

"Live and learn Sam. I wonder if he had the opportunity to divulge our plans to his people. I'm not going to wake him up to find out, but maybe we need to alter our plans some just in case he did."

"Good plan, we can set up two SHTF's on opposite ends of the mining camp and cover them with brush or whatever to hide them. They'll be looking for something in the middle of camp if he did communicate with them. As soon as we're back on the planet's surface I'll get the SHTF's set up and you can orchestrate the villager's departure."

"Sounds like a plan. Take the rover and I'll see to it the villagers are aboard the Varizone by the time you return. Right now we need to get the fuel cell installed so we can get this thing moving. It is priority one."

Sam smiled and raced back to the lab to retrieve the fuel cell, Grant trailed behind.

"I'll be there as quick as I can. This whole, not being able to breathe, is really cramping my style. Go on ahead." When Grant finally entered the lab, the events of a short time ago flashed through his mind. He stopped for a moment.

"You okay, Grant?"

"I'm fine, just a flashback of the look on Delack's face as he was about to do me in. He was happy about it. He was going to enjoy offing me. By the way, how did you get here so quickly?"

"You'll see when we get back to the Terra Aurai." There was minimal damage to the fuel cell, and Sam had the straps undone in record time. "Let's put it back on the bot, it will be a lot less work for us."

"Smart thinking Sam, here's a low bot." The two of them shuffled the fuel cell back onto the bot and Sam jogged beside it as he took it to the Terra Aurai. Once aboard Sam led the way to the engine room and hooked the fuel cell to the loading device. Grant arrived a few minutes later. He was impressed Sam had removed the old cell in such a short time. Without much effort, the new fuel cell was loaded into the receptacle. Suddenly there was a catch and the cell would go no further.

"What now? Can this day go any more awry?"

Sam took a look to see what was catching and found Delack had managed to dislodge one of the small pieces of the cell. It was mangled and pressed into the groove where the cell was supposed to slide. "Gonna have to pull it out, Grant." Sam began the removal process, but the cell refused to let loose from the housing. The small piece was keeping the cell from moving either direction.

"Seriously? I'm struggling to breathe so I'm not of much help and this damn thing won't move. Sam, I have to go to the med room. I'll do a quick heal so I'm at the least not dying and can function somewhat."

"Go, I've got this, Sorry, I should have suggested it."

Grant left for the med room and Sam began banging on the small piece with a hammer and chisel. After about five minutes the small piece broke free and the cell was loose. "About damn time!" Sam was frustrated and beginning to think they may not make it back in time to get the villagers to safety. He began sanding the rest of the piece off of the cell. It finally looked good enough to try again. He hit the button and the cell moved into place like it should. Sam released the clamps, closed the cover, and hit the green button on the side indicating the transfer was complete, and the cell was ready for business. When Sam hit the button the ship's lights came on and everything powered by the cell began to whir, buzz, and chirp. Sam looked around and then thought about Grant. "Oh my God, I hope it didn't have a negative effect on the healing device when I hit the button." Sam raced to the med room and found Grant lying on a table just as he should have, but the healing device was not moving. When he looked at the control panel it said the system was rebooting. "Oh buddy, I hope I didn't just lobotomize you or something." The device flashed a few times, dinged twice, and then initiated, Sam guessed, where it left off. The control panel indicated it would be another 45 minutes before Grant was healed. "Damn it! I have to get Varizone back to the surface. You're going to have to hold on tight, Grant."

Sam pushed a few buttons and straps appeared cinching Grant to the table top. He wheeled Grant, table and all to the Varizone's med room, and anchored it in place. "Excellent, gotta go buddy, see you in 45 minutes." Sam made his way to the bridge.

"Eliot, close the hatch to the Terra Aurai and detach. We need to get to the surface as quickly as we can and gather the villagers. Grant will be in stasis for another forty minutes or so. It's just you and me, let's get this thing moving."

Eliot did as instructed and they were on their way to the planet's surface.

"Eliot, can Delack get out of the brig?"

"No, he cannot bypass the security in the brig nor

can he escape."

It was good news to Sam. "Is he awake?"

"Yes, he woke up ten minutes ago, he is not happy, and is not approachable at this time."

"Thanks for the information. I was going to go have a talk with him to see what other situations he may have created for us."

"It is not advisable at this time."

"Understood, make way for the surface and the village."

The trip to the surface would take nearly thirty-five minutes from their current location and Grant would need another five to get healed. He was going to be pretty useless for at least another hour, if not longer. By then Sam could have the SHTF's installed and be on his way back to the village. He was going to have to appoint someone to lead them onto the Varizone. He prayed Tayana would be there and willing to assist him.

Chapter Twenty-Five

As the village came into view, Sam was surprised to see the villagers were all there, waiting with the necessary items they needed to survive, for what was hopefully, short term. "Well, get a load of that. They are lined up and waiting. They had to have seen us coming." At the head of the line was Tayana and several of her crew. "Eliot, set us down with the lab bay doors facing the villagers. It looks like they could run onboard and we could take off within minutes."

Eliot skillfully landed the Varizone and opened the lab bay doors.

Sam was standing in the door way. He greeted Tayana with a hug and directions. "They need to fill in from the back to the front. Grant and I moved all of the equipment to the front corner to make lots of room. Remember, they are not camping in here, this is just transportation to the Terra Aurai."

"Understood, we will direct them to the location you requested." Tayana told her crew to lead the villagers to the back of the lab and fill in to the front as Sam instructed. The crew was quick and efficient. Within minutes the lab bay was filling up with supplies and bodies. One overzealous villager tried to bring a Chotuk onto the shuttle. He was quickly persuaded to release the beast and board the shuttle with his other belongings. He mumbled as he entered the lab, "I'm sure going to miss good Chotuk flank." Most of the villagers seemed excited to journey off the planet, but some had deep reservations and preferred to stay on the ground.

"We could all die or worse, never see our pods again." All in all it took about twenty minutes to get the villagers and their belongings into the shuttle. As the last few made their way in, Sam and Tayana came back together for a quick chat.

"Where is Grant?"

"He was injured and is healing."

"What? What happened?"

"Delack is a traitor and tried to kill him while I was working in the Terra Aurai. You can visit him in the med room."

"Is he going to be all right?"

"Yes. Have you seen the girls?"

"Kyera and Dyanta will be here shortly. They had a special errand to run before boarding the shuttle."

"Special errand?"

"Something for you I would imagine." She said with a smirk. Sam blushed.

He wondered what his two crazy beauties were up to. "Please tell them to come to the bridge when they arrive."

"I shall let them know."

With the loading going so smoothly Sam didn't need to leave and come back, he would take the villagers with him and head to the Terra Aurai when he was finished planting the SHTF's. He went to the bridge to converse with Eliot. "Change of plans, Eliot. We are going to the mining camp to set the charges, then to the Terra Aurai. We will take the villagers with us, it will save us a lot of time."

"What about the rover?"

"No room, we will retrieve it after the battle, if we're able."

Kyera and Dyanta came rushing into the bridge and jumped into Sam's arms covering him with kisses, letting him know he was theirs, and they were his. Sam was delighted to see them and swore they looked more beautiful than he remembered. He had not seen them in over a week.

"Take a seat over there and buckle up. We are going to take off in about three minutes." The girls quickly buckled in, excited about what was about to happen. "I'll be right back," Sam said and kissed them before he left.

Outside the shuttle Tayana and her crew were mounting their C-Rexes. "Tayana, where are you going? You need to be in the shuttle. We cannot make a return trip for you before the Anotokians arrive."

"We are staying, we will be fine. We have our cloaks and other means of staying safe."

"I'm not sure you understand the plan. We are going to ignite the entire planet at helium fall and wipe them off the face of the planet, along with everything else. That includes you!"

"We will be safe. We have been herding animals of all kinds into the caves over the night and most of the morning. We do not need everything sustaining us destroyed. We have taken some of the healer's herbs into the caves and many other items to keep us alive and healthy. You have your plan, I have mine." With what appeared to be a blush, she told Sam, "Tell Grant if we survive this, I am his."

The look on Sam's face said it all, but he added words anyway, with a broad smile and a wink, "Well, it's about time. He was going to tell you the same thing. A match made in the heavens."

"Stop, you're making me feel like a girl."

"Go on, do what you have to do, but remember, if there are lots of Anotokians on the planet when helium fall comes, this whole place is going to be engulfed in flames."

"I know Sam, and thank you for worrying about me, but I have a plan and it only works if you set the place ablaze."

Sam was perplexed, but he had to get moving. He gave Tayana another hug and wished her luck. She replied in kind. Tayana and her crew took off in a rush. "Eliot, close the lab bay doors and get this thing in the air."

Sam entered the bridge and let the girls know they were making a short stop before going into space. They seemed disappointed, but still excited. Sam strapped into the captain's chair and they were on their way.

"Five minutes to the camp."

"Thanks, Eliot. We need to set down in the middle of the camp, close to the bunker."

The girls looked amazed at the speed of the shuttle and how everything was growing smaller as it zoomed by the view screen. "Enjoying the ride girls?"

Dyanta shook her head. Kyera seemed excited and a little afraid at the same time. "This is amazing. What is it going to be like farther up?"

"You'll see. It is one of the most beautiful things you will ever see." Both girls giggled and glued their eyes to the view screen.

"Arriving in thirty seconds."

"Thanks, Eliot. I have the SHTF's and a couple other surprises for our guests carted and ready to go. I will only be a few minutes."

Eliot landed the shuttle with ease, as always. Sam gathered the cart and went to deploy his weapons. The plan was a central SHTF and a remote detonation. Thinking Delack may have tipped off his captain, Sam made for the corner of the bunker. It was not directly in the center, but about twenty yards to the west. He planted a common military mortar behind some vegetation next to the entrance, then placed another one near the back edge of the bunker, just in case they decided to be sneaky and not come in the direct route. He then went to the center of the mining camp and placed a wreath of flowers there. He knew if they knew there was a bomb in the middle of the camp they would safely blow it up from a distance, sustaining no casualties. The SHTF's were then placed, one inside the bunker, and the other two on opposite sides of the camp. They would easily destroy anything within the boundaries of the camp, and then some. Those would be detonated by remote once a substantial number of Anotokians were in the camp. It took him longer than expected, but he still had plenty of time to get to the Terra Aurai and off load the villagers. He would have to wake Grant if the healer was not finished by the time they needed to get him to the Ebony Belle. Sam rushed into the shuttle and Eliot closed the doors without having been asked. Sam was beginning to believe Eliot really was learning, and if they made it out alive he was going to work with him on a regular basis. "To the Terra Aurai, Eliot. Everything is in place, receivers are set on the SHTF's, and once we get into space, I'm going to check on Grant."

"Good plan, we will dock with the Terra Aurai in thirty-three minutes."

"Excellent! I sure hope they're not early."

"They appear to have slowed their approach. They may have discovered Delack is no longer in communication with them."

"Good point, Eliot. Maybe it will give us the few minutes we need to safely get the Terra hidden behind a nearby planet out of harm's way, and Grant safely to the Ebony Belle.

"We will be entering space in two minutes."

"Girls, once we are in space, I'll open the view screen, you will be amazed." They giggled with anticipation and held each other tight. Sam looked over at them and shook his head, how could he be so lucky? How could he be getting ready to do battle with a superior foe and still be thinking about sex? He would eat, sleep, and make love for the rest of his life and nothing more, if the opportunity arose. He prayed it did.

"We have left the atmosphere and are now entering space."

"Girls, you can unbuckle and step up here with me." Sam unbuckled and stood directly in the middle of the view screen. They hurriedly did as he instructed and wrapped their arms around him as the screen opened. Their mouths dropped open at the beautiful sight before them. The twinkling of the distant stars was more pronounced without atmosphere. Small tears rolled from Dyanta's eyes and down her cheeks. Kyera mumbled something about the most beautiful thing she had ever seen. She squeezed Sam tighter and they both thanked him with lots of kisses. "I told you you would be amazed!" Sam and the girls stood there in wonder for a long time.

"Docking with the Terra Aurai in four minutes."

"Better get buckled in until we complete the docking." The girls headed to their seats, eyes still glued to the view screen. From their vantage point they could see their planet in the near distance. They never knew it was green and brown with lakes, streams, and mountains scattered around.

"Docking complete, you can now disembark the passengers."

Sam made for the connecting hatch to be sure it was secure. He determined it was and opened the outer door. He ran down the gangway to the outer door of the Terra Aurai and opened it as well. "Eliot, have the villagers come across to the Terra Aurai."

Sam heard Eliot instruct the villagers to make their way to the gangway hatch and proceed to the next ship in an orderly manner. The villagers began moving across and Eliot instructed them to place their belongings in the large open bay in the center of the ship.

Once across with belongings dropped off, Sam directed them to the various empty cabins onboard. The captain's quarters were reserved for him and the girls. He hoped it was nicely appointed like the rest of the ship. He had not checked it out, but assumed it would be nicely appointed. Sam remembered he forgot to check on Grant so he made his way back to the shuttle. Once in the med room he checked the control panel. Grant still had fifteen minutes before he could be woken up. How could that be? He should already be out of stasis. He would have to wait. "Eliot, I will be back on the bridge in two minutes, are the girls still there?"

"Yes, they are waiting impatiently."

When Sam reached the bridge the girls gave him their pouty looks and he melted. "Come on, I'll show you our room." They unbuckled and stuck to him like ticks. He loved it, but wondered how long he could take their clinginess. "Eliot, Grant's healing is taking longer than planned, please keep an eye on him. Make sure no one goes in there without my permission."

"Yes, Sir."

Sam and the girls headed to their quarters for what could be their last rendezvous. "Going to have to be a quick one, I've got a planet to save ya know." They had not been together in weeks. It may be the best fifteen minutes of his life. No way was he turning it down. Seventeen minutes later, Sam emerged from his quarters smiling from ear to ear. Not even an Anotokian battle ship could remove the smile.

Eliot shook him loose, "Sir, the Anotokian ships will be able to detect the planet's surface within the next two hours. The cloaking device must be functioning before then. If not, the Ebony Belle will be their first target."

"Thank you, Eliot; I have to check on Grant." Sam headed to the med room and found Grant sitting up on the edge of the table, groggy, and speaking unintelligibly. "Whoa there buddy, you're not supposed to get off the table without assistance." Grant gave him a look of who the hell are you and what are you saying to me. He looked like an old drunk being ran off a park bench, only he was naked, and there was no park. "Grant, you've been in stasis, but you're healed, at least I hope so. Let's get you dressed and get some food in you. Grant grunted and appeared to understand as he allowed Sam to dress him, without a fight. Sam was pleased there was no fight. Grant, despite his being battered and bruised on numerous occasions, was six feet two inches of muscle, and a formidable opponent when challenged. Sam wrangled on the last of his clothing and escorted him to the galley. He ordered a double protein drink, some fruit, and a bowl of cinnamon sugar oatmeal. Grant was going to need all the strength he could get in just a few short hours, or less. "All right Grant, time to fuel up and get back to being the you you're supposed to be." Grant understood and began to eat the oatmeal and chugged half of the protein drink, the fruit was a bonus. When Grant finished he asked Sam for a large glass of ice water. Grant had never asked for a glass of water in the many years they had known each other, and he gave him a sideways look of questioning. "I'm thirsty, been in stasis, feeling dehydrated. The water will help clear my head and help me digest the food quicker."

"Oh, so ten minutes ago you can't even gurgle out your name and now you're a nutritionist. Welcome back buddy!" They exchanged smiles and Sam filled him in on what had transpired while he was in stasis.

"Sam, is everything is in place? Does Tayana and everyone know what to do?"

"Yes, we've been waiting for you to heal so we can get you to the Belle."

"Shit, where am I?"

"On the shuttle. We're still docked to the Terra Aurai. I will captain the Terra Aurai and you will captain the Belle. Once I leave the shuttle you need to dock with the Belle and get the cloaking device installed and functioning. You need to be hidden before the Anotokian ships get within range."

"All right, gotta go, don't want to get my ass shot off again!"

Sam chuckled, "No doubt. Get moving, and good luck. He gave Grant a hug. "I can't lose you my friend; life wouldn't be the same without you."

"Same here, be safe, and no heroics, understood?"

"Understood." Sam exited the shuttle and Grant made his way to the bridge.

"Eliot, we need to get to the Belle, now. Pull up the schematics for the cloaking device. I need to know how to install it."

"Good to have you back."

"Thanks Eliot!" Eliot had never shown care towards him or Sam. This was a good step in his growth. Grant was feeling better by the minute, but time was running out. Within minutes they were at the Belle and docking.

"Dock this thing in short order, I'll be waiting by the hatch." Without another word Grant made his way to the hatchway, cloaking device in hand. He felt good; better than he had in many years. The healing table did a number on him, he liked this feeling. He felt strong and capable, his mind was clear, and he was determined to kick some Anotokian butt.

Sam had filled him in on Delack trying to kill him and he was in the brig on the Terra Aurai. Grant was thankful to not be anywhere near Delack. It would be too soon before he saw his face again. The hatch opened and Grant was off like a rocket. He headed straight for the engine room and tried pulling up the schematics he requested from Eliot. "Eliot, where are the schematics I asked for?"

"There are no schematics for the cloaking device, it is a hybrid made by the captains of the Terra Aurai."

"How the hell am I supposed to install it without instructions?" Eliot began to answer, but Grant cut him off, "It was a rhetorical question." "Grant looked over the device and noticed a small plaque on the side. The inscription read, "Just plug it in!" There was a small recess in the back of the device for a power cable. He found the cable and plugged it into an adapter on the fuel cell housing. The device came alive. There was a flash of bluish light and then just a green light on the device, staring at him. I guess its working?"

"Sam, can you still detect the Belle?"

"Uh, no, we cannot, awesome!"

Eliot broke in, "Captains, the Anotokian ships are within range. They have not detected either ship."

"Sam, radio silence until we have no other choice, but to talk. Run silent as well, and keep the villagers quiet, our lives depend on it."

"Will do, catch you on the other side my friend." Grant and Sam were scientists, not trained military. They were apprehensive about what was going to happen.

"Sam, I know we need to be running silent, but we never gave Tayana a way to communicate with us."

"Oh crap! We'll have to rely on Eliot to be our eyes and ears."

"Yep, damn it! No offense, Eliot, I made a huge mistake."

On radar they could see the Anotokian ships coming into view. There were three large warships, four times the size of the Ebony Belle, headed their way. The sight of them made Grant's blood boil. He was ready for some payback for Delack trying to kill him. "Gonna get yours, you Anotokian bastards." He could feel his blood pressure rising. He had to get himself in check or he could end up killing a lot of innocent people. The ships came into view on the view screen. They were warships, but they were in pretty rough shape. Grant assumed they were the bottom of the barrel sent out to take care of the natives. Little did they know the natives had some new friends, smart ones.

The ships closed on the planet and settled into orbit. Grant was amazed at how close they were. He was concerned debris from a missile explosion might cause damage to the Belle.

The Anotokian ships began launching shuttles to the planet's surface. Grant guessed each shuttle carried a large number of soldiers. He wanted to break cover and race to the surface to save Tayana, but he knew it would only get him killed and most likely everyone else. He held his ground and waited impatiently.

Sam noticed the shuttles too and felt bad he had not thought to give Tayana a communicator. She could not call for help. She was alone and seriously out numbered. Sam maneuvered the Terra Aurai to the back side of a close moon and waited for Grant's call to arms. The villagers were settling in and were pretty calm considering most of them had never left the planet's surface and were on board an alien spaceship. Sam was confident they had not been detected and were at the moment, safe from harm. Grant on the other hand was practically making out with them he was so close.

Tayana and crew were about to get even closer.

Chapter Twenty-Six

Meanwhile on the surface, Tayana and crew prepared for what was coming.

"Stay cloaked. Do not engage the Anotokians until I give the signal."

Tayana was a fierce warrior, not so much battle hardened, but a fierce protector of her village, her family. Her crew was well trained and loyal. Fierce as she was, her mind drifted to Grant lying on the healing table in the Varizone, unaware of what was happening around him. Not being able to say the things she wanted to say, and knowing they may never get the opportunity. She saw Grant in pain or dying too many times and was determined to tell him how she felt. Grant and Sam had neglected to give her a means to communicate with them while they were orbiting the planet. She was cut off and on her own. Thankfully she had her crew and a good plan. She was a survivor and a warrior.

The Anotokian shuttles began landing in strategic locations, but farther away from the mining camp than she expected. There were a couple hundred soldiers at a minimum, she stopped counting. The Anotokians unloaded rovers much like Grant and Sam's, only theirs were loaded with weapons and angry soldiers ready to kill anything moving. She and her crew were cloaked and could not be detected. She felt safe, for the moment. The rovers began to organize and fill with the rest of the soldiers.

Tayana turned to her core crew, "We need to get closer to the mining camp, now. Let the others know we ride when they do. Keep out of sight and behind them.

We can hide behind the boulders for protection once we're there, move!"

The crew made their way out of view and began mounting their C-rexes, readying for their ride. A war was about to begin, Tayana and her crew were ready. They trailed behind the rovers, making good time. It was only be a matter of time before the fireworks began. Her thoughts drifted to Grant, she did not know if he was recovered. Had they executed all of their plans? Was her family in trouble, were they in space? She shook herself and regained focus.

The Anotokian's slowed as they approached the mining camp, then came to an abrupt stop, causing some of Tayana's crew to separate from the group. She was not concerned; they were trained, and knew the plan. They made their way to the boulders, about fifty yards away from the mining camp. They were elevated enough to see the bunker clearly and not draw attention to themselves.

The Anotokian warriors carefully made their way into the camp. They spotted the wreath Sam had left behind and dispatched it with a single shot. No explosion, just a poof of dust and wreath debris scattered about. They advanced further into the camp and looked around.

The plan was for all of them to come into the camp, and the plan was working. The Anotokian's began exploring the mining equipment and several ventured over to the bunker. The majority of them stood like they were waiting for something to happen so they could fire their weapons and kill something.

Grant and Sam monitored the Anotokian's progress. With Eliot's help, they had a clear picture of what was happening. The first shot fired was the claymore mine Sam had set near the bunker. It killed five or six of the warriors, and caught the others completely off guard. All hell was about to break loose. Tayana motioned for her crew to duck and cover. They made themselves as small as possible, up close to the large boulders. They knew what was about to happen, the Anotokian's had no clue. Eliot signaled Grant, it was time to fire the first SHTF. Grant pushed the button detonating the SHTF. The lag in transmission through atmosphere made for a long and awkward pause. Then it happened. Grant, Sam, and Tayana saw the bright flash from their respective positions. The explosion was tremendous and the damage was beyond belief. The boulders Tayana and crew were hiding behind took a beating of biblical proportions. All the trees in and near the mining camp were eradicated. The blast took out nearly half of the Anotokian warriors. Tayana's crew weathered the first blast and prepared for the second. They shifted positions to be out of the angle of the next SHTF. Grant fired the remaining SHTF's. The planet shook like it had no intentions of stopping. Tayana and crew once again hunkered down and survived the blast. Now was the time for them to execute their plan. If it breathes, farts, or smells like it did or could, kill it. Close to all of the remaining Anotokian regiment was taken out by the blast. The few survivors were not in the best shape, but still dangerous. They could use small arms and fire on the crew at any time.

Tayana gave the signal to advance. Under their cloaks they began systematically slitting throats and burying their swords deep into the hearts of wounded warriors. It was hard to tell if they were dispatched successfully. Their hearts were not located where a human heart would be, causing some intense moments. They began stabbing the warriors repeatedly trying to find the right spot for a quick kill. Once they found the right spot they made light work of the remaining Anotokians. The ground was littered with bodies and parts. Tayana signaled her crew to head back to the village. They knew more warriors would come if they knocked out the first team of Anotokian warriors. And come they did.

Unaware of the new load of warriors being shipped down, Tayana and crew were nearly crushed by Anotokian rovers making their way to the mining camp. Their cloaks hid them and their C-Rexes from the eyes of their enemies, allowing them to continue their trek back to the village.

Nearing the village they saw the Anotokian's had landed in their front yard. "We need to go around the back side of the falls and get the dome activated quickly. We do not know when Grant will ignite the hydrogen, but it will be soon, helium fall is beginning.

Sam and Grant celebrated in their respective crafts at the nearly complete destruction of the Anotokian ground forces. Sam almost broke radio silence when several more blips appeared on the view screen. The Anotokians sent more troops, a lot more troops. They would wait until the majority of the warriors were away from their crafts. When helium fall began they would return to their rovers, and not a minute sooner. Sam knew Grant saw the same thing, hundreds of new warriors joining the fight.

Tayana and crew made their way around the back of the falls to the dome generator. She fired it up. The initial noise caught the attention of the Anotokian's guarding the shuttles. She pressed the button and the dome began to form. It was visible until it was complete and the

Anotokian warriors began firing at the dome, Tayana, and her crew. "Fire back, make them pay!" Swift arrows of the villagers pierced the neck coverings of the Anotokian's and several were quickly dispatched. The rest advanced with hesitation, but met the same fate. With the dome securely in place all went clear. From the outside there was nothing to see but forest. Helium fall was nearing its apex and the Anotokian's began heading back to their crafts.

Grant had to ignite the hydrogen. He had given Tayana every chance to get to cover.

On a whim, Sam thought of Tayana and how she had entered his mind. He thought of where she might be, but nothing came into view.

He must think hard enough to catch her attention.

Within a minute she was there, in his mind. "We are safe, ignite the gasses."

Sam broke the radio silence, "Grant, Tayana is safe, fire now."

Without hesitation Grant pushed the button on the remote. What happened next was beyond their imagination. Grant, Sam, and Tayana witnessed one of the greatest natural forces they had ever seen and would likely never see again. Tayana and crew were instantly engulfed in flames. The dome rattled and shook violently. From space the whole planet became a giant ball of swirling fire.

The spectacle was more than they bargained for, "Tayana, please survive this, please." For the first time in his life, Grant was terrified. He may have blown up the woman he loves, and destroyed a beautiful planet at the same time. Her death would haunt him forever, but there were other matters to deal with.

The Anotokian ships were a short distance away, by space standards. Taking a risk and hoping for the same outcome as the planet below, he signaled Sam. "Fire on the ships, fire on the ships."

Sam maneuvered the Terra Aurai around behind the Anotokian ships. "Firing now! Wasn't it the coolest things you've ever seen? I've never seen a planet burst into flames. You made it happen, Grant. Good job!"

"Shut up and fire!" Grant was in no mood for games.

"Firing!" Their missiles impacted on the Anotokian ships, and exploded. There was no damage. Both men freaked out.

"What the hell do we do now, Sam?"

"Uh, I don't rightfully know. I thought the missiles would do more damage, any damage."

"Think Sam, we have less than five minutes before those three maneuver to firing positions. We have lifted the veil, so to speak, they know we're here."

Sam stared at the Anotokian ships wondering what type of metal could withstand a direct missile hit and not have a scratch on it, and then it occurred to him, the alloy. *Did they discover the same alloy and patch their busted ships with it?* "Grant, crazy idea, you need to load some of the Ebony Belle's water tanks into an outer hatchway. Then jettison them in the direction of the Anotokian ships."

"Sam, that's crazy, and insane. Why would we do that? We're not a mobile ship wash. They aren't going to back off because we cleaned their windshield, what the hell are you thinking?"

"The alloy we created. Their ships look like they're made of same alloy. Just do it! If I'm wrong, well...good knowing you!"

"Fine, last ditch effort, could work, could get us killed, I'm in." Both ran to their labs and located full water barrels. Sam poked a few holes in the top of his and advised Grant to do the same. He wanted it to explode easier once it hit their hull. Grant loaded his into the outer hatchway. "Sam, pressurize your compartment. When the hatch blows, the barrels will be forced out in a hurry. It won't be lethal, but it may buy us some time."

"Good idea, Grant, pressurizing now."

"I'm headed back to the bridge Sam, I hope this works."

"Me too, it was my idea. This is going to be a close one, buddy!"

"Dear God let this work!"

They returned to their respective bridges just in time. "We must make evasive maneuvers captain."

"They're moving faster than I expected, Eliot, thanks for the heads up. Move us forward five hundred yards. We need to launch the barrels before we get to their ship. We have one shot at this."

"Sam, you've gotta get out of there, hopefully you loaded your barrels on the starboard side of the Terra."

"Sure did." Making a quick run to stay out of their direct line of sight, they cannot see us, we're cloaked!"

"I totally forgot, we just have to stay out of their way and hope the barrels hit the front of their ships."

"I loaded six. I should be in firing position in thirty seconds."

"Right with you, Sam. They know someone is here, but they cannot detect where we are. We could cat and mouse them for days, but we need them to go away, one way or another. Get ready to fire on my mark."

"Oh, Grant, this is either going to be one of our

greatest hours or sensationally, one of our worst."

"Blow the hatch Sam, blow the hatch." Grant released the outer hatch. With an audible bang, the barrels launched on a direct path toward the Anotokian ships.

Sam's experience was similar, but not the same. He had a situation. "Grant, um...I think I over pressurized the hatch."

"What do you mean Sam, what happened?"

"Well, there was a loud bang and then a smaller one right after it. I think I ripped the outer door off of the Terra. I need to do some damage control."

"How bad is it?"

"Not exactly sure, but my barrels are outpacing your barrels three to one."

"Holy crap, you tore a hole in the hull, didn't you?"

"Possibly, but we need to focus on not getting shot out of space. We can deal with the issue later."

"So now it's an issue? There's always something with you. Your barrels should make impact, in three, two, one..., there was no explosion, no fire, and no major holes ripped through the side of the Anotokian ship. Just a slick spot running down the side of the ship.

It was a direct hit. Sam had failed. "Car wash it is, let's get the heck out of here before they find us. We can try to out run them." About then the other barrels began having an impact on the Anotokian ships.

"Sam, you need to look at this, their ships appear to be melting."

"What? Are you kidding?"

"Nope, where your first barrel hit there was a slick wet spot, but now there are holes forming, lots of them."

"On my side too. Oh look, they're starting to veer off,

they're running scared!"

"I wish we had more water barrels, Sam. Those Junkers are falling apart."

"But the next batch they send will be armored and packing. It won't take them long to return with a lot more fire power."

"Seven ships have dropped out of hyperspace two thousand miles behind us."

"Holy crap, Grant, I meant they'd be back with better firepower later, like a week, or a month, not fifteen seconds."

"Sirs, they are our ships."

Eliot's clarification brought an abrupt halt to their conversation. "Our ships?" Grant was stunned, incapable of understanding the concept of "our" ships.

"Your message got through, sir."

"Thank you, Jesus! Whoo hoo!" Grant was excited and not so excited at the same time. The ships, the villagers, and he and Sam were saved, but Tayana was still in great danger, if she was still alive. "Welcome to the fight Gentlemen."

"Captain Goodwine, this is Captain Park Lane aboard the Magnolia. We should have them out of here in short order."

"When did you receive my signal, I sent it almost two weeks ago?"

"The signal was received one week ago. We gathered men and supplies, and then made a mad dash through space to get here. I thought we'd arrive, shoot up a few alien ships, and be heroes. Looks like you had them on the run before we arrived. You didn't really need us."

"Glad you received my message and glad you're here. We may still need your assistance on the planet surface."

"We're spacers, captain, not landies."

"I know, but we just obliterated the planet below. There may be survivors. We request an escort to the surface to check on some friends."

"Friends? You mean there are more bad guys surface side?

"Well, they are not bad guys; they are another intelligent civilization desperately needing our help."

"First run out and you two hit the jackpot, lucky bastards!"

"We need to be planet-side yesterday, Captain Lane, if you know what I mean. I'll launch my shuttle in five minutes, an escort would be appreciated."

"Yes sir, we will escort you to the surface, on your mark."

"You might bring a few fire suits, to be safe."

"Captain Goodwine, this may be a dumb question, but where the hell are you? We knew you were in the area because of the radio transmissions, but have yet to locate you."

Grant laughed, he had forgotten about the cloaking device. "I'll be there shortly." He ran to the engine room and turned off the cloak. The ship instantly appeared three hundred yards away from the Magnolia.

"How in space did you do that? You popped out of the black like a pimple on a fat lady."

"Something we will have to discuss when we return to the PSAD. First, we need see what we can do to help or who we can rescue."

"What did you drop on the surface to ignite the entire planet?"

"Long story, I'll fill you in later. Launching shuttle in

three, two, one..., see you on the surface, Captain Lane."

"Right behind you, Captain Goodwine."

"Sam, stay put. Captain Lane and I, along with one of his platoons, are deploying to the surface as we speak. We need you where you are in case the Anotokian's return."

"This is Captain Westboro of the Broadmore. They shouldn't be a problem, sir. We blew their ships into space dust about four minutes ago."

"Thank you, Captain Westboro! My guess is they got a message off before it happened. We need to be on alert. They will return and they'll come back packing." Grant felt things were far from over.

"We'll be vigilant sir, good luck on the surface."

"Thank you, Captain Westboro, going to need all the luck I can get." Grant re-engaged the cloak on the Ebony Belle before departure, leaving Eliot instructions to move the ship to a safe location away from the planet and any ships, friend or foe.

It was going to be hell when he landed, but Grant was not prepared for what he saw when he popped into the lower atmosphere. There were no trees, not a single bush, flower, or blade of grass. The planet was barren as far as he could see. He headed to the mining camp where the battle was fought. As he approached, his heart sank. The bunker, the mining equipment, even some of the rocks, had completely melted. He hovered over the sight trying to find signs of life, anything to give him hope Tayana was alive.

Captain Lane and his platoon arrived and were also surprised by the barren landscape before them. "Captain Goodwine, I'm hoping this is how it looked before the battle?"

"Yes and no. It was barren in places, but it was also very lush. There were tall trees, lush vegetation, and plenty of wildlife. I don't think anything survived."

"I'm sorry to hear that Captain, let's keep looking, maybe we'll get lucky."

"Thank you, Captain Lane. Let's head to their village. I hope it fared better. Its environment was different than the rest of the planet due to its location in a valley."

"Then let's go see if we can be heroes." Grant appreciated Captain Lane's sense of adventure.

Chapter Twenty-Seven

Tayana and her crew huddled close as the gasses ignited. It shook violently and all was engulfed in flames. When the fire dissipated and the smoke cleared, Tayana and crew uncloaked. Their village was safe. All the pods, trees, and buildings were intact. There remained a few smoldering tree stumps outside the dome. Steam from the super heated water around the village created wild patterns as it rose past the dome. It was surreal. Tayana and crew had not seen any Anotokian's for the last fifteen minutes. She decided it was time to remove the dome and venture out. She had no idea what the atmosphere was like now and she had no way to communicate with Grant. Then she remembered Sam, she could communicate with Sam. She thought about Eliot and wondered if he could tell if the air was ok to breathe.

Sam moved the ship some distance away from the planet and had stopped close to another life sustaining planet nearby. A vision of Tayana crept into his mind and he began to concentrate on the vision. It was not clear and he could not make out what she was saying, but he caught enough to know she was alive. "Eliot, can you hear me?"

"Yes, Sir."

"Can you tell if the planet's atmosphere is breathable for Grant and Captain Lane?"

"The gasses have burned off and the oxygen levels are at twenty-five percent. There are no longer trees to produce oxygen."

"Can they breathe the air on the planet?"

"Yes. It will be like breathing thin air on top of a mountain. They will be short of breath and recovery will take longer."

Sam tried to contact Tayana to let her know it was safe, but taxing. He thought as hard as he could but there was no answer. "Damn it! I sure hope she understands what's happening."

"Grant, come in, Grant."

"I hear ya, Sam, what's up?"

"Tayana is alive, I'm not sure how. She spoke to me in my mind again."

"We're headed to the village, Sam."

"Be warned, the oxygen levels are at 25 percent and it will feel like you're on top of a mountain."

"Thanks, we'll be at the village in two minutes. I'll let you know what we find."

Tayana pushed the button to retract the dome. The good oxygen she had inside quickly mixed with the thin, charred oxygen of the planet. They began taking quick breaths and thought they were suffocating.

"Tayana, we need to get back in the dome, there is no oxygen left out here."

"There is oxygen, but it is thin. We will have to move slowly and with purpose. The Anotokian rovers were just ahead of us in the clearing. We need to see if there are any survivors, and then dispatch them if there are." The crew made their way to the clearing and found nothing left of the rovers. There were no bodies to be found either. The heat from the flames turned them to dust and the wind blew them away.

As Grant neared the village, there were no landmarks, or trees, with the exception of one clump in the distance. He located the now dry streambed that once fed the large waterfall in the village. The village came through the explosions and fire unscathed, but how? There was no sign of Tayana. The smoke was thick and Grant would have to land in order to search for her. Through the smoke he saw the tops of the village trees. He set the shuttle down as close to the village as he could. Captain Lane landed fifteen yards away.

"Gentlemen, be prepared for anything. Do not fire unless it has four arms, four arms."

Grant exited the shuttle. His nose was assaulted by the acrid smell of burnt everything. He became light headed and held onto the rail of the bay door to steady himself. He caught his breath and called out Tayana's name.

She and her crew hid behind the large outcrop of rock in the middle of the village when they heard the shuttles landing. She was uncertain if the landing parties were friend or foe. "Shh, did you hear that?"

"Hear what?" Her crew had not heard Grant call out.

"Listen!" All were quiet and trying to refrain from breathing, but the low oxygen made it next to impossible, they felt faint.

"Tayana, are you here, Tayana!" She heard her name this time and took off in the direction of the call. Through the mist she made out his outline and he made out her silhouette.

"Grant, I am here." They walked faster. A full out run would have taken them to their knees, breathless as they passed out. They embraced tightly, Tayana kissed him, full on. Grant did not hesitate for a nanosecond, he kissed her back. The kiss was passionate. They felt each other's soul.

As they pulled away from each other Grant could not help himself, "Oh my God, you're alive. But how? How did you survive the explosion and the flames? There is literally nothing left, except the village, how?"

"When you went to the Ebony Belle my crew and I went to the caves and retrieved a device my father made for this occasion. He called it the protector, and protect us it did."

"Let's get you and your crew into the shuttle."

"Wait, there may be Anotokian's who survived the blast, we need to dispatch them at once."

"Tayana, nothing but you, your crew, and the village survived the blast, nothing. We'll go back to Ebony Belle and see what we can do later. It's getting late, night will be here soon. Let's get you out of here."

"All right, let's go, for now. We must come back and tend to the village. It will need care in order to survive. We will have to find a water source and ..."

"Tayana, there is nothing left, no animals, no grains, no fruits or vegetables. This planet has lost its life. There will be no coming back here. You and the villagers have to relocate. Let's talk about this later. We need to get you to safety. The Anotokian's may return and if the planet is once again barren, they may leave it alone."

Tayana had a different opinion. "We are going to discuss this later, but for now I need to see my people and I need to speak with Sam."

Grant was puzzled that she needed to speak with Sam, but he let it go and they made their way to the Varizone.

The trip back to the Terra Aurai was uneventful and Tayana was soon reunited with her people. She broke the news to them that the entire planet surface was destroyed and the village was the only thing left standing. There were tears and wailing as Tayana spoke about the possibility of having to relocate to another planet.

"But this is our home, how can we live anywhere else?"

"We can figure it out; they will return us to our home."

Tayana, Grant, and Sam were all at a loss for words as her people dealt with the loss of their homes, the loss of their planet. "We will talk more later after I have some discussion with Sam." Tayana motioned to Sam to follow her and she led him out of the lab bay. "Where can we speak in private, Sam?"

"We can go to my quarters, if it works for you."

"It will be fine, it is private, and we will not be interrupted."

Sam was becoming concerned as to her intentions but went along with her anyway. "Uh, what are we doing?"

"I need to know what you know and what you've seen on this ship. It is of the uttermost importance, Sam."

"Alright, what do I need to do?"

"Be still and let me into your mind. I will view the ship through your memories. If I find what I'm looking for there may be hope for my planet and my people."

"Sounds pretty serious, I'll do what I can to help." Tayana had Sam sit quietly at his desk chair while she paced around the room and gently entered his memories. Sam was not acutely aware of her presence in his memories, but he had a feeling he was being watched, only this time it was from the inside. The silence was enough for Sam to drift off to places he loved and missed. He missed the girls, the pool, and his home. He knew Tayana could read his mind as well as his memories but he was not bashful about any of it. She was in his mind on several occasions and it now seemed almost normal to him. He couldn't hide anything and she was good about not calling him out on what she saw. Sam drifted to a rather erotic memory of a night he shared with the girls before the battle began. The three of them were naked and oiled head to toe, and they were rubbing all over one another and—

"Sam, Sam! I know where we need to go and what we need to do!"

"Oh damn, I was just getting to the good parts."

"Get your manhood in check and follow me, we have a mission and we have to act fast."

"Go, I'm right behind you, hobbling like a three legged man." Tayana paid him no mind and led the way to the lab bay on the Terra Aurai. Grant and Sam had done a cursory examination of the ship when they boarded to install the power cell. Tayana made her way through the ship as if she was there before. Once in the lab bay she pointed to the large white plastic tanks lined up near the back of the lab. Sam had not noticed them when he was looking for drums of water to launch on the Anotokian ships. These tanks were much larger, about the size of a small recreational vehicle.

They were too big for Sam to maneuver alone so he discounted them, earlier. "What are these?"

"Sam, these are the seeds of life. These are the capsules my father launched into the atmosphere, releasing their contents as they circled the planet. They fall to the surface when they are empty."

"Seeds of life? What do you mean?"

"These capsules contain the seeds, DNA, and whatever else is needed to populate a planet. I must tell you, I have not been honest with you. I know more than I have led on. These were developed by my father and his team to bring life to new worlds, my world. I am a product of the Genesis Project."

Sam looked puzzled, then fully realized what Tayana said.

"You were created by one of these?"

"Not directly. My father and his team seeded this planet and some others. When they completed seeding they returned here and were astonished to see how rapidly everything was growing. As a joke, they added some human DNA into the mix as fertilized human eggs, wondering if it would create humans in a new environment. It worked. When they returned five years later they were greeted by young adults. My father and his co-captain were mesmerized by the beauty of the planet and the creatures they created. They mated with them. I was born here, along with others."

Sam's mind was a whirl, so many thoughts, so many questions. "So if they left Earth three hundred years ago at approximately the same age I am, seeded the planet, and returned five years later, then conceived children, it would make you approximately 163 years old. It can't be."

"Sam, it is true. I lost count of my years, but on this planet years do not mean what they mean on your Earth. I am physically the same age as you, but my mental abilities are more advanced, I've had longer to practice. My father was a great teacher and a great man, I mourn his loss daily."

"I'm sorry you lost your father. From what I gather he was an intelligent man. He knew you'd out live him and he planned accordingly." "How did you survive the fire on the planet?"

"My father invented a device, it created an impenetrable barrier. It encompassed the entire village. I had the villagers leave because I was unsure I could retrieve the device and make it function. It is a complex device, thankfully, with fairly simple instructions. The village is intact, but there is no life left there to sustain us. No animals, no plants, and no water. It will replenish over time, but we would not survive until then."

"So, why did you bring me here?" Sam knew part of what Tayana told him. He and Grant had discovered much of it in the crashed shuttle.

"Sam, we need to launch one or two of these containers over the planet. If I'm correct, it will take a few years for our planet to return to what it once was. Will you help me do this, for me, for my people?"

Sam could not deny it, her idea was good, but where would they go in the interim? "We need to discuss this with Grant. He is my captain and I cannot make the decision without him, but I'm sure he will be on board with your plan."

"Thank you Sam!" She gave him a huge hug as tears of joy rolled down her cheeks. "I feel I have let my people down, I have to make things right for them."

"I understand, Tayana, I'm on your side!"

He tapped his communicator, "Grant, please come to the lab on the Terra Aurai." His tone was direct and his intentions were true.

Grant felt the urgency and made haste. "So, what's been going on in here?" He was trying to be light hearted, but his voice was tense.

"Grant, Tayana has a great idea and I agree with her, Tayana."

"I called Sam into a private meeting to read his memories. He was aboard this ship longer than you and I needed complete silence to find what I was looking for.

My father described these containers to me when I was younger." She pointed to the large containers. "They contain what is needed to create life on the planet below. We need to launch a couple of them into the upper atmosphere. They will empty while they orbit the planet. The seeds, DNA, and everything else will begin rebuilding the planet. Sam thought it best to include you in the decision. The planet will be livable within two to three years, and then we can return. What do you think?"

Grant pondered for a moment and said, "Where will you stay for the next two to three years? The seeds are over 200 years old, we do not know if the release mechanisms will work, and we do not know the procedure or sequence to make them work properly." With a shrug and a sigh, "We fly by the seat of our pants on a regular basis, I'm all for launching them with no instructions."

Tayana was delighted; she mashed her body against his in a tight embrace. "Thank you!" With a quick look at Sam, "both of you!"

"With the Terra Aurai cloaked we can launch the containers. The other ships might detect the containers since they are large, but they'll see liquid in them and leave them alone. Let's get moving. I pray this works. We need to determine where you and your people will live for the next two to three years."

Sam gave it some thought and offered, "Grant, Tayana told me her father seeded several other planets in the region, they could relocate on one of them."

"Great idea Sam. We can continue our research."

"We can also continue the research Captain's Coke and Morgan began so many years ago. In many ways they were more advanced than we are, so long ago. We have a lot to learn my friend."

"Sounds like a plan, what are your thought's Tayana?"

"It's a good idea. We can live there then return to our planet when it is time."

"Sam, ready the containers. How many are we launching?"

"For now, two. We could be seeding our own planets. There are a dozen of those things back there. I'm not sure how many they started with, but two seems like a good start." As they prepared to launch he thought about what Tayana said earlier. Her father put fertilized human eggs in the mix. What did it mean for the other planets? They were not guided by their creators? He kept the thought to himself.

He remembered the egg shaped vessel he found in the Gemo2 and the warning with it."I'll be right back, gotta use the head."

Grant gave him a quizzical look as he left the lab bay. He let it go and readied the containers for launch.

Sam raced to his quarters to retrieve the vessel. "Grant would be pissed if he knew what I was up to." He opened the vessel and retrieved a vial of the accelerator Captain Morgan had described. The instructions were clear. 'Do not break or open the vial. Insert one into the container via the valve. The vial will dissolve into the solution.' Again, there was a warning. 'This has not been tested. We do not know the full outcome of introducing it to the solution. Good luck!' He closed the vessel and returned to the lab.

"Whew, couldn't hold it any longer. Is everything ready? I'll check the valves to make sure they're functioning properly." He climbed a ladder to the valve on top, opened it, and gently inserted the vial. "I pray I'm doing the right thing," he said to himself. He released the vial. He quickly checked the valve on the other tank and gave them a thumbs up.

Helium Fall

Chapter Twenty-Eight

"Container away!" They successfully launched the first of two containers full of the seeds of life. When the planet rotated one hundred and eighty degrees they launched the second one and prayed they were doing the right thing. Grant felt good about what they were doing. He knew losing your home was devastating and he did not want to see Tayana and the villagers displaced any longer than they needed to be.

He made his way to the bridge and checked in with the captains of the other ships. It was time to have a meeting and determine their next steps. "Captain Lane, please contact the other captains and have them meet us on the Ebony Belle in three hours."

"Hello, Captain Goodwine, glad to see you're still making things happen, it would be my pleasure to host the meeting aboard the Broadmore. You and your crew have been through much, it is the least I can do for you."

Grant did not hesitate and accepted his offer. "Thank you; we will meet you and the other captains in three hours." He was relieved he didn't have to put on airs to accommodate the other captains aboard the Ebony Belle.

"Sam, we have a meeting in three hours with Captain Lane and the other captains aboard the Broadmore. We need to get to the Belle, shower, change, and get ready to go. Tell Tayana she is welcome to come. I'll meet you in the Varizone."

"Will do, Grant. Headed your way in ten minutes. Gotta finish this game of soccer with the kids, find Tayana, and get the elders together to let them know what's happening. Could be more like twenty, if you know what I mean."

"Get moving Sam, we don't want to be late, I called this meeting."

"Gotcha, I'll get Tayana and meet you at the Varizone."

The trip to the Belle was short and sweet, no incidents, and a smooth docking. We have two hours, Sam; meet me on the bridge in two hours!"

"Alright, I'll meet you on the bridge in two hours. It was two hours, wasn't it?"

"Smartass! See you then."

"Tayana, you can shower in our guest quarters. I'll find some suitable clothing for you."

"Thank you, Grant!" Grant showed her to the guest quarters then proceeded to find her some clothing. He found an assortment of women's clothing in the guest quarters two doors down. Some were formal, leaving nothing to the imagination, and some were motherly. He found the perfect items for her and returned to the guest quarters. "I found something you may like and it is suitable for the meeting."

"Tayana came out in nothing but a towel, oozing sexy from everywhere.

Grant nervously and slowly backed out of the room. "I'll go so you can get ready. Let me know if you need anything." He closed the door and retreated to his quarters, tail between his legs, feeling like a loser. "*What were you thinking? She was almost naked, oozing sex, and you left the room! OMG, you deserve to be alone.*" Grant undressed and continued kicking himself as he got into the shower. It had been nearly a week since he showered, the water felt good on his tired and aching body. He stood with water pounding on his back, and then felt another sensation. He quickly turned around and Tayana was standing in front of him, naked, and wet. She was beautiful. This time Grant did not hesitate. He took her in his arms and kissed her the way he should have kissed her a long time ago. The passion rose as did his manhood. Her body was smooth and strong, yet supple and delicate. He ran his hands over her body as she ran hers over his. Their bodies were slipping and sliding across each other, lubricated by the water. Tayana kissed his neck as he caressed her breasts. The passion grew and Grant reached for her woman parts. He was surprised how they felt; they were different than Earth women's. She moaned with pleasure, grabbed his manhood, and guided him in.

"Grant, two hours! I'm in the Varizone, alone, and waiting. You said two hours!"

"On my way, Sam, got a little sidetracked."

"You dog! Did you?"

"Later, we'll be there shortly." When Grant and Tayana arrived neither one could erase the smile off their face.

"You two! Congratulations! Should have happened months ago. Eliot, take us to the Magnolia please. You know you're going to have to stop smiling when we get to the meeting, right?"

"Sam, I could smile forever."

"Me too!" Tayana held Grant tight, and for the first time Sam saw a much softer side of her. She was truly in love with Grant and he with her. Life was never going to be the same.

They soon docked with the Magnolia and were met by Captain Lane. With a firm handshake he welcomed them aboard the Magnolia.

"Glad you could make it. We haven't had visitors in quite a while, please make yourselves at home. I can give you a quick tour if you'd like. Meeting isn't for another hour or so." So far the ship looked like any other PSAD ship, pretty plain and unadorned, for the most part.

Grant replied, "Sure, sounds like a great idea, lead on." As they passed through the airlock into the receiving vestibule, Grant was impressed with the decor. "Wow, I was not expecting anything this elaborate. I was expecting a plain, drab, typical PSAD vessel with little to no personality, I'm impressed." The walls were a rich taupe and the curtains were cobalt blue patterned with planets, stars, and solar systems. The fixtures were brushed nickel. Low backed couches lined the walls and looked inviting, but were designed to be sat on only for brief periods. The rest of the ship followed form and they were all amazed at the detail. The bridge was large and well appointed. The seating was comfortable and inviting with long term sitting in mind. They were plush and comfortable. Sam was sure they had vibrating, heating, and cooling features installed on them. He wanted to check them out when the occasion arose, and it did.

"Please have a seat; we have ten minutes before the meeting begins. I will be back shortly." Captain Lane exited the bridge to freshen up before the meeting. Sam took advantage of his absence and began checking out the chair. One of the crew noticed him, "Have you misplaced something, sir?"

"Uh, no, I was uh, looking to see if these had any um, comfort features."

The crewman smiled, "They're under the arm on the left side, you lift it up to see the controls." He turned back to his duties, chuckling as he did.

In a weak and almost defeated tone Sam offered his thanks. He leaned towards Grant, who was chuckling as well, "Well that was embarrassing!"

Tayana could no longer contain her laughter and laughed out loud. "Only you Sam, you're like a child, having to push buttons and flip switches. Do you want to sit in the captain's seat as well?" The whole bridge erupted in laughter and Sam's face turned crimson.

He had never been embarrassed by a woman before and hoped to never be again. "Ha, ha, too funny, and yes, I'd like to sit in the captain's seat." Another round of laughter began.

The crewman looked at Sam and with a look of disapproval, slowly shook his head, "No!"

Captain Lane returned in time to save him from more embarrassment and another round of laughter. "Please, follow me." They followed him to a large conference room. It looked like outdoor patio, not a conference room. One wall looked like a meadow with deer and other wildlife milling about. Trees and a forest adorned two walls, and a small stream ran through the remaining wall.

Captain Lane said, "The walls are holographic. We thought you'd be more comfortable in a natural setting, Tayana. I hope you feel more at ease in a here than a closed room."

"Thank you, I am pleased with your choice."

Grant called the meeting, so he addressed Captain Lane first. "Captain Lane, you are somewhat familiar with the situation at hand, but I wanted to reiterate, and ask for your assistance. Tayana and her people have been displaced. Their planet, Antaya is lifeless and they cannot return to their homes for what may be several years.

There is now a high threat the Anotokian's will return seeking revenge. The Antayan's have no means to defend themselves against a superior enemy. What I am proposing is this; we relocate the Antayan's to a nearby planet, one populated by the work of Captain's Morgan and Coke. These are habitable and have the necessary flora and fauna to sustain them. I also propose we establish a base on the planet, or on Antaya, to protect them. Per PSAD law we are responsible for the safety of these newly discovered life forms."

"Grant, let me stop you there. When we heard new life was discovered and it was under attack, we immediately formulated a plan to protect them. Two ships in our convoy will stay and establish our presence. We will build a base of operations on the opposite side of the planet. We do not want to interfere with the lives of the people. We will allow them to develop independent of our influence. We will establish a base on Antaya and other inhabitable planets. Does this meet your specifications, Captain Goodwine?"

"And then some, thank you, Captain Lane."

"Don't thank me; thank the cantankerous old man who sent you on this mission."

Grant knew he meant Major Abram T. Aboy, his mentor and boss. "I will thank him the next time I see him. When do we begin the transition to the alternate planet?"

"As we speak, we have crews investigating planets in the area most closely matching the conditions on Antaya before you destroyed it." He gave Grant a wink and continued, "It will be a few days before we can begin the transfer. In the mean time, we will show you to your quarters, so you get some rest and freshen up before dinner."

"Fine with us. Tomorrow we'll take Tayana to the planets you've selected and get her input. She is the resident expert and knows her people's needs. She will have a voice in this decision."

"Agreed, Captain Goodwine, I expect nothing less. Dinner is at seven in the dining hall, see you there."

"Captains, if you will follow me, I will escort you to your quarters." The young man led them to level three and to their quarters. "The dining hall is on this level, down the hall to your right; it will be on your left. Enjoy your stay with us."

With a yawn, Sam said, "All right, Grant, I'm going to catch a few Z's. I'll meet you in the dining hall, don't be late, again!"

"Whatever." Grant looked at Tayana with passion in his eyes. She grabbed him by the hand, pulling him into the guest quarters. She kissed him deeply and passionately, in a 'yes, we're going to be late', sort of way.

Dinner time came quickly. Grant and Tayana hustled to get their acts together. How could a woman make Grant forget his responsibilities and duties so willingly? He did not want or need an answer to the question. He was glad she existed, and she was his.

They got dressed after another close encounter and quickly made their way to the dining hall.

"About time you two made it." The slight blush on their faces told the whole story. "You two really need a vacation, alone and uninterrupted."

"Sam, I couldn't agree more."

Tayana could not wipe the smile off her face or let Grant out of her sight.

Dinner was a feast beyond compare. They ate to

their hearts content, and then ate more.

Tayana was making her way to the dessert table when Grant caught her midway. "You know what chocolate does to your people!"

"I guess I better steer clear, for now." She gave him a wink and opted for a sumptuous piece of lemon cake instead. When he wasn't looking she stuffed a couple chocolate bars into her pocket. Dinner concluded and they made their way to their quarters. This time, they slept. They were so full anything else would have been a disaster.

Morning came early. Captain Lane was moving slowly and methodically as he bumped into Grant in the corridor. "Good morning, Captain Goodwine! Glad to see you're up so early."

"Captain Lane, you look as if you had more of a night than you cared too."

"I ate too much and drank beyond my limits. I'm headed to the med room to get a remedy for this hangover."

Grant chuckled and felt his pain, "Can I accompany you to the med room?"

"Sure, what's on your mind?"

"I appreciate all you've done for us, and for Tayana and her people. I also want to say Tayana and her people are a free people. We do not own them."

Captain Lane looked at Grant in a questioning manner, "What are you trying to say Captain?"

"Merely we cannot make decisions for them and we cannot force them to do anything they do not wish to do. We are their first contact and I do not want there to be any, off color dealing with them."

"Grant I assure you we have considered all of their

ways, cultures, and needs. We have no intentions of conquering them. Do you feel we are disposed that way?"

"I heard some talk last night at dinner, it made me question some of the crew's intentions, that's all."

"That's all? This is serious. We do not tolerate any injustice to Tayana or her people. Thank you for bringing this to my attention. I'll take leave of you now. We will meet in the bridge at eight."

Grant was unsure he made the right decision letting Captain Lane know what was overheard. Too late to take it back now. Hopefully something would be done and there were no hard feelings.

Grant swung by his quarters and gathered Tayana for their journey to the planets. They met Sam in a corridor. "Bridge at eight, Sam!"

Tayana, I ran into Captain Lane earlier, we meet in the bridge at eight, and then to we go planet shopping."

"Shopping, what is shopping?"

Tayana had never heard of shopping so Sam took the opportunity to enlighten her. "Shopping is like picking flowers, you see something you like and you pick it."

Tayana made an unpleasant face, "Sounds like bringing something to its end. I'm not sure I'm going to like, shopping!"

"You're welcome Grant; I just saved you tons of money in the future."

"Tayana, shopping is where you look for something you need to accomplish your goals. We are looking for a planet to best suit you and your people's needs."

"So shopping isn't all bad, it's like picking the fruit you want off of the buffet?"

"Exactly!"

Grant gave Sam a look and Sam laughed. "I could

have saved you tons of money, but no, you have to be Mr. Straight Forward. Good luck!"

They laughed and entered the bridge. Captain Lane looked better than he did earlier. "Captain Lane, good to see you again." Captain Lane's expression was not what Grant had expected.

"Have a seat, please." The captain's from the other ships entered the room much to Grant and Sam's surprise. "I have called the captains here to address what you heard at dinner. Please tell them what you told me."

Grant was not sure he wanted to tell them anything; their dispositions were not the most promising. He had opened his mouth and was now committed. "I overheard several of the crew discussing Tayana and her people. The comment that caught me off guard was, "These backward ass aliens are perfect slave material. They'll be our bitches as soon as the rest of the ships leave orbit."

The captains were taken back. One of the captains took the lead and said, "This will not be tolerated in any manner, we will review the feeds. The spacers involved will be punished and likely discharged. I have never heard such talk in all of my years."

Another proposed a lie detector test and imprisonment for any who failed. Captain Yurslick of the Charlotte offered to let things play out and see what transpired. "It was tough talk and nothing more. Why bring attention to the matter? Let it play out, nothing will come of it, you'll see. These men are rough and came here looking for a fight. They're full of aggression and have not been able to let it out in combat. Cut them some slack, they're military."

He was not received well and left the bridge in a huff. "We need to keep an eye on him as well." Captain

Lane said, and made notes in his compad. He raised his hand to quiet the room. "This is serious and we will not go lightly on anyone bringing harm to these people. Tayana, you have been most gracious and have not said a word, please share your thoughts with us."

Tayana was now the Tayana, Grant and Sam encountered at their first meeting. She was the huntress, intense, determined, and capable. "Captains, the crew members in question assume we are slave material. I assure you we are not. Any attempt to enslave my people will be met with force. We will be silent death in the dark and a plague in the light. They will neither see us, nor enslave us. We are warriors and will defend our home to our death. Be warned, we are not as simple as we appear."

There was barely a breath in the room when she finished. The captains looked at one another.

Captain Lane broke the silence. "Tayana, it will never come to that. We will take care of this before it becomes a situation. Please believe me when I say, we are with you."

Tayana's fierce dark eyes lightened a shade and her disposition smoothed out somewhat. She, along with Grant and Sam, doubted any person in the room wanted to be on the receiving end of her wrath.

Captain Lane reassured Tayana, "We will put an end to this, mark my words. If we can move forward, please, let's go shopping for you a new home, shall we?" The group rose in unison and made their way to the shuttle. Tayana gripped Grant's hand tightly. He spread his fingers to let her know he needed his circulation back. She relaxed her grip and put on a better face for the trip. The first planet they visited was overgrown and would not be suitable for them to farm. The second was too hot and barren over most of the surface. As they approached the third planet they could see the distinct blue of water on its surface and the snow capped peaks of mountains in the distance. There were small bands of plains and lots of green space. Tayana became excited, "This is the best so far, we may have found our new, temporary, home."

The emphasis on temporary caught Grant's attention, "Yes, temporary. We have seeded Antaya and pray it will have new life soon." The shuttle touched down in a green space near a waterfall. The trees were reminiscent of those on Antaya. It was as close to perfect as they were going to get. The same pods they used as their dwellings were growing nearby.

Tayana made her decision, "This is where we will relocate my people. We will make this our temporary home."

Captain Lane instructed the pilot to return to the Magnolia. "We have some work to do." The trip back to the Magnolia was quicker than the trip out.

Tayana could hardly contain her happiness. She desperately wanted to see her people and give them the news.

The hours transferring from the shuttle to the Magnolia, from the Magnolia to the Varizone, and then the trip to the Terra Aurai, seemed like days. When the Varizone docked with the Terra Aurai, Tayana was waiting at the hatchway, ready to run to her people with the news. Once onboard she ran to the lab bay and shouted to her people, "We have found a temporary home, the planet is named Bandores." Cheers went up all around. The villagers were excited they were going to once again be on the ground. "Gather your belongings and leave nothing behind, not even a crumb. We will leave for the new world in the morning." It was late in the day so Tayana determined morning would be the time to go. They needed a whole day to get settled in, and prepare for the night and what it may bring.

"Tayana, your people love you. You have proven you are their leader. They will follow you anywhere."

"They are my world and I would go anywhere for them. Tomorrow will be a good day to relocate, yes?"

"Yes, it will be fine. We will make it happen."

It was a sleepless night for all. Grant and Tayana, of course spent the evening cuddling. Sam, Kyera and Dyanta were reunited so they were going to have a sleepless night anyway. Morning once again came too soon. Everyone moved slower than normal, but were excited about the move.

"Sam, coms on?"

"What?! It's early and you're waking me after fifteen minutes of sleep, what gives?"

"Sam, it's eight o'clock, time is wasting. We need to get the villagers moved and settled as soon as we can. Meet me in the lab bay."

Sam was not fond of mornings, especially not fond of mornings involving getting up and moving. "Damn it! I need two or three hours of sleep, is that asking too much?" Kyera was first to emerge from the covers and slowly make her way to the toilet, followed closely by Dyanta, who never seemed to be more than a few steps away.

"Girls, we need to move quickly or Grant will be up here knocking on the door. He was greeted with a couple hmpfs and what he thought was a growl. "Ladies, it's moving day! If I can get moving, so can you, let's go!"

They dressed and looked presentable. Upon arrival at the lab bay they were greeted by a rather enthusiastic young man, apparently coordinating the move process. "Good morning sunshines! What are your names and where are your belongings?"

"Kyera and Dyanta, our things are there." Kyera pointed to a pile of bundles and what appeared to be a small tree.

"Um, I do not believe the tree can go with you."

"Spacer, the tree goes."

"And you are?" he said in a snarky, defiant tone.

"I am the captain of this ship and you are?"

"I am letting the tree go, yep, that's who I am. You two will be in the first group, gather your things and move to the loading area, quickly, please," he said with a sideways glance at Sam. It took several trips and more hours than expected to get the villagers and their belongings moved to the shuttles and the planet surface.

Grant and Sam spent most of the day planet side assisting villagers with their belongings and helping plan the village layout so everything would be close to normal. The waterfall, river, and pods were too much of a coincidence, but Grant understood the nature of the seeding and assumed the pod seeds naturally grew by the stream. Evening drew close and Grant expected helium fall soon. He wasn't sure the village set up would protect them. The valley was smaller and the trees were farther apart. He positioned the shuttle close by so in the event of an emergency they could board the shuttle for safety. The helium fall never came. The villagers were free to move outside the village without fear of getting caught in the gasses.

Sam, Grant, and Tayana met up to recount the day as

night approached. "It's been a busy day, Grant. You two doing all right?"

"Thanks, Sam. Tayana and I are fine. We're pleased we've accomplished so much. Life in the village will be back to normal sooner than you think."

Tayana was happy, but this wasn't home. "We will survive until we can return home." She watched villagers hurry to and fro putting things in their places. She noticed construction on the dining hall was coming along rapidly. The pods were claimed, and Salbola and Emara came by to give their thanks and express their appreciation. Tayana was tempted to throw them a chocolate bar, but decided not to feed their addiction.

"Sam, I'm going to head back to the Belle and do some—reporting."

"Tayana would you like to accompany me?"

"Yes, I'd like to see your—reporting."

With a smile they took their leave of Sam who was now eyeing his brides and making plans of his own. "Catch you two tomorrow afternoon! Do not call me before one o'clock, Grant. It won't be pretty if you do."

"I hear ya, Sam, get some rest. I'll see you tomorrow; we do have some things we need to discuss." Grant planned to sleep as late as possible.

"Sure, I'll let you know...when I'm available." Sam said.

"Tayana and I have some reporting to do, Eliot, to the Belle, please."

Helium Fall

About the author

Darren Robison has loved writing for most of his life. He discovered his passion in his high school Creative Writing class. Each week they had to write a new story and it truly sparked his imagination. Life was tough after high school and his dream of writing waned, life had taken over. In 1996 while attending college he was assigned a writing project. With full time work being the priority he put it off until the last minute, an hour and a half to more precise. When he received his graded work his professor complimented him, having given him the only A in the class. His professor asked how long it took him to compose his writing and was at a loss when he was told an hour and a half. He commented it had to have taken him weeks to get it to this level. Again, Darren's creativity was sparked and he dreamt of writing once again. Twenty one years later he was challenged to enter a writing contest. No prizes, no parade, and no book deal for the winner. He accepted the challenge despite his reservations. The rest is history, or was it the beginning. This writing is a result of the challenge.

Darren grew up in Liberty, MO in the last neighborhood at the edge of town along with his parents and siblings. After graduation he left family and friends behind and took up residence in Florida for a few years. He met some great friends, but it just wasn't home, he moved back to Liberty. One evening he called a friend who invited him to a birthday party and she introduced him to the woman who would become his wife. They were married in 1993 and have two children. At the time of this writing they have two granddaughters. Darren and his wife reside in Kansas City, MO.

Darren Robison's mission statement: "I want to capture my reader's attention and draw them into the world of my imagination. Giving them the opportunity to use their imagination and escape into the pages with me."

Made in the USA
Columbia, SC
21 June 2019